About the author

Kathryn is a single mum of two boys. Originally from Sheffield she now resides in a small market town in Lancashire. As well as writing, she runs a small crafts business from the indoor market. She enjoys many creative pastimes including cross stitch and knitting. She enjoys watching football and Formula One. She also likes to travel and explore new places.

This is a work of fiction. Names, characters, businesses, places, events and incidents are either the products of the author's imagination or used in a fictitious manner. Any resemblance to actual persons, living or dead, or actual events is purely coincidental.

LIVES ON THE LINE

KATHRYN PANA

LIVES ON THE LINE

Vanguard Press

VANGUARD PAPERBACK

© Copyright 2022
Kathryn Pana

The right of Kathryn Pana to be identified as author of
this work has been asserted by her in accordance with the
Copyright, Designs and Patents Act 1988.

All Rights Reserved

No reproduction, copy or transmission of this publication
may be made without written permission.
No paragraph of this publication may be reproduced,
copied or transmitted save with the written permission of the
publisher, or in accordance with the provisions
of the Copyright Act 1956 (as amended).

Any person who commits any unauthorised act in relation to
this publication may be liable to criminal
prosecution and civil claims for damages.

A CIP catalogue record for this title is
available from the British Library.

ISBN 978 1 80016 366 9

Vanguard Press is an imprint of
Pegasus Elliot MacKenzie Publishers Ltd.
www.pegasuspublishers.com

First Published in 2022

Vanguard Press
Sheraton House Castle Park
Cambridge England

Printed & Bound in Great Britain

Dedication

For my two wonderful boys who are the light of my life.

For my dad, for all you have done for me.

For Grandma K for believing in me in all my endeavours.

For Pastor Pauline and everyone at New Life Christian Centre in Colne for every prayer and all the support they have given.

Prologue
Two years earlier

Alpha team had gone for a drink after work, the three newer members of the team, Bennett, Palmer and Hill, were over by the pool table in Charlie's bar, Tom was sat at a table and Will was getting a drink. It had been a rough week, and as it was Saturday and they didn't work Sundays, they had decided to go for a drink. Harvey had gone straight home, he was the only one with a family, and so didn't go out drinking much with the others. Though it wasn't often Will and Tom went either, Tom had a wife and Will was usually busy with his never-ending supply of women. Will went and sat with Tom.

'So what's wrong with you? You have been quiet all day.'

'Nothing.'

'Come on, Tom, I have known you since we were at school, so I think I know when something is bothering you.'

'It's personal.'

'And I can't help unless you tell me.'

'You can't help us anyway.'

Will looked at Tom, had a drink but never looked away.

'OK, Lynne was a week late, we thought she was pregnant, but she isn't.'

'Really? Again, isn't that five times this year?'

'Yeah.'

'So what did the doctors say?'

'They have said we need to go to a fertility clinic.'

'So that's what you are going to do?'

'No.'

'Why not?'

'It costs too much, it's thousands for all the tests and if we needed IVF that's thousands more and we just don't have that.'

'So money is the issue.'

'Yeah, pretty much.'

'Then it's not an issue, just get them to send the bills to me.'

'No.'

'What? Why not? Tom, it's not an issue you know that I don't mind.'

'But I do.'

'If it solves the issue, I can't see the problem.'

'Will, you don't see a problem because you have money to burn, you will never understand the concept of having nothing. I have been considered your charity case for years by your circle of rich friends and I refuse to live the rest of my life like that.'

'OK, but if you change your mind, you know where I am.'

'I won't, now can we talk about something else please.'

'Sure, so what do you think of that group of ladies that are stood by the bar?'

'That they don't stand a chance with you around.'

Will laughed.

'What are you trying to say, Tom?'

'That you go through more women than anyone else I have ever known.'

'I am just enjoying life.'

'Or hiding from commitment.'

'I'm not hiding, but I just don't see me as the getting married and having kids, kind of guy is all.'

'You used to.'

'And we know how that turned out.'

Will turned and looked at the others in the team.

'Hill's a good officer isn't she.'

'Yeah, she is, so keep your hands off.'

'Tom, she is on my team, you know I don't break my own rules.'

'Yeah, and I also know what a good-looking woman docs to you.'

'OK well I am going to buy that group of ladies a drink, and you should go home to your wife.'

Will got up and went to the bar where the women were stood. He flashed his charming smile and immediately got their attention.

'Hey, can I buy you ladies a drink?'

'Yeah, why not,' one of them responded.

Will ordered in a round, one of them was more interested in talking to him than the others, she was tall with long blonde hair and a pretty smile.

'So what do you do?' she asked.

'I'm a cop.'

'Really so is my dad, he is a lieutenant at the fifth precinct.'

'Really, what's his name?'

'Don Walker, do you know him?'

'You could say that.'

She looked at him curiously, Tom walked past, he was going home.

'See you Monday, Will.'

'Yeah, see you then,' Will said to Tom and then he turned back to her.

'Will, that's your name?'

'Yeah.'

'Not Will Falco by any chance.'

'Yeah, that would be me.'

'My dad told me I should stay away from you, if I ever met you, said you are arrogant, reckless and that you have different women all the time.'

'Of course he did, should I go now?'

'He didn't tell me, however, how handsome and fit you were, and I am not looking for anything serious right now anyway.' She smiled.

'You have your own place.'

'Yeah.'

'You want a lift home? I have my motorcycle right outside.'

'Sure, why not?'

'Let me just let my team know I am going then, and we can go.'

Will walked over to the others, still playing pool.

'Well as much as I would love to go on to a club with you guys, I have had a better offer so I will see you all Monday.'

'Have fun Sergeant,' Bennett said as he walked back to the bar.

Kathy Hill watched him leave with the beautiful young woman on his arm.

'Our sergeant can seriously get any woman he wants it seems, I would love to know how he does it,' Bennett said.

'Yeah, it's as though they are queueing up,' Palmer replied.

'He has to be good in the sack or something, mind you, some of them don't stay around long, bet she only lasts a night,' Bennett stated.

'Why, she seems nice?' Kathy asked.

'Because she is just a bar hook-up, it's the classy ones he keeps around.'

'How do you know so much about his private life? Do you stalk him or something, Bennett?' Kathy joked.

'No, I just pay attention to who he is photographed with and who he talks about, is all.'

'And you want to be just like him, right?'

'I wouldn't mind just half the action he gets.'

'Well let us go to that new club, and see if we can hook you up with someone then, Bennett, get rid of some of that frustration,' Kathy answered. They left, laughing and talking about the night ahead.

Chapter 1

Sergeant Will Falco, was sat in his office, it was dark outside, and he was starting to miss the bright summer days and it wasn't even Christmas yet. Will was the alpha team leader in the New York SWAT unit, he loved his job and now he and Sergeant Kathy Hill had been engaged for nearly four months and she had officially moved into his place, he wondered if life could possibly get any better. It had taken him a long time to be this happy, but now he had found that he wasn't going to let it go. The office was pretty much empty, his team and Kathy's had finished their reports and gone home, their paperwork was a little more extensive. He looked out of his office door, the SWAT office wasn't too big, but it had eight groups of five desks and offices all the way round the edge, one for each sergeant, the three lieutenants and Captain Bridge. The alpha desks were by the door, but Will's office was at the back, next to the captain's. Kathy's was by the door, and her team's were next to Will's, they worked well together and were an extraordinarily strong unit.

Captain Bridge appeared at his door and snapped him back from his thoughts.

'Sergeant, I am glad you are still here, I need a word with you.'

Will got up and followed the captain into his office. Captain Bridge was in his fifties, was five foot nine and was slightly balding, he had served on SWAT for most of his career and Will respected him a lot. Will shut the door and sat down. The captain's office was one of the biggest, he had several filing cabinets down one wall, a large window with a plant either side, a large desk with his chair on one side and two facing him. The captain sat down and leaned back in his chair.

'Now, Falco, you won't be happy about this, but I am informing you now, so it isn't a shock in the morning.'

'OK, Captain.'

'I am not going to be here for the next month.' He put his hand up to stop Will from interrupting. 'The chief is good friends with his counterpart in Detroit, so I am swapping places with their captain for a month.'

'What? Why?'

'Because we are one of the best performing units in the country, and they, at this time, are one of the worst, this is an observational swap only, she is coming to get a look at how a successful unit works to enable her to make the changes that are needed back in Detroit. She is not going to be changing any of the daily operational running of this unit.'

'Well, that's something at least.'

'And she won't have access to your file either, the chief agreed with me on that one, we don't know the woman, she is new to the rank and the job, she has never served on SWAT either. She is also extremely ambitious.'

Will's personal file was only accessible to three people, himself, the captain and the chief. His parents were murdered, and they had been multi-billionaires. Will had taken his mother's maiden name when he joined the force, so people didn't make the connection. His team now knew limited information about him, except his number two and best friend, Tom Hargreaves, no one else at work, not even Kathy knew everything.

Will observed the captain for a brief moment.

'I get the feeling that's not all you wanted to tell me, Captain.'

'No, it's not, I need you to do me a favour.'

'And what's that?'

'I want you to watch my unit for me, keep your ear to the ground, if I am right and she is up to something you need to watch out for what that could be.'

'Shouldn't Lieutenant Planter and the other lieutenants be doing that, Captain, I mean I am just a sergeant and up against a captain what chance do I have?'

'Planter is good police, but he plays things by the book and I need someone who isn't worried about upsetting things if needed. I need someone who is prepared to push the boundaries and do what it takes to protect this unit. Falco, I trust you to do this for me more than anyone, you have been here for fifteen years, nearly sixteen now, and I know it means as much to you as it does to me.'

Will sat for a moment and then smiled.

'All right I'm in, but I can't guarantee I won't have to break a few rules along the way.'

'I will pretend I didn't hear that, Falco, but do what you have to.'

'Can I see her file?'

'I printed you a copy off but keep it at home. I don't know if we can trust her, there is something that just doesn't add up, and I'm not sure why she was so eager for this switch, I believe it was her idea.'

Will picked up the file, got up and walked to the door.

'Don't worry, Captain, I will always have your back.'

'Thanks, Falco, I will see you in a month.'

'You can count on it.'

Will left and headed over to Kathy's office, she was just finishing up her work and packing things away.

'Are you ready to go home?'

'Yes, just give me a minute.'

Will walked in and sat on the edge of her desk and watched her.

'I just had the weirdest conversation with the captain.'

'Really, what about?'

'We can talk about it at home when I have a drink in my hand.'

'OK, then let's go home.'

***

Will had inherited his parents' apartment, it was a penthouse on Park Avenue, it had an exceptionally large open plan living area including an extensive kitchen. His bedroom had an en suite and a walk-in closet, it had a gym next to his bedroom with all the workout gear Will could ever need. There were three other bedrooms, all a very generous size with their own en suites, and then a cinema room. It also had a large roof terrace with a bar and barbeque. Part of it could be covered in winter. Will had grown up there and moved back in when his parents were killed — it was his haven.

When they got home, they both showered and then Will ordered dinner, he knew all the local restaurants and none of them minded delivering to him, he rarely had time to cook for himself because of his work hours. He often found himself after shift completing all his paperwork, it really wasn't his strong point or his favourite part of the job and often got behind with it, he had spent many days off catching up.

Over dinner Will filled Kathy in on what the captain had told him and what he had asked of him, Kathy was surprised by the whole thing and wasn't sure what to make of the situation that had now presented itself. After they ate, they sat on the sofa, Will had a strong drink, but Kathy stuck to juice.

'So why did the captain agree if he doesn't really trust this woman?'

'I don't think he had much of a choice from what he said to me.'

'I just don't understand why she wouldn't observe the captain in his job to see how he handles it.'

'Maybe they don't have anyone to look after her unit if he stayed here, I don't know, it was her idea too and the whole thing just doesn't make much sense unless she is up to something.'

'Like what?'

'Maybe she wants to take control of our unit.'

'How would she get away with that, the switch is only for a month.'

'I have no idea, I only know what little information the captain gave me, I have her file, but I had a look when you were in the shower and there isn't much there to go on at all.'

'Well, this could be an interesting month then, and he must have known you would tell me, right?'

'I would presume so.'

'So he knows we will both do this for him because I'm definitely in.'

'Good, we can brief alpha team at Charlie's after shift tomorrow.'

'Just alpha?'

'Yeah, I think it will be best for now to keep it just between a few, less risk of conversations being overheard, she will be in the office tomorrow and I don't want her to know that we are tasked with keeping an eye on the unit, that way she is likely to make mistakes.'

'OK, sounds fair enough, I will brief bravo later if we need to.'

'That's sorted then, now we are done with work shall we go to bed for the pleasure.'

'I'm a bit tired actually, was a long day today.'

'OK, do you want to head to bed then, I will just clear up then I will be in.'

'Yeah, OK.' Kathy kissed him and went to bed.

Will got another drink and sat on the sofa thinking about all the captain had said. He wasn't sure what to expect but he was used to working in difficult situations and he would do everything to protect the unit.

Chapter 2

The next morning Will and Kathy got into the office early, as always. Lieutenant Planter was just coming out of the captain's office, he walked over to them as they were getting their morning coffee. The coffee machine had been a very useful introduction to the office, Will had brought it in when he joined the unit and no one was complaining.

'Good morning. Sergeant Falco, Captain Ashborne wants to see you.'

'OK, but can't it wait while I am actually on shift, I haven't even had my coffee yet and it is literally fifteen minutes.'

'I would say not, she is keen to get organised and meet everyone and you are first on her list.'

'Fine, let's get it over with.' He followed Lieutenant Planter across to the captain's office.

The lieutenant went in first and Will followed, the lieutenant shut the door behind them and stood by it. Will stood behind one of the chairs opposite the captain.

'Captain Ashborne, this is Sergeant Falco, our alpha team leader.'

She stood up and walked round the desk and offered a hand to Will. He shook it but didn't move, he barely even looked at her. She wasn't what he had expected, she was around five foot eight, was quite thin and had dyed blonde hair cut into a bob, dressed relatively smartly, not like a SWAT unit leader, that was for sure.

'Sergeant Falco, nice to meet you, sit please.'

'I'm good thanks.'

'OK.' She walked back round the desk and sat. 'So Sergeant Falco, I have been looking at the rotas for the unit, I see your team and bravo always do the main shift on a six-day pattern, usually taking Sunday off.'

'Yeah, we do.'

'Why are the teams never moved around?'

'Because we are alpha and bravo, the best teams in the unit, so we work the busiest shifts, on the busiest days.'

'But bravo are new, and just how are the other teams supposed to improve if they just stay on the quieter shifts?'

'That's what training is for and I don't know of any team unhappy with how the rotas are done. Captain Bridge worked with all the team sergeants to do them and the other teams are quite happy for us to take those shifts.'

'Well, I am thinking we may have a move around.'

'Captain Bridge said that you wouldn't be changing anything operational, and you are just here in an observational capacity to learn from a more successful unit, to enable you to improve your own.'

'Did he now? Well, I am your captain now and will change what I see fit and I think it will be good for you to work a bit differently, for a while at least.'

Will folded his arms, he towered over her. He was taller than all the lieutenants and Captain Bridge, standing at six foot four, he was muscular, he had jet black hair, brown eyes, and an overall Latin appearance. He observed her for a moment sitting back in her chair looking smug.

'Are we done?' Will asked.

'For now, Sergeant, can you send Sergeant Hill in, please.'

Will walked out, moments later his office door slammed making Captain Ashborne jump. Kathy knocked on her door.

'Sergeant Hill, come in.'

Kathy stepped in and the lieutenant closed the door.

'So, Sergeant Hill, I hope we have a better start. I have been reading your file, very impressive. You earned your sergeants pretty quickly since you moved here, that's very good and shows how dedicated you are to your job.'

'Thanks, and yes, I am but then I did learn from the best.'

'The best?'

'Yes, Sergeant Falco taught me everything I know about this job.'

Captain Ashborne stood and walked round her desk and leaned on it in front of Kathy. Kathy was only five foot four, she had long blonde hair and blue eyes, not really the usual type of SWAT officer, but the position suited her. Captain Ashborne watched her for a moment but Kathy didn't move or give anything away.

'So I was telling Sergeant Falco, I will be moving the teams around a little bit, trying you all on different shifts.'

'I thought you weren't changing operational things and you are here to observe the unit, to see how a successful unit works.'

'It appears the sergeants here are well, if not misinformed.'

'With all due respect, Captain, if you are only here for a month, why change what works?'

'To see how you all work in different circumstances.'

'We work fine as we are Captain, that's why this unit is one of the best.'

'Well, your opinion is noted, Sergeant, a much better response than Sergeant Falco, I must say.'

'Well, you will just have to hope that he calms down or gets an hour in the gym before he gets a shout.'

'What do you mean by that, Sergeant?'

Just then Kathy's beeper went.

'I guess you are about to find out, Captain.'

Kathy left, the teams had just walked in. Will walked out of his office. Captain Ashborne watched from her doorway.

'We have shots fired at a bank so let's move,' Will said as they left.

Captain Ashborne went back into her office and sat behind the desk. Lieutenant Planter was stood by the door.

'Lieutenant, please can you tell me why I can't access Sergeant Falco's file.'

'I don't know, only Captain Bridge and the chief can.'

'OK, I will ask the chief then, but first what can you tell me about him.'

'He has worked on SWAT for nearly sixteen years now, eight almost nine in charge of alpha. He is more than capable of running incidents and handling multiple teams on a shout, though he has never been interested in promotion. He is not a guy to piss off that's for sure, used to have real anger issues, but since being with Sergeant Hill he has calmed a lot.'

'That's calm?'

'For him, yeah.'

'So he is dating Sergeant Hill?'

'Actually, they got engaged about four months ago.'

'And they work alongside each other.'

'Yes, though not all the time, they often get separate call-outs, but they work very well together, she was on alpha till she passed her sergeants, so they are used to the way each other work.'

'Thanks Lieutenant, if you will excuse me, I need to make a phone call.'

He left and closed the door. Captain Ashborne picked up the phone and called the chief.

'Good morning, Captain Ashborne.'

'Good morning, Chief, I wanted to ask you about Sergeant Falco.'

'What about him?'

'I can't access his file.'

'I'm sorry, Captain, you aren't authorised to.'

'But I'm his captain.'

'No, Captain Bridge is his captain, you are here to observe the department.'

'But I want to know the officers I am working with.'

'I'm sorry I can't authorise that, and also I hear you are wanting to change the team's rotas around.'

'Yes, I thought it would be good for them.'

'Well, Captain, it's not good for my city, so leave them as they are, and that's not a request, it's an order.'

'Yes, Chief.'

'Anything else?'

'No.'

'OK then, goodbye.'

He hung up. Captain Ashborne slowly put the phone down, she was furious that she had been overridden. She sat back wondering what she was going to do now.

Chapter 3

The teams arrived at the Westgate bank and they got out of the truck. Will walked over to the sergeant in charge when a PD officer shouted to him.

'Hey, Sergeant, make sure you don't rob the place this time.'

'What?' Will said as he walked over to him.

'I said make sure you don't rob the place this time.'

'Wow you're funny.' Will stepped closer to him. 'Maybe we should send you in instead.'

'That's not my job,' he said, shocked.

'No, it's mine, and seeing as you are too scared to do it, why don't you keep your mouth shut.'

'Or what?'

'I may have to make you.'

'Sergeant Falco,' Kathy shouted.

Will walked back to the sergeant in charge and got the information. Back at the truck, alpha team were ready to go, but bravo had been watching what was going on. Will and Kathy walked back over to the truck. Will looked at bravo team still getting ready.

'OK, as you lot aren't ready you can watch the street. Two minutes to get ready at a call, it's now four and you aren't even close. I don't expect this to ever happen again,' he shouted, furious. 'Alpha team let's do this.'

Alpha team followed Will to get into position.

'Shit, sorry, Sergeant,' Fremont said.

'Well congratulations guys, side-lined for a shout, it's not what I expect from you, but you should all know by now what Sergeant Falco expects and this is not acceptable,' Kathy responded.

Will sent Harvey, Bennett, and Palmer to the front door, they kept low underneath the windows, which was tough for Harvey and Palmer, each being six feet. It was an older building so didn't have the full glass front that some banks had, but it was still quite low. Will took Tom and Stanson round the side, he remembered the manager left his window open and he hoped that would still be the case in the colder weather. They got round the side, and sure enough, it was open a fraction. He pulled it open and climbed through, being so tall had its advantages sometimes. Tom and Stanson followed. Will went to the door and listened to see if there was anyone there, he couldn't hear anything so he opened the door slowly and went down the corridor to the security door.

'Alpha blue we are in position, enter on my count, one… two… three… go.'

They went through the door and the others entered through the front.

'NYPD, put the weapon down, and put your hands on your head.'

The man with the gun looked around at the team and lowered his weapon, he slowly put it onto the floor.

'They are just blanks, I didn't want to hurt anyone, I just wanted to stop the foreclosure on my house.'

Will moved closer and slid the handgun away with his foot towards Tom, who took it and checked it.

'Yeah, they are blanks, Sergeant.'

Will lowered his weapon and checked the suspect for another, he didn't find one, so he handcuffed him.

'I understand your situation, but this isn't the way to go about these things, you can't go holding up a bank because you haven't paid your mortgage.'

'I didn't have an option.'

'There are always other options before this.'

'I guess so, I will definitely lose it now'

'Control, we are all clear, send in an officer to take the man into custody.'

'Received.'

When the PD came in, Will and his team exited the bank and they headed back to the truck. As they were packing their gear away, Will spotted the same officer that had confronted him, smoking behind the truck. He went around the back.

'What the fuck are you doing?'

'What is it to you, Sergeant?'

'Well, you shouldn't be smoking on duty, never mind next to a SWAT truck.'

'What's so special about your fucking truck?'

Will walked right up to him.

'It is full of live ammo and you are not meant to be smoking next to it.'

'Get a grip, Sergeant, who cares?'

'I care.'

Just then, Stanson appeared.

'Sergeant we are all ready, just waiting for bravo.'

'OK, go and sit in the truck.'

Stanson took Will's arm and pulled him back from the officer.

'Sergeant, he isn't worth it.'

'Yeah, listen to your girlfriend,' the other officer chipped in.

Stanson turned around.

'What?'

'You heard.'

Stanson smiled then punched the officer, breaking his nose and he fell to the floor. Will looked at Stanson.

'Nice one, Stanson,' Will smiled, 'Now let's get bravo and go.'

They were stood by the truck when bravo appeared, alpha got in and bravo headed for the cars. Kathy noticed an exchange between Will and Stanson, Will was about to get in when she stopped him.

'What happened?'

'What do you mean?'

'You and Stanson.'

'It's probably best you don't know, see you back at the office.' Will smiled.

***

They got back to the office and Captain Ashborne was waiting for them.

'Sergeant Falco, Officer Stanson, my office.'

They followed her and went into the office. She closed the door, they both stood opposite her desk.

'Well, I found out what Sergeant Hill meant.'

'I'm sorry,' Will said.

'Never mind,' she shouted. 'I just got a phone call from a sergeant at the scene you just attended, one of his officers had his nose broken by Stanson, after you, Sergeant, confronted him twice.'

'Really, I don't remember that Captain, I spoke to him after he made a smart remark, and then when he was smoking next to the truck, I asked him to move away from it, but that's all,' Will replied.

'You expect me to believe that, when after you spoke to him, he appeared with a broken nose.'

'He had an issue with us, he probably fell and saw it as a chance to get us in trouble, Captain.'

Stanson and Will were both struggling to keep a straight face.

'As I can't prove anything and your two stories contradict his I have no choice but to let it slide, but I will be watching you two very closely from now on. Stanson, you can leave.'

Stanson left and went and sat with the rest of alpha to write up his report. Will didn't move.

'Well, Sergeant, I don't know how you have so much influence in this unit and the whole PD, but I spoke to the chief and he has put a stop to my rota changes. I know it was you that reported it to him, and I am not happy you went over my head, it had better not happen again.'

'It wasn't me, Captain, I have no idea what you are talking about, how can I possibly have any influence over the chief.'

'I don't know, Sergeant, and I know it was you because there is no other way he could have found out.'

Will stood silently and didn't move an inch.

'Anyway, next week my alpha team will be arriving here, and they will be shadowing teams in the unit.'

'Charlie and delta are good for that.'

'I was thinking more alpha and bravo.'

'OK, they can shadow my team, if they can match them.'

'This isn't a negotiation, Sergeant.'

He looked at her and made a judgement call.

'OK, you match me on the range, and they can, or I could call the chief.'

'OK, but I am an excellent shot.'

'We will see.'

***

They went down to the range. Will followed her, she walked so confidently but Will was not worried at all.

The captain stood at one of the firing points and Will stood at another.

'One clip, best target wins,' Will said.

She nodded, she aimed and fired. Will did the same. They retrieved the targets. Will put his next to hers on her booth. She looked at Will's target then turned to him. He smiled.

'Charlie and delta, it is then, Captain.' He turned and left, still smiling.

'Damn it,' she shouted banging her fist on the booth, angry at herself for underestimating him.

Kathy stopped Will as he went back into the office, and gestured that he join her. He went in and closed the door. She went behind her desk and he sat opposite in the chair.

'You want to tell me now, what went on at that call-out.'

'I told you it's best you don't know.'

'Why?'

'Because you will just get pissed off.'

'Will, just tell me.'

'OK, Stanson punched that officer that was giving me shit, broke his nose.'

'What?' she shouted. 'So you are dragging Stanson into your bullshit now?'

'See and that's why I didn't want to tell you.'

'You could both have been brought up on charges.'

'Well, we aren't, because it's our word against his.'

'So, you lied.'

'I told her a different story so Stanson didn't get in trouble is all, that officer was smoking by the truck I told him he shouldn't be, he got mouthy.'

'And that makes it OK.'

'I didn't ask Stanson to punch him.'

'You don't have to ask anyone for anything, they just do it anyway.'

'I think we have bigger things to worry about right now than my team being too loyal, Kathy. Ashborne just told me her alpha team arrive on Monday, now what do you think they are coming for?'

'To take over the unit?'

'Exactly, I have delayed that process, but they will continue to try, so watch your back.'

She stood up and walked round her desk, he stood up.

'I will be OK, I have the best man in the unit to watch my back.'

He went to kiss her, but she stepped back.

'You best go, the captain will be watching for an excuse to get rid of you now.'

The rest of the shift was busy, and Kathy was tired when she got home, she made her excuses and went to bed early. Will was starting to wonder what was going on, she hadn't been near him in weeks.

Chapter 4

The next morning Kathy arrived at work with Will and went straight into the dispatch office to see her friend Gina. Gina was only five feet, her parents were from the Caribbean, she was bubbly and lots of fun. She had worked in SWAT dispatch for ten years and was one of the senior members of the team. She loved her job especially on busy days, she knew the teams so well and which to send to which call. She had been the first real friend that Kathy had made when she joined the unit and they had been best friends ever since.

'Hey babe, how are you?

'I have a serious problem,' Kathy answered.

'Talk in the corner or the ladies' room, kind of problem?'

'Ladies' room kind.'

'Must be serious, hold on.' She went over to another controller, spoke to him, and came back to Kathy.

They went into the ladies' room, Kathy checked it was empty.

'OK, what's up?'

'I think I might be pregnant.'

'What seriously? Aren't you on the pill or something?'

'Yeah, but about eight weeks ago I missed a few days because I ran out, I didn't have time to pick any up, anyway I hadn't mentioned it to Will so…'

'You had sex?'

'Yeah, a lot.'

'Oh, I know what he can be like, so have you told him.'

'No, he will freak out and I haven't even done a test.'

'OK, then when I get my break, I will go and get you one.'

'OK, thank you.'

'I will come and find you when I have it, OK.'

'Yeah.'

Gina hugged her and they left, Kathy went into the main office. Will was getting the coffees.

'Hey where did you disappear to?'

'I needed to speak to Gina.'

'OK, made you a coffee.'

'Thanks.'

Kathy walked off into her office, Will followed her and closed the door. He sat on the edge of her desk, she started to organise some papers. He took her hand and moved her in front of him.

'Are you OK?'

'Yeah, why?'

'You have just seemed a bit distant these last few weeks.'

'No, I'm fine.'

He pulled her closer and went to kiss her, but she moved.

'Not with the new captain around.'

'Come on one kiss isn't going to hurt, and we aren't even on shift yet, at least not for another five minutes.'

'Later, OK.'

'All right, I guess I best go do some work then.'

Will walked out and went into his office. Kathy had been pushing him away for over a week now because she thought she was pregnant, she was terrified that she would be and now it was beginning to affect their relationship. Since getting back together, they had quite a physical relationship, it had been amazing and she was certainly not complaining. She knew Will would notice eventually that she had been making excuses but she didn't know what else to do until she knew what was going on. She had also been feeling a bit sick for the last few days and though she had managed to keep herself from being sick, it had been hard work.

Just then the teams walked in and she could hear them talking. They had changed the meeting about Captain Ashborne to their place tonight to include a movie and a barbeque, only alpha were coming, but Kathy wasn't really in the mood. But it had been Will's idea and she hadn't known how to get out of it. After all, them having people round more was her idea and she had pushed Will into opening up his life to his team, so she couldn't really change that now. Even Stanson was part of it now and she didn't want Will to go back to how he was and shut them all out again.

'Morning Sergeant,' Fremont said as he passed her door.

'Morning,' she replied.

She sat at her desk doing some paperwork when Captain Ashborne appeared.

'Sergeant Hill.'

'Captain, what can I help you with?'

'I was wondering where everyone goes to socialise after shift.'

'Charlie's, it's just over the road from the PD.'

'Do you all go there often?'

'Sometimes, I think some of the guys go more than me and Sergeant Falco, though.'

'Are any of you going tonight?'

'I don't think so.'

'Oh, OK, maybe another night then.' And with that, she left.

Kathy wasn't sure what that was about, the higher-ranking officers never had drinks with the teams. Just then her beeper went off, the teams got up and Will came across.

'We have an armed robbery at a jewellery store, let's go.'

***

They pulled up at the scene and Will got out, he walked over to the lieutenant in charge.

'Sergeant, we have three suspects, and around ten hostages.'

'Do we have any other entry points except for the front door?'

'There is a back door.'

'OK, do we have any plans at all?'

'Yeah, I will just get them for you.'

Will glanced across at the teams, they were all ready to go. Kathy had stayed with the truck, he knew something was going on with her, but he couldn't figure out what it was, he was just hoping that things weren't starting to go wrong.

The lieutenant came back with the plans, Will looked at them and considered the options. He wasn't sure he needed both teams for this, but now they were all here he would utilise them. It was unusual for dispatch to get it wrong, maybe Gina was distracted by her conversation with Kathy, so it must have been serious. He went back to the others.

'Tom and Harvey, I want you on that rooftop to cover with your snipers, Webb and Walker take the left side street, Blain and Ford take the right, Palmer and Bennett, I want you to cover the front. Stanson with me through the back door and Fremont you will accompany Sergeant Hill through the front.'

They all got their appropriate weapons and got into position.

'Control alpha and bravo are in position.'

'Received, you have an all clear and a green light.'

'Received, green and blue, you have a green light, do you have a clear shot?'

'That's a negative at this time.'

'Received. On my count we go in one... two... three.'

Will kicked open the back door and he and Stanson cleared the back rooms before going through into the main store. Kathy and Fremont were in but in a stand-off with the suspects.

'Put the weapons down,' Will ordered as he went in.

The suspects turned around, they could see that they were now outnumbered and decided to give up and lowered their weapons. Fremont and Stanson took them and made them safe.

'Control, this is alpha team we are all clear.'

'Received alpha team.'

Will walked over to Kathy and smiled at her.

'Well done, Sergeant.'

Kathy nodded, and as the PD came in to take the suspects into custody, the teams walked back to the truck and cars. Just then, Captain Ashborne appeared.

'Good work, Sergeant, I thought I would come down, and see just how you guys' work.'

'Thanks, Captain, but it isn't always that easy.'

'Well, I am glad I saw it anyway, maybe I will attend a few more, to get a real sense of how things work.'

'As long as you attend and not shadow, I don't care, Captain.'

'Fair enough, see you all back at the office.'

***

When they got back to the office, Gina was sat in Kathy's office waiting for her, they left and headed to the ladies' room. Will saw them leave and wondered what was going on. In the ladies' room, Kathy did the test in silence and then she and Gina stood waiting without saying a word at all. After a few minutes, Kathy looked at the test.

'Oh shit, it's positive.'

Chapter 5

Kathy and Gina stood looking at the test for a minute in complete stunned silence. Gina put her hand on Kathy's.

'What now?' Gina asked.

'I have no idea,' Kathy replied.

'Well, maybe see a doctor to be sure.'

'Yeah, that's a good idea.' Kathy was still staring at the test.

'Do you want me to call?'

Kathy nodded. Gina walked to the other end of the ladies' room and Kathy could hear her talking to the receptionist. She slid down the wall and was sat on the floor, tears started to roll down her cheeks and she started shaking. When Gina was done, she rushed over.

'Are you OK?' she asked as she crouched in front of her. 'I got you in Monday morning, it's the first they had.'

Kathy nodded.

'Probably better on Monday as Will is at work.'

Gina leaned forward and hugged her, and she held her for a few moments.

'I best go before Will notices how long I've been gone.'

Gina helped her up and she washed her face and took a deep breath. They left the ladies' room and hugged.

'If you need me, just shout, OK?'

'OK, thank you.'

Kathy went straight into her office without looking at or speaking to anyone. A few minutes later Will walked in her office.

'Hey where did you go? I turned round and you weren't there.'

'Just talking to Gina if that's OK.'

'Yeah, of course, I was just asking.'

'I'm sorry, I'm just really tired.'

'Well tomorrow you can sleep in all you want.'

'That sounds good to me.'

***

All the team were on the terrace, Will had heaters out for the winter months and part of it could be covered which made it quite cosy. the team were sat around talking as they ate. Will explained what Captain Bridge had said to him and the goings on of the last two days.

'So we keep our eyes and ears open and protect our unit.'

'And her team arrive on Monday?'

'Yeah, Palmer, they do, so be on your guard, they could be very well trying to take our jobs.'

'We will help you, Sergeant. Captain Bridge always has our back, we will gladly watch his,' Bennett stated.

They were eating and drinking so long they decided against watching a movie. Kathy was stood talking to Selena and Lynne, she enjoyed their company, the guys could get carried away and it was more her type of conversation outside of work. Suddenly she felt sick and ran off through to her and Will's bathroom. Selena and Lynne followed quickly, they found her being sick. Selena leaned down and held back her hair and Lynne went back to the bedroom door to watch out for Will coming. When she was done, Selena passed her a cloth for her face.

'So how many weeks are you?'

'What?'

'You're pregnant, right?'

Kathy didn't know what to say.

'Sweetheart, I have three children, you think I don't know the signs?'

'I don't know, I only did a test today, I have a doctor's appointment on Monday.'

'I am taking it Will doesn't know.'

'Not yet, I wanted to see the doctor first.'

'OK, so do you need someone to come with you to your appointment?'

'Really, you don't mind? I was nervous about going alone.'

'Of course, just let me know when and where and I will be there.'

'Will's coming,' Lynne shouted.

Kathy got up and washed her face and mouth, she followed Selena out of the bathroom to find Will in the bedroom talking to Lynne.

'Hey, are you OK?' he said as he walked over to Kathy.

'Yeah, fine, just feel a bit off, that's all, probably tired.'

'OK, well the guys are all leaving now, so we can go to bed.'

'OK, sweetheart, we will see you soon and get some rest,' Selena said and then her and Lynne headed for the door.

Will saw everyone downstairs, Kathy went into the kitchen and made some tea, she sat on the sofa and when Will got back upstairs, he sat next to her.

'You should have said you felt ill.'

'I'm OK really, I had a good evening and didn't want to spoil it.'

'OK, well, finish your tea and we can head to bed and you can have a good rest tomorrow.'

***

Monday morning, Will was up and ready when Kathy came out of the bedroom, she went into the kitchen and Will poured her a coffee.

'Good morning,' he said giving her a kiss and handing her the coffee.

'Morning, listen I'm not going straight in I forgot to tell you I have an appointment at nine a.m.'

'An appointment?'

'Yeah, just a check-up is all.'

'You have a doctor's appointment and you didn't tell me.'

'It's my female check-up, nothing serious, it completely slipped my mind is all, and these things are routine.'

'Oh, OK, do you need me to sort you out a cab?'

'No, it's OK, you get going.'

'OK, see you soon.' He kissed her and left.

Kathy exhaled deeply. How was she going to tell him?

***

Kathy and Selena were sat in the doctor's office waiting for the doctor to come back in. They sat quietly for a few moments, then she came in.

'Well Kathy looking at the test results and the scan, you are pregnant, and you are eight weeks.'

Kathy couldn't stop the tears from rolling down her cheeks, the doctor handed her a tissue.

'I am guessing this wasn't planned.'

'No, I haven't even told my fiancé yet, what do I do now?'

'Well, if you intend on continuing with the pregnancy, we will need to see you again in about four weeks.'

Kathy looked at Selena then back at the doctor and nodded.

'If you need anything before then just come in or give me a call and I will answer any questions you may have.'

'OK, thanks.'

They stood and left the doctor's, they walked down the block to Selena's car.

'You want a lift?'

'Yeah, thanks.'

They got in and Selena turned to Kathy.

'Are you OK?'

'Yeah, still in shock I think.'

'So what are you going to do?'

'Now I have to tell Will and see what he wants to do I guess.'

'How do you think he will react?'

'I have no clue, he said he wanted kids one day, but neither of us was planning this now.'

'Well, you let me know if you need anything.'

Chapter 6

When Kathy got back to the office, she went straight in to see Gina.

'Hey how did it go?' Gina asked quietly and pulled her into an empty office.

'OK.'

'What did they say?'

'I'm eight weeks, and I need to go back in four.'

'So you are definitely keeping it then?'

'Yeah,' she smiled. 'I was thinking about it and I am really happy about this, the timing isn't great, but when is it ever? I will do it alone if I need to, but I really hope I don't but then I really don't know how Will is going to react.'

'So when are you telling him?'

'Tonight, I just want to get it over with.'

'Oh, my goodness, I am so happy for you.' She gave her a big hug. 'But you best get back to work, because the teams are on their way back.'

'See you later.'

Kathy went into the office, there were six officers sat at the on-call desks, she didn't recognise them. She got a coffee, and Captain Ashborne walked over to her, with one of the officers.

'Sergeant Hill, I would like you to meet my alpha team from Detroit, this is the team leader, Sergeant Sutton.'

'Hi,' she said.

'And good morning to you,' he replied in a flirtatious manner.

'Sergeant Sutton and his team will be here for a week or so to observe.'

'Yes, Sergeant Falco said.'

'Of course he did.'

Kathy went into her office with her coffee, just then alpha and bravo came back in from a call.

'Sergeant Falco,' Captain Ashborne called.

He walked over to her.

'This is Sergeant Sutton and his team, my alpha team from Detroit.'

Will looked at him for a moment, he was quite tall nearly six feet, he was broad but wasn't muscular like Will. He had a thin face though and had dark hair that was going grey.

'OK, is that it'? Will said, obviously unimpressed.

Will then walked off and went into his office. Tom and Harvey tried not to laugh as he did so, Captain Ashborne looked furious. She walked off back into her office.

Kathy came out of her office a moment later, she went over to Fremont to have a chat about the call. Sergeant Sutton walked over to Kathy, as she turned round to face him, he was extremely close to her. Will saw him from his office and got up and moved to his doorway.

'So what do you say you and I go for a drink later,' he touched her arm.

'Sorry, I'm busy.' She turned away.

He put his hand on her backside.

'Come on, sweetheart, I promise we will have fun.'

'I said no,' Kathy said and walked off into her office.

Will walked over to Sutton and got really close before he spoke.

'I see you touch a female officer like that again and we are going to have more than a problem.'

He then went into Kathy's office and shut the door.

'I don't know how anyone gets anything done with her walking around.'

Stanson stood up and went over to him.

'What? That's one of our sergeants you are talking about.'

Tom came over and whispered something to Stanson, he sat back down, and Tom stood in front of Sutton.

'Listen, if you know what is good for you, you will stay away from Sergeant Hill. As you can see, we won't allow anyone to disrespect her at all, and she is engaged to Sergeant Falco and believe me when I say you really don't want to piss him off.'

'They're engaged?'

'Yeah, so why don't you go and sit down and wait for delta team, they will be in soon.'

'Delta team?'

'Yeah, you are shadowing charlie and delta teams.'

Sutton walked off and went straight into the captain's office.

***

'You OK?' Will asked as he sat on the edge of her desk.

'Yeah, guys like that don't bother me any more, I have been on the force too long.'

'How did it go at the doctor's?'

'Yeah, good, we aren't doing anything tonight are we?'

'No, except relaxing with a beer on the sofa.'

'Good, I need to talk to you.'

'Really, sounds intriguing.' He pulled her closer and kissed her. 'Why can't you tell me now?'

'Because we are at work.'

'OK.' He kissed her again. 'I best get my report done.' He got up and went to the door. 'You aren't dumping me though, right?'

'No, of course not, now go and get some work done.'

He left, and just as he was about to go in his office, Sergeant Sutton and Captain Ashborne stopped him.

'Why won't you let us shadow you and your team?' Sutton asked.

'I came to an understanding with your captain on Friday.'

'Which was?'

'You shadow charlie and delta.'

'But you hadn't even met us then.'

'And now I have, believe me, I haven't changed my mind.'

'You do realise that we are alpha too right?'

'Yeah, but that's in Detroit and I run alpha team here.'

'But it's the captain's choice on who we shadow not yours.'

'Till she bet she could beat me on the range and lost.'

Sutton looked at Captain Ashborne and then back at Will.

'Sergeant Falco, why don't you let them shadow you for just one call out?' she suggested.

Falco looked at her for a moment, she was trying to get out of their agreement. He looked at Sutton.

'No one shadows my team, they get in the way, but what I will do is let you take our next call, if you pull it off then I will reconsider.'

'Deal, piece of cake,' Sutton said smugly.

'Captain, is that OK with you?'

'Yes, of course, I trust my team, they are more than capable of handling a call.'

Just then Will's radio went.

'Control to alpha team.'

'Go for alpha.'

'We have a hostage situation at a store on Madison Avenue.'

'Control, on Captain Ashborne's orders, the alpha team from Detroit will be taking this one. Call sign, delta alpha.'

'Received alpha team.'

Captain Ashborne handed Sutton a radio.

'Control to delta alpha.'

'Go ahead control.'

'We have a hostage situation at a store on Madison Avenue.'

'Show us attending.'

'Received.'

Sergeant Sutton signalled his team and they left. Captain Ashborne went into her office, smiling. Tom came over to Will and they went into his office.

'Was that a good idea Will?'

'Just wait, and you will see, Tom, I'm not having them anywhere near alpha and bravo and this will put an end to it all.'

'If you are sure?'

'If I'm not right, then I will give you all a job,' Will joked.

***

About an hour later Sergeant Sutton and his team walked back in, heads down, not so confident as when they had left. Will watched them as they sat down, he was sat talking to Tom at Tom's desk, he had a gut feeling that he had been right and they had messed up. Five minutes later, the chief walked in, it was rare that he ever came over to their offices.

'Falco, Sutton, join me in the captain's office would you,' he shouted.

Will got up and followed and so did Sutton. The door was closed behind them. The teams looked at each other, wondering what was going on.

'Captain Ashborne, why did you authorise for your team to attend a call alone, that was an alpha call?'

'Chief, they are an alpha team and more than capable.'

'Capable, is that a joke?' he shouted.

'No, sir.' She looked at Sutton questioningly.

'Your alpha team who are so capable, just shot and injured five hostages, my on-call teams are better than that.'

Will couldn't believe what he was hearing and was visibly shocked.

'Falco and his team haven't injured or killed a hostage in over four years now. I don't expect your team to answer another call and they are to stay with charlie and delta. Who knows, they might learn something, like how to aim. I am starting to see why your unit is down at the bottom of the pile, Captain.'

'But Sir.'

'But nothing, Captain, this is my city and I expect better.' He turned to Will. 'Can I have a word with you in your office, Sergeant.'

'Yes, Sir.'

They left and went into Will's office under the eyes of the teams. The chief shut the door behind them.

'I have a feeling that you instigated all this, Falco.'

'It was more of a suggestion really, sir.'

'And they fell for it because it's all their egos would allow them to do.'

'Something like that.'

'A dangerous game, Falco, even for you, but it stops them taking over your place in the unit which I am guessing was the point.'

'Yes, it was, Chief, was just looking out for the unit.'

'But now I have a problem, five injured and possible lawsuits.'

'Yeah, I didn't think they would hit five hostages, but consider it taken care of.'

'Good, and if there are any more issues, let me know.'

'Yes, Chief.'

The chief left and Will walked across the office to get another coffee. He needed one after that. Tom walked over to him.

'Well?'

'They shot five hostages, and we are free and clear of them shadowing us.'

'Five hostages, shit that's bad.'

'Yeah, just a bit and now I have some phone calls to make to prevent any lawsuits.'

'What? Why?'

'Request from the chief, as it was my idea.'

'Fair enough, best let you get back to it then.'

Will took his coffee back into his office and shut the door.

Chapter 7

About an hour later, the teams got another call. Will came out of his office.

'Alpha and bravo let's go, we have armed suspects entering a warehouse.'

The teams left, they took the truck and a car to the scene. When they arrived, there was only one squad car who had cordoned off the street. The teams got ready and Will obtained what little information they had.

'OK, we don't have much information on this as it has just happened. Two armed men were seen going into the warehouse following another man who isn't armed. So we go in and search the whole place bit by bit, these guys may have gone but let's be vigilant. There is the main floor and some offices and back rooms, we don't know what this is so watch each other's back. Pair up, Stanson you're with me.'

They got into pairs and headed to the main door and split up and started to search the building. It was full of crates but there was space to walk in between them. Kathy was with Fremont. Suddenly Kathy was tackled to the ground by a man, she hit the ground hard. Fremont reacted instantly pulling the man off Kathy, and aiming at him.

'NYPD put your hands on your head.'

'You're police, oh thank God, I thought you were the two that were chasing me.'

'Alpha red, I need you at my location,' Fremont radioed through. 'We are on the third row.'

Will appeared after a few moments, he hadn't been far away. The man was sat on the floor handcuffed and Fremont was looking over Kathy.

'What the fuck happened?'

'This guy tackled Sergeant Hill to the floor, she hit the ground pretty hard, Sergeant.'

'I didn't know you were cops, I thought you were the ones who chased me in here.'

'Because armed men tend to wear police uniforms,' Freemont said.

'I was hiding, I just saw shadows and thought it's me or them.'

'Who are they?' Will asked him, standing over him.

'I don't know. I saw them shoot someone a few blocks away, they heard me and started chasing me, thought I could lose them in here.'

'Are they still here?'

'I think so, but I don't know.'

'OK, I have a plan. Fremont take Sergeant Hill outside sit her in the car.' He then radioed his team. 'Alpha team, the armed suspects may still be in the building, I am on the third row, five crates down, meet me here fast, bravo stay alert.'

Alpha team all headed to Will's location.

'OK, Tom and Harvey go a crate down left, Bennett and Palmer go one right, Stanson go opposite stay out of sight.'

They all got into position. Will sat the man on the floor with his feet showing, so the suspects would see him and walk right into Will's trap. It wasn't long before Will heard them coming, they prepared themselves.

'Hi there, you two are under arrest.'

They were about to run but the team surrounded them, so they gave up.

'Control, this is alpha team we are all clear, we need PD down here, there are reports of a shooting a few blocks away, so need some extra officers.'

'Received, alpha team, we have them on way to you now.'

They were cuffed when the PD arrived and their weapons secured and handed over for evidence. PD walked them out and took over the scene, both teams met at the truck. Will walked over to the car where Kathy was sat, Fremont was stood by the car door.

'Are you OK?' Will looked at her.

'I think so.'

'She hit the ground pretty hard, Sergeant.'

'OK, wait here,' Will said before walking over to Tom. 'I am going to the ER with Kathy, that guy tackled her pretty hard before, I am sure she is fine, but it shook her up.'

'No worries, hope she's OK.'

Will walked back to the car.

'Fremont, bravo is yours, take the sergeant's weapons back and book them in.' He turned to Kathy. 'I'm taking you down to the ER to get checked over.'

'OK,' she replied, a little surprised.

'Control, this is alpha, we are all clear. Officer Fremont has bravo team, I am on comms if required, I am taking Sergeant Hill to the ER for a check over.'

'Received, alpha team.'

Kathy got into the car, Will closed the door, and then got in the driver's side. As they set off, he glanced over at her, she looked a bit shaken but smiled at him, when she realised he kept glancing over.

'I'm fine Will.'

'I know, but he was a big guy and it's better to have you checked over.'

'He was a big guy, but ER is a bit unnecessary.'

'Then why agree to go?'

'Because I know you and I wasn't in the mood to argue.'

Kathy got a text from Gina.

What happened? Are you OK? I will come to the hospital now as just got off shift.

I will explain all when I see you, Kathy texted back.

Will pulled into a parking space and walked Kathy inside. He explained what had happened to the nurse, she took Kathy over to an examination room straight away. She stopped Will at the door.

'You need to stay out here with those,' she said, gesturing to his handguns.

A doctor went into Kathy's room and was in there for a while. Will paced up and down outside the room, he wasn't sure what could be taking so long if she were OK. After some time, the doctor came out.

'Hey, doctor, what's the prognosis?'

'You're her fiancé?'

'Yeah.'

'OK, she is a bit bruised and shaken up, we want to just monitor them for about an hour or so, but they will both be just fine.'

'I'm sorry?'

'Kathy and the baby, they will both be fine.' He smiled and walked away.

Will stood for a moment trying to take in what the doctor had just said. He sat down on a nearby seat for a few moments, then his radio went.

'Control to alpha team.'

'Go for alpha.'

'We have an armed suspect in a bar on 54th Street.'

'Received, we are en route.' He called Tom. 'Tom did you get that?'

'Yeah, we are on our way, will meet you there.'

Will hung up and then stood, he paused for a moment outside Kathy's door, then left without saying a word.

Chapter 8

Will arrived at the bar, Tom and the team were already there and ready. Will got out of the car and walked over to Tom. There was a lot of people around, many talking to PD, others watching what was happening.

'What we got Tom?'

'So there are two guys in the bar, armed and pointing them at each other.'

'What?'

'According to a witness one guy came in waving a handgun around, shouting at the owner, so the owner pulled out a shotgun from behind the bar. Everyone else got out, so the fact they were allowed suggests he was only after the bar owner.'

'OK, Tom and Stanson with me, rest of you watch the street.' They walked towards the door. 'Tom, stay by the door just inside, Stanson, you and me are going to have some fun, just follow my lead, let's see how fast we can get them to give up.'

They went through the door and the accounts were accurate. There was the owner behind the bar with a shotgun and another man on the other side of the bar with a handgun.

'NYPD put your weapons down and put your hands on your head,' Will said as he and Stanson moved forwards.

'I'm not putting it down till he does, he will shoot me if I do,' the bar owner stated.

'You slept with my wife,' shouted the other.

'This is over a woman, really?'

'She's my wife,' he shouted.

'So Stanson, they aren't complying, so what part do you want to go for today, shoulder, leg or head?'

'What?' the bar owner shouted.

'Well, you see, we take it in turns based on how it would appear to have gone down, you know for the reports, because our bosses don't like it when things don't look right to what our reports say.'

'But you can't do that.'

'Why not? So Stanson what do you think?'

'Well, we did the leg earlier, shoulder yesterday, and if we swap targets the angles would be perfect for a clear head shot.'

'Yeah, that's good, I think that would work, OK fire on my count one…'

'OK, OK we give up.' The bar owner put his shotgun on the bar and the other man put his next to it.

'Control, this is alpha team, we are all clear, send in PD.'

'Received, alpha team.'

Will went over and took the two weapons, made them safe and handed them to Stanson. PD came in and handcuffed them.

'You know, Stanson, I think that's a new record from stand-off to hands up, well played.'

'You weren't going to shoot us in the head?' one asked as they were led out.

'Probably not,' Will replied, smiling.

The three of them left and met the rest of the team at the truck. Will walked back to the car, he got in and took a deep breath and paused for a second, thinking about what the doctor said. They got back to the office, Tom got a coffee and Will went into his office and grabbed his stuff and went to leave.

'Tom I'm heading out, can you give Kathy a lift when she gets back from the hospital, I don't think she will be long now'

'Yeah, sure, what's going on?'

Will took Tom outside the office and made sure no one was around.

'I need to clear my head, think about some stuff.'

Tom looked at him, puzzled.

'Kathy's pregnant.'

'What? That's great, isn't it?'

'To be honest, I'm struggling to get my head round it, the doctor let it slip at the hospital, he thought I knew.'

'So you haven't spoken to Kathy?'

'No, I need to sort my head out before I do.'

'OK, I will take her home, and say hi to Ash for me.' Tom walked back into the office, smiling.

Will took his phone out and called Ashleigh. She was like a sister to him, their parents had been friends, so they had grown up together, she was a model and actress, but she was always there for Will and he for her.

'Hey, handsome,' she answered.

'Hey, can we meet?'

'Yeah, usual place in twenty minutes.'

There was a taxi waiting when Will pulled up on his motorcycle, he took off his helmet and went over to the taxi. Ashleigh got out, she was six feet, with long hair, which was dyed red for her latest movie instead of her natural chestnut, she had a perfect figure and big blue eyes. They hugged and she kissed Will on the cheek. They walked over to a nearby bench. It was a quiet spot by the river, they always met there to avoid the media and her fans.

'So, what's up?'

'Kathy's pregnant.'

'Really?' she said, excited. 'Wow that is so amazing, I'm going to be an auntie, so when is it due?'

Will sat quietly. She knew something was wrong.

'What's wrong? It is good news, right?'

'I don't know'

'Why not?'

'We only got engaged a few months ago, she said she was on the pill. We had talked about having kids in a few years, I mean she said she wanted to lead bravo for a while before all that, and I have been trying to work out if there was any chance she got pregnant before we got back together, but I don't think so, it's too long ago.'

'It is definitely too long ago, she would already be showing if she were that far along, and honestly I haven't met her, but I don't think she would cheat on you, so it has to be yours.'

'Yeah, that's the conclusion I came to, but it still doesn't explain it.'

'You know she probably didn't plan this right.'

'From what she said I don't think it was.'

'Sweetie, the pill isn't one hundred per cent you know, this can happen, or maybe she missed a day by accident or something. My friend, Amy, she was useless at remembering to take hers and ended up pregnant, you guys are always so busy with work, these things can happen.'

'Yeah, I guess so, it's just a shock.'

'But you want kids though, right?'

'Yeah, of course.'

'And if this had happened in a couple of years, when you two were married would you be happy?'

Will sat for a moment thinking and a smile appeared on his face.

'I would be ecstatic.'

'Then what does it matter that it's now if it's what you want anyway?'

'You're right, it doesn't matter, I love Kathy and I will love our baby so much.'

'OK so let's go shopping.'

'Shopping for what?'

'A few things for Kathy, that she's going to need over the next few months.'

***

When Kathy got back to the office, Tom was the only one there, the late teams had been called out, the officers from Detroit had gone for a drink and Captain Ashborne had just left for the day. Tom was drinking a coffee, he had done all his paperwork so was looking up some information online.

'Hey Tom, where's Will?'

'He had to go somewhere, asked me to wait and drive you home, said he would see you at home soon.'

'Oh, OK, just let me get changed and we can go.'

Kathy got changed and they left the office. She couldn't help but wonder why Will had disappeared, it wasn't like him to leave her at the office, she would have got Gina to wait if she had known, but she hadn't heard from Will since he had left the hospital.

'So how did the call go?'

'Good, Will tried a new approach and it worked.'

'A new approach?'

'Yeah, there was a stand-off in a bar, they gave up pretty quick though.'

'That's good, will have to ask him, when he gets home.'

They got in and drove all the way to Will's place without saying much at all. Tom pulled up by the door.

'Thanks for the lift, I will see you tomorrow.'

'Kathy, Will knows.'

'Knows what?'

'About the baby, the doctor said something at the hospital, he must have thought Will knew.'

'Shit, you're kidding, that's why he left and asked you to bring me home?'

'Yeah.'

'How did he take it?'

'I don't know, he said he needed to clear his head.'

'OK, thanks for telling me.'

'No problem, and Kathy, congratulations.'

'Thanks, see you tomorrow.' She smiled as she got out.

When she got upstairs, she sat on the sofa and put her hand on her stomach, she had been so unsure about what she wanted, but after going to the doctor she knew she wanted this baby. She had been terrified about how Will would react. When they got engaged, he said he hadn't even thought about kids, but she knew he wanted them. She was now sat overthinking about what would happen next, going over every scenario in her mind good ones but mostly bad and what she would do. She knew she could stay with Gina at her house if it went really badly, but she sat there hoping above all that he would want this baby as much as she did and they would be happy.

Chapter 9

Kathy was in the kitchen when Will got home, he walked in quietly and walked over to the kitchen, put down the bag and he held the biggest bunch of flowers he could find behind his back.

'Hey,' he said.

She jumped and turned round.

'Sorry, I didn't mean to make you jump?'

'Will, listen I...'

He gave her the flowers and smiled.

'What are these for?'

'Because the woman I love is carrying my baby.' He stepped forwards to her and kissed her, he put the flowers on the counter next to her.

'So you're OK with this?'

'Couldn't be happier.'

He wrapped his arms around her and kissed her on the head.

'So how is Ashleigh? Can't believe I haven't met her yet.'

'She is fine,' he replied stepping back a little. 'Why do you ask?'

Kathy picked up the flowers, grabbed a vase and went to the sink to fill it up.

'Tom said you needed to clear your head and I am guessing you went to speak to her.'

'You know me too well it seems,' he smiled.

'I know who you trust and her and Tom are top of that list and I figured as Tom brought me home, you must have been talking to her.'

'Then you got it right, she also took me shopping.'

'Really, what for?'

'Mostly stuff for you.' He got the bag and started taking stuff out. 'Tablets for nausea, and you can take them when pregnant, we checked, some chocolates, some herbal tea, some luxury body cream and some comfortable pyjamas.'

'Wow, a pregnancy survival kit, you spoil me.'

'Are you mocking my gift?'

'No, I love it really.' She kissed him.

'And I got a book.'

'A book, what about?'

'Pregnancy, birth and babies.'

'Seriously?'

'Yeah, no need to be so surprised, I want to know it all and be there every single step.'

'Well, that is the sexiest thing you have ever said.'

'Really, shall we have an early night then?'

'I think that's an excellent idea.'

***

The next morning Kathy woke up, Will was already up and she could smell something good. She got up and went through to the kitchen, Will was cooking, she sat on a stool and watched him.

'Something smells good.'

'Well, you need to start eating more and better, so I made you scrambled egg on toast and a tea.'

'Tea, but I need my coffee.'

Will turned round and put them in front of her.

'The book says less caffeine, so tea here and you can keep your coffee at work till we tell people.'

Kathy started eating.

'Is it OK we don't say anything yet, I mean it's so early and I would rather wait till the captain is back.'

'Yeah, but you need to be more careful on calls, not like yesterday.'

'Bad luck was all that was, how often does that happen?'

'Well, I just think you need to start easing off a bit.'

'I'm not giving anyone reason to start speculating, we carry on as normal till the captain is back.'

'OK but…'

'No, buts Will.'

She carried on eating, Will moved behind her, and put his arms round her and put his hands on her belly.

'I just want you two to be safe.'

'I know and we will be, so stop worrying.'

***

They got to the office, they got changed and signed out their handguns, they went upstairs and into the office. Kathy got a coffee and poured Will one, she went into her office and Will followed. Captain Ashborne walked over and knocked on the door.

'Sergeant Hill are you OK after yesterday?'

'Yes, Captain I'm good.'

'OK that's good. Sergeant Falco I hear you have training sheets for different areas of training.'

'Yeah, I use them for my team, and Sergeant Hill has some for her team too.'

'Could I get a copy?'

'What for?'

'For my alpha team.'

Will looked at Kathy and then back at the captain.

'I'm not sure they will help, Captain.'

'No, and why not?'

'I tailor them for my team and Sergeant Hill's, takes me weeks to do them for each person, they are designed for individual needs based on their strengths and weaknesses.'

'Oh, I see,' she replied.

She walked off and back into her office.

'She didn't like that answer.'

'I don't care, it's not my job to train her team so they can take over here.'

'You really think that's what she wants?'

'Yeah, I do.'

'Fair enough, I trust your instinct.'

They heard the teams come into the office, they were chatting and getting coffee. Moments later the first call of the day came in.

'OK, we have an armed suspect at a school, hostages too so let's go.'

Both teams headed out and they took the truck and a car. When they arrived at the scene, Will went and got the information while the teams got ready. There was a lot of police and children huddled together with teachers trying to organise them, the whole scene was quite chaotic as so many school shootings were.

'OK we have a teenager with multiple weapons in an upstairs classroom, he has a classroom full of students as hostages, so here is how we will do this. Tom and Sergeant Hill, I need you on the roof opposite for sniper cover in case we can't end this any other way. Fremont you will take bravo team and clear classrooms on the right side of the building on the upper floor, just keep in mind if you find anyone, they are likely to be scared. Alpha, we take the left, get people out then we will be going in if we can, let's do this right and get those kids out alive.'

Kathy got her sniper as did Tom and she quietly followed him up the stairs. She was furious with Will, but she had a job to do. The others headed to the front door of the school, Will and alpha made their way down the corridor checking classrooms as they went. They got to the one he was in, Will glanced through and stepped back again. He signalled to Stanson where he was and that the door was clear.

'Green and purple do you have a clear shot?' Will radioed.

'Negative.'

'Received.' He signalled to the others that he would go in with Stanson, Harvey would take the door and Bennett and Palmer would cover the corridor.

Harvey kicked open the door, there were screams and squeals as Will and Stanson went in. Harvey stayed at the door aimed at the suspect.

'NYPD put your weapons down on the ground and your hands on your head,' Will shouted.

'Well, well, the pigs are here to save you all, or maybe these ones will bleed alongside you instead.'

'Put your weapons down,' Will insisted.

'Now why should I do that, way I see it I have all these hostages and so you won't fire, because you might hit one of them.'

'I will shoot you if you don't put them down and I haven't hit a hostage in years.'

'So you say but you might have a bad day today, you pigs are always shooting and killing people like me, and like these kids here, and then you make up some bull shit about what we did.'

'I don't want to kill anyone, but if you don't lower your weapon, I will fire.'

He pointed one weapon at a student and one at Will.

'Choices on who to shoot, perhaps both, because that sounds like fun.'

Will fired, hitting the suspect in the shoulder, he fell to the ground dropping his weapons as he did so. Will went over to him and kicked them towards Stanson, who collected them and made them safe. Will stayed aimed at the suspect on the floor.

'Control, we are all clear, we need EMTs and PD for the suspect and PD for the hostages.'

'Received alpha, they are on their way to you now.'

It seemed to take a while for the PD to arrive, Will looked down at the suspect on the floor.

'Told you I wouldn't hit them, and that I didn't want to kill you, all cops aren't bad you know.'

'You're the first I have met that isn't.'

'Well, I am one of many, and it's shit you haven't met better till now'

PD arrived and started to escort the hostages out, then Will got the suspect to his feet and he was escorted out. The teams headed back to the truck. Kathy got in the car without speaking at all, they packed up and went back to the office. Will grabbed a coffee and headed into his office, Kathy followed slamming the door behind her.

'What the fuck was that?'

'What?'

'Sticking me on the fucking roof, we decided this morning I would carry on as normal then you stick me on sniper cover, really?'

'Hang on a minute.'

'No, Will, pull that shit again and we are going to have a serious problem.'

She stormed out and went into her own office, Will followed, and slammed the door behind him. The team sat watching, a bit shocked as to what was going on, they had never argued like this before at work.

'What, so I don't get my say on this?' he shouted.

She turned round and looked at him, arms folded.

'I didn't put you on that roof to keep you out of the way, I put you there because in a room full of students as hostages, there are only three people I trust to make that shot. Me, you, and Tom, and as I had to go in that left you and Tom. Bravo team were clearing classrooms at the other end of the school, not exactly in the line of fire. I would never disrespect you, to do that for anything but professional reasons and I can't believe you think that I would.'

He walked out and left the office, Captain Ashborne watched as he did so. No one heard what was said just raised voices and doors slamming. Captain Ashborne left the office and found him in the gym. He was punching the bag. He had taken off his shirt. She took a deep breath as she walked over, she found herself attracted to him which made her extremely uncomfortable. He glanced across as she approached but continued with what he was doing.

'I thought you and Sergeant Hill kept it professional at work.'

'We do.'

'Really, because that sounded like a domestic to me.'

'It was a disagreement over the last call out is all, nothing personal.'

'Do you do that often?'

'No, we don't.'

'If you say so, Sergeant, but any more of those and I may have to put Sergeant Hill on another shift.'

'Is that all you wanted, Captain? Because I prefer to work out without an audience.'

She walked off, smiling.

***

Tom went in to see Kathy, he closed the door behind him and went over to the desk, she was standing looking out of the window.

'You, OK?' Tom asked.

'Yeah, fine, but can I ask you something?'

'Sure.'

She turned around to face him.

'If you were Will on that last call, who would you have put on the roof?'

'Honestly, me and you.'

'Why?'

'With a class full of students, I would want two damn good snipers up there with the experience to pull it off.'

'Shit.'

'What's wrong?'

'I had a go at Will over it, thought he had put me up there to protect me because of you know'

'That's what all the shouting was about?'

'Yeah.'

'Well, he is in the gym if you want to go and talk to him.'

Just then there was a knock, and Captain Ashborne walked in.

'Hargreaves, can you excuse us please.'

Tom left, closing the door behind him.

'Sergeant Hill, I don't like domestics disrupting my unit.'

'With all due respect, Captain, it wasn't a domestic, and this isn't your unit.'

'I would watch yourself, Sergeant,' she said as she left.

Kathy stood for a moment looking out of her window. She needed to apologise to Will, she shouldn't have gone off at him like that, even if she hadn't got his motives wrong, not with Captain Ashborne watching their every move. She went down to the gym, Will was still at it punching out all his anger.

'Come to shout at me some more.'

She walked over to him.

'No, I have come to apologise.'

Will stopped and looked at her, he was shirtless, and she felt her heart race as she looked at his perfect body as it glistened.

'I overreacted and I shouldn't question you and your decisions on a call.'

He got really close to her and she felt her heart pounding and her breathing quickened.

'Apology accepted.'

He leaned down and kissed her and she responded, she pulled him closer and then stopped herself and stepped back.

'I have to go,' she said quickly.

'Why?'

'Because if I stay here, with you like that we will get into trouble.'

'Really?' he smiled flirtatiously.

'Will, I'm serious, I have to go.'

She left really quickly and took out her phone, she dialled.

'Selena, I have a problem.'

'I'm on my way.'

***

Ten minutes later Selena walked into the garage, Kathy had been pacing up and down.

'Hey what's up?'

They went outside to talk.

'This is a bit embarrassing.'

'Sweetheart, don't sweat it what's wrong?'

'I was in the gym before, Will was there working out, and I could seriously have you know, please tell me this is normal.'

'Oh yeah, it's normal, some women only get really horny in the second trimester, me I jumped on Dan nearly every day.'

'OK so what do I do?'

'Have you spoken to Will?'

'No.'

'Where is he?'

'In the gym.'

'OK I will sort this.'

She walked off before Kathy could stop her, she went straight into the gym, Will was just finishing up.

'Selena what are you doing here?'

'Kathy called.'

'Why? Is she OK?'

'She has a small issue and you are not helping.'

Will sat and gestured to Selena to sit next to him. He had a drink and wiped himself down with a towel, she sat watching him for a moment before she continued.

'See she is experiencing a lot of hormonal changes, that means heightened emotions, but it also means she is feeling horny a lot.'

'What? That's why she left before?'

'Yeah, she was ready to jump on you.'

Will looked at her.

'Will, you are a hot piece of ass, let's just say it as it is and you half naked, working out and getting all sweaty, would make most women horny, but a pregnant woman, like a red rag to a bull, honey.'

'OK, so what do I do?'

'Just don't be all touching and kissing her when you are at work, and keep away from her when you are down here working out and most importantly make sure you have plenty of sex at home.'

'What?'

'Come on, Will, don't get embarrassed about it, just keep her satisfied and she should be OK, I have heard all about you in the bedroom, Will, so I know you are more than capable of that.'

'OK, thanks, I think.'

'Right, I'm going, got to pick the kids up.'

With that she left, Will got his stuff, and went back upstairs, he got a clean shirt and put it on before he went into his office. Kathy appeared with a coffee for him, she went in and closed the door.

'Did Selena see you?'

'Yeah, bit of an uncomfortable conversation, but I get what she was saying.'

'Good, I would have talked to you, but I wasn't quite sure how to put it.'

'Yeah, well Selena definitely doesn't have any problems with that.'

'Yeah, I have noticed, I best get back to my reports.'

Will got up and wrapped his arms around her, he held her for a moment before he stood back and looked at her, he took her hands and smiled.

'This is going to be an interesting road.'

'It sure is.'

Chapter 10

The rest of the week was so busy the teams hardly had time to write their reports. Late nights and awfully long days had taken its toll on Kathy, on Sunday she slept for most of it. When Monday came around, she would rather have stayed home but she got up when her alarm went off. Will was in the kitchen, she came out and her breakfast and tea were ready for her.

'Morning, sleep well?'

'Yeah, did you?'

'Pretty well, now eat up because we have to go soon.'

'You say that every morning,' she smiled, 'and we are never late.'

'And I don't want to start.'

She ate then went and got ready. He was by the door waiting. She stopped right in front of him.

'What?'

'Nothing, I'm just thinking how lucky I am and how sexy you look today.'

'OK shall we go,' he smiled.

They left and got in the elevator.

'I was thinking we should start looking for a car for you soon.'

'Why?'

'Because I reckon in a month or so you will be better in a car and more comfortable.'

'Yeah, I guess so, can we not just use yours.'

'No, you will need a bigger one anyway when the baby comes, and I will still use the bike.'

'Why?'

'Because we may be working different hours when you are at a desk.'

'Never thought of that.'

'Well, we will know more in a couple of weeks when the captain is back.'

***

They arrived at the office, they got changed. As Will was about to put his shirt on, Kathy put her arms around him, he turned round, and she kissed him.

'You, Sergeant Hill are going to get me in trouble one day, now can I get dressed because the teams will be walking in any minute.'

'OK, I will save that for later,' she smiled.

They walked into the office, Sergeant Sutton was getting coffee. Kathy went to make one for her and Will, and Will went into his office.

'Hey beautiful, changed your mind about that drink yet?'

'No, and I'm not going to.'

'Let me guess, the uptight boyfriend won't let you.'

'On the contrary, I just don't want to.'

'Why? We could have some real fun.'

'That I doubt.'

'I bet you don't even know what fun is with that guy.'

'I guess it depends what you call fun.'

'Lots of alcohol, then probably bedroom type fun.'

'Wow you really are a sleaze.'

Just then Stanson walked in, and saw Sutton getting a bit close to Kathy.

'Sergeant Hill, why don't you go in your office and I will bring your coffee in.'

'Thanks, Stanson. Sergeant Falco will have one too.'

'No, problem.'

Kathy walked off to her office, Stanson got closer to Sutton.

'You got your coffee, now piss off back to your team.'

Sutton walked off, Stanson got the coffee, he took Kathy's then Will's.

'Stanson, where's Kathy?'

'In her office, Sutton was hitting on her so I told her I would make the coffees.'

Will stood up.

'I will fucking kill him.'

Stanson stopped him.

'He's not worth it, Sergeant, he wants your job, you going at him will only help him.'

'You're right, so let's ruin him.'

'How?'

'Us against them, in the gym, then on the range he won't say no because his ego won't let him.'

'Sounds good, we can easily take them, half of them can barely run.'

'And we know they can't outshoot us.'

Will walked out of his office and over to Sergeant Sutton. The rest of the teams were just walking in, they got their coffees and watched Will, they knew something was going on.

'What do you say to a little competition, Sutton?'

'What kind of competition?'

'A bit of circuit training and a shoot on the range, your team against mine.'

'What's the catch?'

'Nothing, just straight up contest.'

'OK, you're on.'

'Bravo team can judge the gym race and your captain can judge the shoot.'

'Sounds fair, let's go.'

Will told the rest of the team what the plan was, they were all in agreement and they headed down to the gym. Kathy and her team followed, she pulled Will to one side by the door of the gym.

'I'm not sure I should be here for this.'

'Why not?'

'The issue I have, and a bunch of men especially you getting all competitive is not good for me and you know that.'

'But I kind of need you to help with the times.'

'Can't Fremont do it?'

'You really want to miss us wiping the floor with these guys?'

'No, but don't blame me when I get all excited and jump on you after.'

'I won't.' He walked off laughing.

Will walked over to Sutton.

'OK, twenty push-ups, twenty sit-ups, twenty step-ups, and climb the rope to the top.'

'That's not much.'

'Well, you should beat us then, one from each team at a time, you can pair them up too.'

'As long as I am paired with you, I don't care.'

Sutton got the teams paired up, alpha smashed every single race especially Tom and Stanson. Then it was Will's turn, he took off his guns and his shirt. Sergeant Sutton looked at him, he wasn't fat, but he didn't match up to Will. Will beat him easily, Sutton had barely finished the sit-ups when Will was done. Will stood next to Kathy and had a drink of water, they watched Sutton finish.

'Full house for alpha, so meet on the range in twenty minutes unless you want to give up now.'

'Twenty minutes,' he replied out of breath.

Will walked out and Kathy followed. He went into the locker room upstairs, she followed and shut the door. He was getting a clean shirt out, she walked up behind him and put her arms round him. He turned round, she kissed him, it was passionate and intense. He stopped her.

'Not a good idea.'

'Why, we have twenty minutes.'

He grabbed his shirt and started to walk towards the door, she stopped him and kissed him again. He reacted this time, and pushed her up against the wall, he kissed her neck, her hands were all over him, she wanted him. He picked her up and she wrapped her legs around him, his hands started to move up under her shirt, the kisses intensified.

Just then the door opened, Kathy jumped off him quickly as Bennett stuck his head around the door.

'Shit, sorry, Sergeant, but the range is ready.'

'Be there in a minute, Bennett.'

He left quickly. Kathy looked at Will mischievously.

'Oopps sorry.'

'It's OK I know better,' he put his shirt on. He looked at Kathy and shook his head. 'It's probably a good job he came in when he did.'

He composed himself before he left.

Bennett was stood with the rest of alpha outside the range, they were stood away from the Detroit team.

'Seriously, if I had got there a few minutes later I swear they would have been having sex right there in the locker room.'

'No, way, Sergeant is a total professional,' Harvey said.

'You didn't see them, up against the wall her legs round him.'

'They were dressed though, right?' Palmer asked.

'He had no shirt on, and I didn't look close enough at Sergeant Hill.'

Just then Will arrived, they all went quiet, Will looked at them curiously.

'We ready?'

'Yes, Sergeant,' Bennett answered.

They all went in, but Tom stopped Will at the door when the others had gone in.

'Getting it on in the locker room now?'

'Bennett mentioned it.'

'Yeah, what the hell if that had been the captain.'

'I know, I don't need a lecture, Tom.'

'Then what were you thinking?'

'It's Kathy, since getting pregnant, she has been excessively horny.'

'Excessively?'

'Yeah, like she is wanting it all the time especially it seems when I am half dressed.'

'I wouldn't be complaining.'

'I'm not, well not till what just happened anyway, she is all over me every time we are alone, but I will deal with that later. Now let's go kill these guys.'

'Yeah, let's do it.'

They walked onto the range and the teams were waiting. Will walked over to Sutton.

'Everyone gets two targets, the first is a one-shot target, the other is a standard one, name and sign each one before giving them to me and we will see who is better.'

They all took their turns and Will collected his team's. He named and signed them all, he was happy his team was as good as always. He collected the others and looked at them, he was surprised by how bad they were, he took them upstairs and scanned them into his computer then took them to Captain Ashborne.

'Captain, thought you might want to see these.' He handed her Sutton's team's targets, and gym times.

'What are these?'

'Your alpha team's times in the gym and targets, as you can see only one didn't hit the hostage.'

'You were training with them?'

'Sort of.'

'Would you like to elaborate, Sergeant?'

'We had a bit of a competition.'

'I see, who won?'

'My team.' He then handed her his team's targets and times, and smiled. 'They weren't even close.'

'I can see that, Sergeant.'

'Good news is I can maybe work out a training programme now, forward them to Detroit when they are done.'

'Thank you, Sergeant.'

Will left, leaving her to look over them. Suddenly there was a gunshot, it came from Kathy's office. Will ran over and opened the door. Kathy was standing in the corner by the filing cabinet pointing her handgun at Sergeant Sutton who was on the floor.

'Touch me again and I will put a bullet in your crotch.'

'She is fucking crazy,' Sutton shouted.

Will went slowly over to Kathy, he put his hand on hers and she lowered the gun, then she handed it to him.

'Someone, get him out of here please,' Will shouted.

Harvey pulled him up and they left, closing the door. Will took Kathy round and sat her on her chair, she was shaking. He crouched in front of her.

'OK, what happened?'

'He came in, I was filing something, I turned around and saw it wasn't you. I asked what he wanted he said he wanted me. I said no, but he came right up to me and stroked my face then my arm, I froze.' A tear rolled down her cheek. 'Then he touched my breast and moved his hand across my stomach, he was about to undo my belt, then I thought of you and the baby and I snapped, I pushed him over, fired a shot into the ceiling and then you all came in.'

Will got up and went to the door, he opened it, and shouted to Tom.

'Get Kathy a coffee with plenty of sugar.'

Tom got it and gave it to Will, he closed the door again and came back to Kathy. He put the coffee on the desk and crouched in front of her again.

'Can you write it all down for me, but leave out the baby.'

'Yeah, but what are you going to do?'

'Don't you worry about that.'

Will left her office walked over to the captain's office. Sergeant Sutton was inside, he knocked and walked in.

'Sergeant Falco, Sergeant Sutton here was just on his way to apologise to you and Sergeant Hill.'

'Apologise, you think that's enough? He should be on the first flight home or charged with sexual assault.'

'Hey, it wasn't my fault she's been giving me the come on since I got here.'

'Really.' Will got right up to him. 'I doubt that.'

'Oh, come on, Falco, she slept with one of your team, she loves the attention and she wanted me.'

'That's why she said no and nearly shot you because she wanted you so bad.'

'All right enough you two,' Captain Ashborne shouted.

'You go near her again and you will have a bullet in your head.'

'Are you threatening me, Falco?'

Will walked to the door.

'Hell no, it's a fucking promise.'

Will walked out and across the office. He stopped at Tom's desk.

'I'm going out, but I'm on comms if you need me.'

He went into Kathy's office and got her report then walked out.

Chapter 11

Captain Ashborne shut the door after Will had left. She went back behind her desk and stood with her hands on her hips.

'What the hell were you thinking?'

'I was trying to win her over.'

'By sexually harassing her?'

'No, she wants me I can tell, but she is scared of that fiancé of hers.'

'If you have messed this up.'

'Come on, Captain, this lot can't stop our plan and you know it.'

'Really you think so, he showed me yours and your team's targets and times in the gym, and he will use them to embarrass you, you and your team weren't even close to his team, did you see his target, it's near perfect.'

'I'm not worried.'

'Well maybe you should be.'

'How were we supposed to know how good they were, I mean I heard rumours, but I have never known anyone like him, I would love to get hold of his training schedule, if I could we can be that good.'

'And how do you propose we do that, we know nothing about him, he has influence over the chief and I am not sure how to change that, I haven't been given access to his file and I have no clue why that is because I haven't had that problem before. I am guessing its contents are why he has such influence but I can't be sure, we now need him on side, and you upsetting him is doing nothing to help in the matter.'

'Relax, we will get this unit, Captain, one way, or another New York SWAT will be ours.'

'For your sake I hope you are right.'

***

Will had taken his motorcycle and rode over to the chief's office, he went up and was let straight in.

'Sergeant Falco, something else happened?'

'Yeah, you could say that, but it has just given us a reason to send Sergeant Sutton and his team home, get them out of our city for good.'

Will handed him Kathy's report. The chief sat back in his chair and read it, he put it on the desk when he was done.

'I'm surprised he's still alive, Sergeant, are you going soft?'

Will laughed.

'He nearly wasn't, believe me, but I want him gone and not land myself in trouble in the process if I can help it. This sends them home.'

'Yes, it does, Sergeant. Have you heard any more about what they are up to?'

'No, but I reckon she has to get me on side now, alpha had a little competition earlier in the gym and on the range, we destroyed them and I kept copies of everything. She knows I hold all the cards and once we have got rid of Sutton and his team she will have to try and get me to work with her, if she is after what I reckon she is.'

'What do you think she is after?'

'Taking over the unit permanently, has to be, there is no other reason to bring her team here to try and push my team out.'

The chief sat back in his chair and thought.

'I have called the chief in Detroit, he said she is ambitious and will step on anyone to get what she wants.'

'So how is she still on the force?'

'She got up the ranks pretty much unnoticed and didn't cause any issue, and now she has a loyal team to cover her back whenever she wants.'

'So why send her here?'

'He was wanting her to learn the job, to settle and improve in her unit but now it is obvious she has a different plan in mind but we need to be able to prove it before we can do anything.' He stood up and moved round his desk 'Falco can you get them out of here tonight.'

'Of course I can, if I can borrow your phone.'

'Go ahead.'

***

An hour later Will got back to the office. About five minutes later, the chief followed, he went straight into the captain's office without saying a word to anyone. There were raised voices and Will just leaned on the counter with a coffee in his hand, he was waiting for the next part. After a few minutes they came out. Captain Ashborne walked over to Sergeant Sutton, the chief stayed by her office door.

'Sergeant Sutton, you and your team are going home tonight.'

'What?' he said shocked.

'You are on the nine p.m. flight.'

'Why?'

'After what happened today, Sergeant? My hospitality has run out, and I want you out of my city,' the chief replied.

'But Captain.'

'I can't do anything now, go home and I will sort this,' she whispered to him.

She stood back.

'Charlie team will take you to your motel then the airport,' she continued.

'OK, come on guys, let's go.'

They all got up and headed to the door. Sergeant Sutton stopped by Will.

'This isn't over, Falco.'

'Actually, I believe it is.'

They left and Will went back into his office, he could hear the chief speaking to the captain. He heard the chief leave and then she threw something — this had really got to her.

Kathy and her team came back in from a call, she came to Will's door.

'Hey.'

'Hey, good shout?'

'Yeah, easy one, did you get what you wanted?'

'Yeah, Sergeant Sutton and his team are gone.'

'Really?' She came right in and shut the door. 'My hero, which means you get it all tonight.'

She sat on his desk, he got up and stood in front of her.

'That sounds good.' He leaned forwards and kissed her.

'OK unless you want me to get all hot again, I best go and write my report.'

He kissed her again, she pulled him closer and she started to lift his shirt, she ran her hands across his back. Then his beeper went off.

'That's just not fair.'

'Be back soon.' He left, and she went and got a coffee.

***

Will and his team arrived at an apartment block and they got out of the truck.

'Detective Park, how are you?'

'Good Falco, you?'

'Not bad, we still on for a drink on Saturday?'

'Yeah, for sure.'

'So what you got for us?'

'Armed suspect in a third-floor apartment, firing at anyone who gets close.'

'OK then, sounds fun, do you need him alive?'

'Preferably.'

'OK I will try, but can't promise if he shoots me.'

'Fair enough Falco,' he smiled.

Will and the team went up to the third floor, there were officers in the corridor either side of the suspect's door. Will slowly walked down towards them and signalled them to get back, they moved away and left the floor. Bennett and Palmer stayed at the top of the stairs, Stanson and Harvey went to the other side and kept everyone in their apartments. Will and Tom went to the door. Will considered for a moment what to do.

'NYPD, you need to put your weapons down,' he shouted.

The suspect fired at the door several times, they stayed clear till it stopped.

'How the hell are we going to do this?' Tom asked.

'We need the door open so we can see better.'

'Any ideas with how to do that?'

'How about I kick it open.' And Will did exactly that. The door opened but he started shooting again and one clipped Will.

'Damn it,' he shouted holding his side. He moved to the side.

It had caught his side just below his vest.

'You, OK?'

'Yeah, just a graze, you want to take a look.'

Tom glanced round, the shooting started again.

'OK, he's square on to the door about five foot eleven. You got this?'

'Hell yeah, he's mine.'

Will got ready, then quickly moved, firing two shots then moved to the other side of the door next to Tom. There was a loud thud, and no more gunfire. Will looked, the suspect was down on the floor. He slowly went in, followed by Tom, they kicked the weapons away. Will looked at him, he had one in the shoulder and one in the leg.

'Control, we are all clear, we need EMTs and PD for the suspect.'

'Received, we have PD en route to you.'

As the EMTs and PD arrived, Will went outside. Detective Park came over.

'Thank you, Falco.'

'No, worries,' Will replied holding his side.

'You, OK?'

'Yeah, just a graze.'

'So, is he dead?'

'No, but he is going to need a long hospital stay.'

'Well, you go get that checked, don't want you collapsing again.'

'Very funny, see you Saturday, Park.'

Will walked over to the other EMTs.

'Can you look at my side, he caught me.'

'Yeah, sure take off your vest, and lift up your shirt.'

Will did so and she had a look.

'It's just a graze, I will clean it and dress it and you are good to go.'

'Thanks.'

Tom walked over while she was dressing it.

'So you dying?'

'No, no thanks to you lot.'

'You kicked the door, how is that my fault?'

'Well, I didn't see you volunteering to do it.'

'So, what will Kathy say when she sees that?'

'Probably yell a little, but I'm sure it will be fine.'

After he was patched up, they got back in the truck and Will's radio went.

'Alpha team we have an officers need assistance at a warehouse near your location, can I tell them you are en route.'

'Yes, control we are on route.'

They arrived at the scene and Will headed over to the lieutenant in charge.

'Sergeant Falco, long time no see.'

'Lieutenant Walker, yeah it has been a while, how's your daughter?'

'She is good, engaged to a fireman actually.'

'That's good.'

'Yeah, it is, away from cops like you now.'

'She wasn't complaining two years ago.'

'I'm sorry.'

Will realised he didn't know.

'You slept with my daughter?' he shouted.

'Yeah, but that was a long time ago, Lieutenant.'

He walked right up to Will, he wasn't quite as tall.

'I should knock your head off right now you arrogant bastard.'

'That's not what your daughter thinks.'

Lieutenant Walker swung at Will, but he managed to duck. Two officers stepped in and Tom flew over to stop Will from doing anything stupid.

'Will, what the fuck is going on?'

'He tried to punch me.'

'Why?'

'You remember two years ago when I slept with his daughter, turns out he didn't know.'

'Well why don't you go and stand by the truck and I will get the info because we are here to do a job.'

Will walked away, smiling, and Tom got the information.

Chapter 12

When they got back to the office the shift was over, having another call on the way back. Will grabbed a coffee, when Captain Ashborne appeared at her door and gestured him to go over. He knew what this one was going to be about. He went over and closed the door.

'I just had a phone call saying you got in a fight with a Lieutenant Walker from 5th precinct.'

'Not a fight, he went to punch me, I moved, and I never hit him.'

'Why would a lieutenant want to punch you?'

'Does that matter?'

'Yes, especially if you want to report it.'

'Well, I don't, so can I go, because I have reports to write up?'

'OK, you can go, but I will find out what happened, one way or another, Sergeant.'

Will left her office and walked back over to Kathy's. He went in and sat on her desk as he always did, she finished what she was doing.

'How did it go?'

'They went fine but…'

'But what?' She moved in front of him and put her arms around him.

He flinched in pain as she caught his side. She noticed, then saw the bit of blood on his shirt, she lifted it up and saw the dressing.

'What the hell happened?'

'That was the but, the first call I kicked the door and…'

'You got shot.'

'No, it's just a graze.'

'Like that makes it any better.'

'It's fine didn't even need stitches and had two more calls, no issue.'

'Do you realise what would have happened had it been just an inch to the right.' She started pacing up and down.

'But it wasn't.'

'But it could have been, then what, Will? I can't lose you.'

'You're not going to, but I still have a job to do, just like you.'

'This isn't about me.'

'You think I don't worry about you every time you get a call, what if you had taken that call.'

'I wouldn't have been the one kicking the door open for a start.'

'OK, this is ridiculous.'

'So I'm ridiculous now?'

'That's not even what I said.' He went to the door and opened it. 'Tom, come in a here a minute, would you.'

'What's up?' Tom answered standing in the doorway.

'Could you explain to Kathy here that I had no choice in what I did, and I wasn't at risk during the first call.'

'Well, we needed the door open to see the suspect.'

'Is the suspect now in the morgue?'

'No, Will hit him in the leg and shoulder.'

'Why?'

'Because Park needed him alive,' Will said.

'So, Park is responsible for this?'

'No, Kathy, I did my job.' He pulled her close. 'Now can we drop this please?'

'OK but if this happens again, I won't be happy, you need to be more careful now.'

She kissed him, he reacted, and it started to get passionate.

'OK, that's my cue to leave, you two need to take more cold showers or something.'

Tom left and closed the door. Harvey came over to him, they moved away from the others.

'Can I ask you something, Tom?'

'Yeah, sure.'

'Sergeant Hill, is she expecting?'

'Why would you ask that?'

'When Selena was pregnant with our three, she was as horny as anything, couldn't get enough.'

'OK.'

'Well after what Bennett said this morning and them two as we speak got me wondering, I mean we all know Falco is always so professional, and Sergeant Hill well she is not the type for public displays of affection, so there has to be a reason.'

'All right, yes she is, but you can't say anything to anyone, we can't risk Captain Ashborne finding out.'

'I won't even tell Selena.'

'She already knows, so does Lynne.'

'What? How?'

'Women, mate, they tell each other everything.'

'Everything?'

'Yeah, how do you not know that her best friends will even know your score in bed.'

'No, way.'

'Yes, way and Kathy is part of that now, probably knows all our secrets, I can't believe you never knew this.'

'I guess I never paid that much attention to that, so you're saying Lynne and Selena will now hear all about Sergeant Falco too.'

'Yeah, probably, but they won't break the secrets they discuss.'

'Women.'

Harvey went back to his desk and put his stuff away. The others were packing away too, and they headed out to get changed. Tom thought about knocking on Kathy's office door but changed his mind and left. Ten minutes later, Will and Kathy came out of the office and looked around, but everyone was gone. Kathy smiled at Will.

'Shall we go home and carry on, Sergeant?'

'Yeah, but be gentle.'

Chapter 13

The next morning Kathy and Will were in her office having their coffees. Kathy had already started some paperwork, while Will sat and drank his coffee watching her, she looked up.

'What?'

'Nothing I just love looking at you.'

'Don't you have work to do?'

'Not before the shift starts I don't.'

'That is literally three minutes,' she said looking at the clock.

'Then I will start in three minutes.'

'You didn't finish your reports from yesterday.'

'I know, I will do them today, before I go home.'

'What did Captain Ashborne want you for yesterday at the end of shift?'

'Where did that come from?'

'I was just wondering.'

'Why not ask me last night at home?'

'Because I was deciding whether to ask or not.'

'She didn't want anything really.'

'Will, she didn't ask you in her office for nothing.'

They heard the teams arrive, right on time.

'I best get those reports started,' Will said and quickly left her office.

Will went to get another coffee and their beepers went off. It was just an alpha call, so bravo team got their coffees and sat down. Kathy wondered what he was hiding.

***

The call was at a second-hand shop, it was small and tucked away on a small street in a rough area. Will got out and headed over to the sergeant in charge. When he had the information, he headed back to the team.

'Not too tough this one, a disgruntled customer decided to go back with a gun, so Stanson and I go in, and Tom you cover the door.'

They approached the shopfront, and looked into the window, it was just one suspect and two people behind the counter as reported. He wasn't looking towards them, so they went to the door and went in.

'NYPD, put your weapon down on the ground and your hands on your head.'

The man looked back over his shoulder at Will.

'Not till I get my money back, they sold me a fake and I want my $300 back, but they won't give it me.'

Will looked at the couple behind the counter. He was five foot ten with grey hair and of slim build, she was around five foot five with dyed blonde hair and was quite heavy, they were both quite untidy looking.

'Is this true?' Will asked them.

'We don't give refunds,' she said.

Will handed his weapon to Stanson and walked over to the counter.

'Where's your sign to say that?'

'We don't have one,' she replied.

'OK, my officer and I are just going to stand by the door then.'

'What? You can't do that, he could shoot us.'

'You're right, but I'm thinking you owe him $300, so you could just pay up.'

No one, including Stanson, could quite believe what he said, but he stood there and did nothing else.

'You heard him, you owe me my money, now pay up before I fire.'

"You aren't going to stop him?' the male owner shouted.

'No.'

There was a tense few moments where a look of panic came across the faces of the owners, they looked at each other and then at the man.

'OK, we will give you the money,' she said.

They took the $300 out of the register and put it on the counter, the customer took it and Will walked over to him.

'I will take that though.' He referred to the handgun.

The customer handed it over and they headed towards the door.

'I will go first, so they don't shoot you, but you are free to go.'

'Thanks.'

'No, worries, I hate to see people get screwed over.'

They left the shop, Will shook his hand and he walked off. Will explained to the sergeant in charge that it was all a misunderstanding. As he was walking back to the truck, the female owner came out and walked over and approached him, as Will was putting his gear in the truck.

'Excuse me.'

'What?'

'Can I have your name please?'

'What for?'

'Because I want to inform your superiors about what just happened.'

'Which part?'

'That we were held at gunpoint and you did nothing.'

'Right and don't forget the part about you ripping people off.'

'We don't rip people off.'

'Really, $300 for a piece of glass in a ring.'

She turned and started walking away.

'And my name is Sergeant Falco,' he called after her.

***

Back at the office, Captain Ashborne was waiting for them to get back.

'Sergeant Falco, a word please.'

Will followed her to her office and closed the door behind them.

'Well, I just received a rather nasty call regarding you, Sergeant.'

'Really I can't think why.'

'Standing by and letting a suspect walk away with $300 I believe.'

'See that's not strictly true, I didn't intervene in a customer dispute, they ripped the guy off and wouldn't refund his money.'

'He had a gun.'

'Which he gave to me.'

'I really don't think that's relevant.'

'He wasn't dangerous.'

'Sergeant, you are reckless, and I will have to consider what to do about this.'

'OK, well when you have decided I will be in the gym.'

Will left her office and went over to Tom and Stanson.

'Tom, keep Kathy up here for a while, Stanson get ready, this could be it.'

Stanson left and Will followed. He knew Captain Ashborne wouldn't have a choice in trying to recruit him and this could very well be the opportunity for her to do so, because she was running out of time. Will was only in the gym about fifteen minutes when she appeared. She stood watching him for a few moments, he had his shirt off as usual.

'Can I help you, Captain, or did you just come to watch me work out?'

'As nice as that is, Sergeant, I wanted to speak with you.'

He stopped and looked at her.

'OK, I'm listening.'

'Well, Sergeant, I was thinking, I like New York and would like to stick around for a while.'

'So, what does that have to do with me?'

'I want to take over this unit and I want you to work with me.'

'And what makes you think I will do that?'

She got really close to him and ran her hands down his torso to his belt and started to undo it.

'Because, Sergeant, being on my team could bring you wonderful benefits.'

He grabbed her wrists.

'I'm not interested.'

'Don't worry, Sergeant Hill would never need to know, I know what that fight was about yesterday, sleeping with his daughter, I believe.'

'Firstly, that's none of your business. Secondly, being with Sergeant Hill is not why I'm not interested, I don't like you, I'm not attracted to you, and most importantly, I don't want you in charge of this unit.'

'Are you worried I will find out all your secrets Sergeant?' she said pulling her wrists out of his grip.

'No, I just don't think you are capable of doing the job.'

'Well, when your Captain doesn't come back, this unit will be mine, so with me or not, I will have it and if you're not with me, when I take over you and your team will be gone.'

She walked off and went back upstairs. Stanson came out from where he had been hiding, he had filmed the whole conversation.

'What did she mean he won't be coming back?'

'I don't know, but we need to get Captain Bridge out of Detroit today.'

Just then Kathy appeared. Stanson left and went upstairs. Kathy looked at Will in a suspicious way.

'What's going on?'

'Nothing, I was just working out.'

'Then why was Tom keeping me upstairs?'

Will paused for a moment trying to work out how to word it.

'Well,' she asked. 'You weren't just working out, were you?'

'No, Tom kept you upstairs because I knew you wouldn't like what I was doing.'

'Which was?'

'Letting the captain proposition me.'

'What? Tell me you are joking.'

'No, I needed to know what she was planning, and now I need to go and get Captain Bridge.'

'What did I miss?'

'I will fill you in when I get home tonight, but now I have to go.'

He kissed her on the head and left very quickly.

Chapter 14

That evening, Kathy was at home pacing up and down, as she had been all evening after she had had a shower, waiting for Will to get back. She hadn't eaten, she couldn't, she was too nervous, she hadn't heard from Will at all since he left the office. She had made up a story to tell Captain Ashborne about where they were, luckily, she had bought it. She heard the door open as she was making a drink, it was Will and Captain Bridge.

'Oh, my goodness, I've been so worried,' she said, going over and kissing Will.

'I see that.'

'Hi, Captain.'

'Sergeant Hill, your man did you proud today and he saved the unit.'

'So are you going to explain now.'

They went round to the sofas and sat down. Will sat and Kathy sat leaning against him and he put his arm around her, resting his hand on her stomach.

'It appears Captain Ashborne wanted to make the switch permanent, she brought her alpha team here to try and squeeze out Falco here. She didn't account for how good my alpha team is though. When her team got sent back, she planned something else, she tried to get

Falco on side, and she was planning something for me, but we don't know what yet.'

'So what now?'

'Well, there is a team sat at the captain's motel room to see what happens. The captain will be in the office when she arrives in the morning, and if she needs arresting, she will be, then,' Will answered.

'You know you would think this unit had been through enough this year, but the shit just keeps on coming.'

'When you are the best, Sergeant Hill, people will always target you.'

'Do you want me to show you to your room, Captain, so you can freshen up before we have food?'

'Thanks Falco, I appreciate the hospitality.'

Will showed the captain down the corridor to the last bedroom. He came back and Kathy was finishing making a drink. Will came up behind her and kissed the back of her neck.

'I am going for a shower, do you want to join me?'

'Will, not with the captain here.'

'I doubt he will come in our room.'

'No, now go and get a shower so we can eat, I am so hungry.'

***

As they were eating at the dining table, Will's phone rang, he answered but took it away from the table. He came back a few minutes later.

'Well, they caught Sergeant Sutton and two of his team at your motel room, Captain.'

'What were they doing?'

'Trying to smuggle a dead woman into the room and making it look as though you killed her.'

'Seriously?' Kathy exclaimed. 'That's really messed up, she wants the unit that badly.'

'Apparently so, two detectives are coming to arrest her in the morning.'

'Do they have evidence on her?'

'Sutton told them everything, they said.'

'Well, I think I need a good sleep before facing this in the morning. Thanks for all your help, Falco. Good night.'

'Good night, Captain.'

The captain took himself down to his room and all was quiet.

'So, do you want an early night too?'

'Can we sit on the sofa for a bit, I couldn't even contemplate sleeping right now.'

'I wasn't thinking of sleeping.'

'Will, I just need to relax a bit.'

'OK, I will clean up later.'

They sat on the sofa. Kathy was curled up and laying on Will. She laid there for a while but had to ask the question that had been bothering her all day.

'So, what did Captain Ashborne suggest in the gym?'

'She suggested that if I sided with her, I would get benefits from it.'

'What benefits?'

'Well, she ran her hands down my body and was undoing my belt at the time.'

'What the fuck!' She sat up and looked at him. 'And you just let her undo your pants.'

'No, I stopped her at my belt, then told her I wasn't interested.'

'Oh, OK good, I would hate to have to punch the bitch.'

Will smiled at her.

'What?'

'Nothing.'

'So, are you going to tell me what happened yesterday now or do you want to keep lying about that one.'

'What?'

'The reason she had you in the office, because if you don't tell me, she probably will tomorrow when they come and arrest her.'

'OK, you will just get mad though. A lieutenant from the 5th, tried to punch me.'

'Why?'

'Because I slept with his daughter.'

'And exactly when did you sleep with her?'

'Two years ago.'

'So why did he nearly punch you now?'

'He didn't know, he has always hated me, so I sort of wound him up about it.'

'I see.'

'He had told her to stay away from me, she made a different choice.'

'OK.' She seemed annoyed.

'This happened two years ago, Kathy, before we were together.'

'I know.'

'You're jealous.'

'No, I am mad you tried to hide it from me.'

'Well, you are beautiful when you are mad, can I take you to bed and make it up to you?'

'It had better be a good apology,' she smiled back.

***

The next morning, Captain Ashborne came in. As she got to the office she froze, eyes wide and was shocked that someone was sat at her desk, and Will was sat opposite. Captain Bridge stood and walked towards her.

'You must be Captain Ashborne.'

'Yeah, who are you?'

'Captain Bridge, thanks for keeping an eye on this place for me.'

'You are not supposed to be back yet.'

'Yes, but something urgent came up, so I came back early.'

'When did you leave Detroit? No one told me you were coming.'

'Yesterday, early afternoon.'

Captain Ashborne went very pale, then she saw two detectives coming across the office. She panicked and drew her handgun and aimed it right at them.

'Stop right there or I will shoot.'

'Captain Ashborne, that's not a good idea,' Will said.

'Why, Sergeant, are you going to shoot me?'

'No, but she might.'

Captain Ashborne felt a gun in her back — it was Kathy.

'Drop it. Captain or not, shooting you would come really easy.'

'Sergeant Hill, listen, your fiancé and I, it was all his idea.'

'I've seen the video and it was you undoing his belt, not the other way around.'

'Video?'

'Yeah, your little chat was recorded.'

Captain Ashborne closed her eyes for a moment then put her gun down. The detectives arrested her, and she looked at Will.

'You think you've won, but it's not over, Sergeant.'

They walked her out just as the teams were arriving.

'Can I have a word with you two please?'

'Sure, Captain,' Kathy answered.

Captain Bridge closed the door behind them and went round his desk and sat down.

'So I am presuming you two were going to tell me at some point.'

'About what, Captain?' Will asked confused.

'OK, I will ask you this, how many weeks are you, Sergeant Hill?'

Kathy and Will looked at each other and then back at the captain.

'Nearly ten, Captain.'

'Don't look so surprised you two, I am a police officer and there is nothing more telling than a future parent, a hand of protection on a stomach holding an unborn child.'

'I didn't realise I did that,' Kathy said.

'Not you, it was Falco.'

'Shit really?'

'Quite a few times actually. It's amazing how, when relaxed in our home, our behaviours change.'

'So what happens now, Captain?' Kathy asked.

'Well, I am going to have to think of some options for you and how we can keep you in the department. I will give you a couple of weeks to consider the options, does that sound fair?'

'Yes, Captain.'

'OK now get to work, and congratulations the both of you.'

They left and went over to Kathy's office. Will closed the door.

'I'm sorry I didn't realise I did that.'

'It's OK we were planning on telling him when he was back anyway, and we knew he would take me off active duty.'

'I guess so.'

'I just hope he has some decent options is all.'

Chapter 15

It was Kathy's last shift on active duty. It had been absolutely crazy, they had back-to-back call-outs for most of the day. They hadn't had time to tell the teams all day, so she and Will had invited both teams to Charlie's to make their announcement, to let them all know what changes were going to happen. They got the drinks in and everyone sat down.

'So we have asked everyone here because we have some news for you all,' Will started. 'It's going to affect you all, at work anyway.'

He put his arm around Kathy and smiled.

'We are going to have a baby.'

'Wow, that's great, Sergeant, but how does that affect all us?' Bennett asked.

'Because, as of now, I am off active duty till the baby arrives at least,' Kathy answered.

'So as of now, Tom will be leading bravo, and alpha will be getting Turner from the on-call teams,' Will said.

'Turner, as in the hot one?' Bennett asked.

'Well, she is the only female, so I'm guessing we are talking about the same person, Bennett.'

'Nice one.'

'You realise I don't allow relations within the team right.'

'Yeah, but I definitely don't mind being her partner.'

'Bennett, you need to find a girlfriend,' Stanson chipped in.

'Ryan, you haven't seen her, she is so hot, ask anyone.'

'OK, moving on, Sergeant Hill will still be in SWAT, but she will be in charge of dispatch and training to take some of the pressure off the captain and lieutenants.'

'That's good that you will still be around, Sergeant,' Fremont said.

'Yes, and I can keep track of your progress and training.'

'Don't you trust me with your team?' Tom joked.

'They couldn't be in safer hands.'

'Really?' Will said.

'Yes, really. Tom's more laid-back than you.'

Tom laughed, as did the rest of alpha.

'Always good to know what your other half thinks of you,' Will smiled. 'Just one other piece of news, because of the changes, I need a new number two, and that will be Stanson.'

'Really? But I'm the newest.'

'But ready for this, you are good and Tom and I have been checking you are ready these last few weeks, and you are.'

'Definitely and Stanson, good luck.' Tom started laughing.

Will went to buy another round at the bar, Stanson came over to him.

'You really think I'm ready to be your number two? I mean, Harvey is much more experienced than me.'

'Harvey is more experienced, but you are more number two material.'

Stanson looked surprised.

'Listen, Stanson, you are an amazing shot, you listen and learn all the time, you have progressed so much since you joined and you remind me of me when I joined SWAT. If you keep working hard you will have your own team one day for sure.'

'Wow, thanks, Sergeant. I won't do anything to let you down.'

'Good, now you want to help me with these drinks.'

They carried them over to the tables. Will sat down next to Kathy and they were all chatting, when Will was tapped on his shoulder. He turned round to see Lieutenant Walker's daughter stood there.

'Can I have a word please?' she said.

Will stood up, avoiding eye contact with Kathy, and they went over by the window so they couldn't be overheard.

'Leanne, what do you want?'

'You are really asking me that, it took me two weeks to find out what had gone on at work, for my dad to be suspended, and imagine my surprise when it involved you.'

'He was suspended?'

'Yeah, something about trying to punch you, and then he tells me that you had informed him we slept together.'

'I didn't know, he didn't know.'

'You think I would tell my dad that I had sex with you?'

'Leanne, it's two years ago, I didn't realise it would still be a problem, I mean I am engaged and so are you I hear, plus my fiancée is pregnant. We have both moved on, right.'

'Yeah, but can you please try and sort it out at work, so they let my dad go back?'

'OK, I can do that. I will have a chat with my captain on Monday.'

'Thanks. Well, I best go, and Will I won't forget the night we had, ever.'

She hugged him and kissed him on the cheek before she smiled and left. Will went back to his seat and everyone looked at him.

'What?'

'Who was that?'

'An old friend,' he brushed off.

Kathy was still wondering but the conversation moved on and they enjoyed the rest of the night. They went home earlier than the others. When they got home, they sat on the sofa.

'So who was she?'

'Who?'

'You know who, the woman tonight in Charlie's.'

'That was Leanne.'

Kathy was quiet for a moment.

'She's the lieutenant's daughter, isn't she?'

'Yeah, she wanted me to get her dad off suspension.'

'And why should you do that?'

'Why not, it wasn't just his fault, I was baiting him.'

'Of course you were, I don't know why I am surprised.'

'What's that supposed to mean?'

'Nothing, I think I am going to go to bed, I am exhausted, and we have the doctor's in the morning.'

Will got a strong drink and went out on to the terrace. It seemed that his past relationships were always going to interfere with this one.

***

Sunday morning, Kathy woke up early. Will was up earlier, and in the kitchen when she got up. He had her breakfast ready and her tea. She sat down and started to eat.

'So, today we are going to the doctor's, then we are going to get you a car and then a bit of Christmas shopping.'

'A car?'

'Yeah, we talked about this before, and now you are doing shorter shifts it makes sense, and I'm not comfortable you being on the motorcycle, so after we get it, you will not be on it again, until the baby is here.'

'Do I get to choose it?'

'Of course, but I get a say too, I want you and our baby safe, so I am thinking an SUV.'

'That's very practical.'

'Which is what we are going to need. Now we have to be at the doctor's in an hour, so go and get ready because we have to get across town.'

***

An hour later, they were at the doctor's office, she checked Kathy over, took some blood, checked her weight, and then did a scan. Will couldn't believe what he was seeing. He held Kathy's hand as their baby moved, the doctor put the sound on so they could hear the heartbeat. Will smiled and kissed Kathy. After the scan they went back into her office.

'OK, Kathy, everything looks really good, baby is growing well, so we will see you again in a few weeks.'

'That's great, thanks doctor.'

'Do you have any questions before you go?'

'No, I don't think so.'

'OK, if you do, just call.'

They left and walked down the block and then stopped when they got to his motorcycle. He held Kathy for a moment and took a deep breath. Kathy looked at him.

'Are you OK?'

'Yeah, I'm just really happy.'

'Good, that means you won't notice all the money I am about to spend on Christmas presents.'

'And a new car.'

'Yeah, that as well.'

'Shall I just give you my bank card now?'

'Yeah, good idea.'

They got on the motorcycle and went to their next stop.

***

It was about five hours later when they arrived back home. Will was carrying a lot of bags and Kathy had none, he wouldn't let her carry any. They parked the new car next to his bike and Mustang and they walked round and through the door. Her mum and dad were sat waiting in the lobby.

'Dad, what are you doing here?'

'Will invited us.'

She turned to Will.

'It was a surprise,' he smiled. 'With Christmas and everything.'

'Where are you staying?'

'Here, but just for a couple of days.'

'Mom, how are you?'

'Good, Kathleen, better now you are back though.'

'Yeah, sorry we got a little carried away with the Christmas shopping,' Will answered.

'I see that,' she replied, somewhat angry.

'Well, let's get upstairs.'

Chapter 16

They got upstairs. Her parents sat on the sofa and Will went into the kitchen to make a drink, and Kathy followed him. He started making some coffee then got the cups out, he turned around and she was right behind him.

'Why did you invite my parents?'

'Because it's nearly Christmas and I thought we could tell them about the baby in person rather than on the phone, because I wasn't exactly sure how they would take the news.'

'You know she will start on about me quitting again.'

'I know, but I will be here the whole time.'

She put her arms round him, and he held her tightly. He finished making the drinks and went over to the sofa.

'So, Will and I have some news.'

'Really? What's that?' Debbie asked.

'We are having a baby,' she said, tentatively.

'Wow, that's fantastic news, congratulations you two,' Frank said, excited.

He got up and hugged Kathy and shook Will's hand. Debbie just sat drinking her coffee.

'Thanks, Dad, we are really happy about this.'

'So am I, I get to be a grandfather, I was worried I would get too old or miss out.'

'Dad you're not old.'

'That's why I'm happy it's now.'

Kathy looked at her mom who was yet to say anything. She sat down on the chair and Will sat on the arm next to her.

'Mom, you are quiet.'

'I think your father is excited enough for everyone.'

'But aren't you happy?'

'About being a grandmother? Of course I am.'

There was an awkward silence for a few moments.

'I presume this will mean that you will be leaving the police force now.'

'I am off active duty for a while, but I have no intention of leaving.'

'You intend to run around shooting people while pregnant?'

'No, mom, I have a different role now until I have the baby, I will be staying in the office.'

'Well, I should think so, and after you have the baby, you will be able to stay home and look after it.'

'Actually, Kathy is intending to return to work, the captain has arranged cover, but bravo is still her team,' Will stated.

'You must be joking,' Debbie said, obviously angry. 'A mother's place is at home.'

'Well, I think that's my choice, Mom, and if I want to go back then I will, and we have already talked about the possibility of having a nanny.'

'No, that's not acceptable.'

'I'm sorry, this is mine and Kathy's decision.'

'If you intend having someone look after your child, then surely it should be family, and nannies cost so much money.'

'Money is not really a concern,' Will replied.

'No, of course not, well not now anyway, but children cost a lot of money and your bank balance will soon go down and then what?'

'My bank balance, is my concern.'

'If it affects my daughter and grandchild, then it is my concern.'

'Well, I can promise you now, I will always take care of my family.'

They sat in silence, the atmosphere was very tense. Will put his hand on Kathy's to reassure her. Debbie finished her coffee and stood up.

'I am feeling rather tired, I think I will have a lay down before dinner. Where are we sleeping?'

'I will show you.'

Kathy got up and walked her mom down to the last bedroom, she took her inside and showed her the bathroom. Her mom sat on the bed. Kathy was about to leave.

'I can't believe this, Kathleen, I thought you had more sense.'

'What do you mean by that, Mom?'

'Tying yourself down like this to a man like Will.'

'What's that supposed to mean?'

'You know, he is an immigrant.'

'Mom, he was born here in New York, he is American.'

'But his mother wasn't, what if your children look like him?'

'Has that been your problem all along? That his mom was Brazilian.'

'Well, I don't think he is a suitable match for you.'

'Wow, Mom, I never saw you as a racist.'

'I am no such thing. I have no problem with any of them.'

'As long as they don't get your daughter pregnant, right.'

'I just think…'

'It doesn't matter what you think, Mom, I am having this baby. I will marry Will, because it's my life, and I love him.'

'Kathleen, you have just destroyed your chances of ever meeting a decent man, you really weren't thinking, were you?'

'Will is a decent man, he works hard and loves us.'

'He is a policeman, Kathleen, that's all, this charade of having money will end all too soon, and then what?'

'What is wrong with what he does, it's no different to being a fireman.'

'Tony has ambition, he has been promoted and one day will be captain.'

'And what makes you think Will won't?'

'Maybe he will, but I don't like that he encourages you to risk your life especially now, when that baby arrives, you should be at home.'

'I will do what I see fit, Mom, I will let you know when dinner is here.'

She walked out, and saw her parents' case by the door. She went through to the kitchen. Will was stood leaning on the counter eating some fruit, Kathy walked over to him. He carried on eating till he had finished, they stood in silence. Before she could speak, her dad came over.

'I'm going to go and get a shower before dinner, give us a shout when it's here.'

'Sure, Dad.'

He left and went down the corridor, she heard the door close.

'So what's for dinner,' she asked.

'Chicken.'

'Great, listen, I don't know if you heard before.'

'Yeah, I did.'

'Will I'm sorry.'

'What for, it isn't you that feels that way.'

'I didn't even know she did.'

'Don't worry about it.' He looked at her and she looked really pale. 'Are you OK?'

'Not really, I feel a bit weak.'

'OK, come on.' He led her over to the sofa. 'Lay down and take deep breaths.'

She did so and watched him as he went off to the bedroom, and came back again with his phone and some headphones. He put some music on it, and passed it to her, she looked at him curiously.

'Put them on.'

She did, it was relaxation music, she smiled. He went and fetched a small bottle and sat at her feet. He took off her shoes and began to massage her feet, Kathy closed her eyes and relaxed. She soon fell asleep, so Will covered her up with a blanket. He walked out onto the roof terrace and poured himself a scotch at the bar. He stood looking at the view, thinking about what Kathy's mother had said, he had never seen how he looked as an issue before. His mother had been so beautiful, and he thought he had been lucky to inherit her jet-black hair and Latin looks. He stood and drunk his scotch wondering if he would ever be accepted in her world, and in fact, if she would ever be accepted in his.

Chapter 17

The rest of the evening was somewhat tense, but quiet. Will decided to go in his gym for a while, he disappeared after dinner. Debbie and Frank sat on the sofa and Kathy sat in the chair.

'So what is your new job?' Frank asked.

'I am supervising dispatch and training.'

'Sounds interesting.'

'Yeah, my days won't be as long either so that's good.'

'How will you be getting to work?'

'Will got me a car today, he doesn't want me on the motorcycle now.'

'I should think not,' Debbie exclaimed. 'I'm not sure I am happy about you being on one of those things anyway.'

'It's perfectly safe, Mom, I have been riding into work with Will for months, he is not reckless on it.'

'Yes, well I am still allowed to be worried, Kathleen, you are my only child.'

'I know, Mom, but Will looks after me.'

'Yes, I am sure he does, like all the others before you, I am sure.'

'What's that supposed to mean, Mom?'

'Well, I presume he has had relationships, and I doubt he was a virgin, Kathleen.'

'MOM.'

'Well, I am going to bed, Frank are you coming?'

'Good night sweetheart,' Frank said to Kathy.

'Night, Dad.'

They went down the corridor and Kathy got up and went into the gym, she stood at the door watching for a moment, enjoying the view.

'They have gone to bed, it's safe to come out now'

Will looked over and smiled.

'You know they aren't the only reason I came in here, right? I haven't been in here for ages, and I need to get fit again.'

'Get fit, Will you are fitter than anyone I know.'

'Yeah, and it takes work to stay that way.'

'Well, I'm not complaining, I could look at you working out all day long.'

Will stopped and looked at her. He moved towards her, she felt her body reacting before he was even close. She moved forward and kissed him, he put his arms round her and she moved towards the wall. Her hands moved across his muscular back and down to his shorts. He kissed her neck and his hands moved under her top. He paused, looked at her, and smiled.

'I need a shower, you want to join me?'

She smiled and followed him into their room.

***

The next morning Will awoke with new conviction, he made Kathy's breakfast and got ready for work. Kathy got up and ate, Will put his arms around her and kissed on the back of her neck.

'I will see you in the office soon.'

'Yeah, sitting behind a desk.'

'I thought you were OK with this.'

'I am, but I am going to miss being out on call, looking at your behind in those uniform pants.'

'You can still do that, you are only in the next office,' he laughed.

'Yeah, but I have work to do too you know.'

'OK I have to go, love you, see you soon.'

'Love you too, see you soon.'

Will left and Kathy continued to eat. Her dad appeared at her side.

'That looks good.'

'Will makes me breakfast every day, he insists I eat properly now, not just coffee.'

'Good on him, he's taking good care of you then.' He got a coffee and sat next to her.

'Yeah, he always has.'

'Yeah, I know but I like to check.'

'Mom not up yet?'

'No, she's awake but I think was waiting for Will to leave.'

'Yeah, and so she should after what she said yesterday.'

'Kathy, you know your mom loves you and she wants what is best for you.'

'No, she doesn't, she wants what's best for her, Will is what is best for me. I have never felt this way about anyone, and he doesn't try to control me, he supports and encourages me and that is love. Now if you will excuse me, I have to get ready for work.'

Kathy got ready, it was the first time she had not worn her uniform, but it was already getting tight. She came out of her bedroom and she saw her mom sat next to her dad with a coffee.

'OK, I will see you later,' she said.

'Kathy before you go, we wanted to ask you something.'

'Make it quick.'

'Well now you are staying here, we were wondering what you had done with your grandmother's house.'

'Well now I'm living here, I rent it to a friend. Why?'

'Because your dad and I have been thinking of moving here permanently.'

'What?'

'Well, you aren't coming home so we thought we would move here.'

'Well, you will have to find something else then, I have to go. Call Jimmy if you want to go out.'

She left, she got in her car and took a breath, why the hell did they want to move here?

***

Kathy went through to her new office, Gina was busy. She opened the door to find Will stood there with a bunch of roses. He stepped towards her, kissed her, and gave her the flowers.

'To celebrate your first day in your new position.'

'Thank you, they are beautiful.'

'Well, I have to go back to work, stuff to sort out for Turner.'

'OK see you soon.'

Will left and went back into the team office. Kathy saw that Gina was quiet and went over to her.

'Gina, what do you know about Turner?'

'Not much, she's not around much being on a call-out team. Why?'

'She's starting on Will's team today, and Bennett says she's really hot.'

'OK, so?'

'So she's working with Will and…'

'And nothing, did you not see those flowers, he has it bad and it isn't for Turner.'

Kathy sighed.

'I don't know what's wrong with me, any other women near him and I freak out.'

'It's called being protective of your man, especially as he is such a hunk and it's probably hormones, too.'

They laughed, it was going to be so much fun working with Gina.

'OK, I have to go and see the captain and find out exactly what he wants me to do.'

She walked through and past Will's office. He shouted her.

'Missing me already?'

'I'm going to see the captain.'

'OK, will you come see me after?'

'Maybe if you are still here.'

She went into the captain's office and was in there for about an hour. She then came back to Will's office.

'Sergeant Falco, I need last month's training for your team putting into the system.'

'When for?'

'Today preferably.'

'Today, all of it?'

'Yeah, and maybe you should do it weekly to keep it up to date, you guys do a lot of training so it's easy to get behind.'

'Yes, Sergeant.' He got up and closed the door. 'You know how sexy you are when you get all authoritative.'

'Will really, I'm trying to do my job here.'

He put his arms around her and kissed the back of her neck. She melted to his touch and turned around and kissed him. She suddenly stopped.

'You need to get your training records done, Sergeant.'

She opened the door, and left. He watched her walk across the office. Captain Bridge came over to him with Turner.

'Falco, you remember Turner.'

'Huh? What?'

'Turner, can you get her settled.'

'Sorry, yeah sure.'

Captain Bridge went back to his office.

'Stanson, get Turner here sorted, I will be back in a minute.'

He left the office leaving Turner still stood by his office. Stanson walked over to her.

'Hi, I'm Stanson, Sergeant Falco's number two, welcome to alpha team.'

'Is he always like that?'

'Only when it comes to Sergeant Hill, she's his fiancée and she just went on desk duty as she's pregnant.'

'Right, that's why I got moved up.'

'Yeah, because Tom is leading her team for a while.'

'Isn't she the one that got kidnapped earlier this year?'

'Yeah, he saved her life.'

'Wow real fairy-tale type thing.'

'Yeah, I guess so.'

Will went into Kathy's office and shut the door, she was putting a file away. She turned around.

'What are you doing in here?'

He took hold of her and kissed her, she reacted and went to lift his shirt but stepped back.

'Will, we can't keep doing this at work, we are going to get in serious trouble if we do.'

'Maybe.'

'Not maybe, what is wrong with you, you are never like this?'

'I know, but something about you right now makes me want you every time I see you, especially when you tell me off.'

'Well restrain yourself in the office because with my hormones I can't cope with this.'

'You're right, I'm sorry, I will go back and do my training records.'

Just then his beeper went off.

'OK, they will have to wait, see you later.'

Chapter 18

The call was at an office block. Will got out and went to speak to the lieutenant in charge.

'Sergeant, we have armed suspects on the 35th floor, a witness says there was seven of them, we don't know what they are after, it's a financial investment company.'

'Is the rest of the building clear?'

'No, the owners didn't want to cause a panic.'

'OK give me a minute.' He walked away, pulling out his phone as he did so. 'Nick, it's Will, I am down at one of my buildings, a hostage situation. I am going to need to clear the rest of the building so I can do my job.'

'OK, Will, if you need it clear, it is yours after all, I just didn't want mass panic.'

'Well, if I pull the fire alarm, though it will alert the hostage takers, it will clear the remaining floors pretty quickly.'

'No, problem do it and let me know how it goes.'

Will hung up and walked back over to the lieutenant.

'OK, we have a go, we can clear the building using the fire alarm, when I do, I am going to need to move quickly so I need some more teams down here. When the fire alarm goes, I will need officers to move the people away from the building, and we will probably need your help to keep the fire brigade outside till we are done.'

'OK, Sergeant, it's your scene, however you want to play it.'

'OK thanks.' He walked back to the team. 'Control, this is alpha team, we are going to need bravo and charlie down here, ASAP.'

'Received alpha team I will page them now.'

Will went inside and spoke to the business manager, the fire alarm was sounded, and a steady stream of people began to appear from the stairwell, Will had disabled the elevators. The PD got them to move away from the building to an area that was a safe distance, the numbers were slowing as bravo and charlie teams arrived.

'OK, charlie team, I want you in the lobby to secure the entrance. Stop the brigade coming in and the suspects going out if they get past us. Bravo, I want you on the stairwell and hostage evacuation. Alpha, we take the offices on the floor that they are on, stay sharp and let's move quickly we can only hold the brigade so long, and the suspects will now know we are coming.'

As they were heading through the lobby, they heard the fire brigade arriving. Sergeant Moss, charlie team leader, stopped them at the doors.

'Sorry guys can't let you in.'

'There is a fire alarm and we need to check the building.'

'Sergeant Falco has a hostage situation on the 35th floor and once he is done you can go in, until then I have my orders to keep you outside.'

'What if there is a fire?'

'There isn't, Falco got the manager to sound the alarm, to clear the building.'

'You do realise we have to check that.'

'Sure, when he's done, because I am not going to be responsible for you going in there, and messing up this shout, when Falco has point, and if you had any sense you wouldn't want to go in anyway.'

'And why is that?'

'We have armed suspects and alpha team in there, not to mention bravo, you wouldn't want to get caught in that crossfire.'

'So you expect us to sit and wait?'

'Go and speak to the building manager, he is just over there, he will clarify what I have said.'

The fire brigade, Captain walked off, unhappy.

The teams were checking every floor, they had to move quickly, but had to be thorough. On the 20th floor they shot and killed a suspect who was heavily armed. Will knew he was the lookout after the alarm had been sounded. When they got to the 35th floor, they stopped at the door, Will opened it a fraction to see what the situation was for entry. There was a suspect just a step away, he had his back to the door. Will closed the door again and signalled instructions to his team and bravo, he would take this one out and they would clear the floor as they went.

Will opened the door and fired one shot, the suspect was down. Shots were fired in their direction. There were two more suspects approaching them as they went in, they were firing shots, but they missed. He signalled to Stanson, they took one each. It fell quiet, they went across the office slowly checking every inch of it checking for more suspects, Will knew there was at least three more. They could see a lot of hostages hiding under desks and huddled in corners.

'Bravo, let's start clearing these hostages,' Will radioed.

'Received, alpha.'

Will went across the office he could hear voices. He headed down a corridor, the voices got louder, they were coming from a meeting room. Will signalled to Stanson that they were to enter, and he counted down from three on his fingers. Stanson kicked the door open.

'NYPD drop your weapons.'

There were three with guns, two pointed at them and one on a man with a laptop.

'You are outnumbered, officer, so I don't think so.'

'That's not a disadvantage, that's a challenge,' he replied. 'So drop your weapons or I will drop you.'

'He will be dead before we are.'

'He sounds fairly sure, doesn't he?'

'Yeah, sure does, Sergeant, but I reckon we can take them.'

Will nodded, there was three shots in quick succession, all three suspects were down.

'Control, this is alpha team, we are all clear, we need PD and a coroner up here, there are seven suspects fatally wounded.'

'Received, alpha team.'

Will guided the hostage from the meeting room out into the main office and he followed the other hostages making their way down the stairwell, bravo checking everywhere for more and sending them down. Ford and Blain were in the stairwell making sure that everyone was OK. Will walked over to Tom.

'First call as bravo boss, how's it feel?'

'It's OK, not something I want to do permanently though.'

'Why not?'

'I'm not you, Will, I would rather take the orders than give them, you know me.'

'Yeah, well it's only for a year or so then you are mine again.'

'But will I be number two?'

'Of course, why wouldn't you be?'

'Stanson is a good officer, Will, and is doing a great job.'

'He isn't you though.'

'No, and being good friends as we are helps us read each other for sure but over the next year you and Stanson will have that too.'

'Maybe I can have two number twos.'

Tom laughed.

'As long as someone has your back, Will, it doesn't matter who it is. I can work with Stanson when I am back on alpha.'

All the hostages were out so the teams set off down too. As Will walked out of the building, the captain of the fire crew, came over to him.

'Can we go in now and check the building?'

'Not yet, well perhaps if you avoid the 20th and 35th floors until PD and the coroner are done.'

'How long are they going to take?'

'I don't know, I don't work for them.'

Will started walking away, but the captain followed him.

'So you pull the fire alarm, and we can't even go in and clear the building, we have been sat round for a while now.'

'There isn't a fire.'

'But we have to check the whole building, it's procedure.'

'Then I guess you will be here for a while.'

'So because of you there are less firefighters to respond to an actual fire.'

'I needed to evacuate the building and it was the quickest way.'

'And people could die because of your actions.'

'Thousands are alive because I inconvenienced you and your crew.'

The captain walked right up to Will, he was of a similar height. Will handed his weapon to Stanson to put in the truck.

'Sergeant, you really are as arrogant as they say, aren't you? You just don't care how your actions affect others.'

'Guess it depends on how arrogant they say I am. I would say more confident than arrogant though.'

'Next time you need to clear a building, don't pull the fire alarm.'

'I will if I need to, if we had cleared each floor, dozens would be dead, and I just won't risk that.'

'But you will take us away from people who may need us.'

'Yeah, because there are more of you to cover an emergency, now if you will excuse me, I have to go.'

The captain walked off then. Will turned round to see Tony stood there.

'Will, you really do make an impression on people.'

'Tony, what are you doing here?'

'I'm looking round fire houses in New York, I might move here with Debbie and Frank, they are like family to me.'

'How delightful.'

'So where is Kathy, isn't she working? Would like to say hello.'

'She is on desk duty.'

'Why what happened to her? Did she get injured again?'

'You don't know do you?'

'Know what?'

'Kathy's pregnant.'

'Pregnant! With your baby?'

'Yeah, maybe we will see you around.'

Will got in the truck and drove off, he couldn't help but smile.

Chapter 19

Will and the others got back to the office. They were all tired after all the stairs. Charlie had finished shift and delta had been called out already. Will got a coffee and sat on the end of Stanson's desk.

'You did well today, first shout as number two and it was a tough one, takes a lot to impress me, but you managed. Well done.'

'Thanks, Sergeant.'

The captain came to his door.

'Falco, do you have a minute?'

Will walked over and went into the captain's office. Captain Bridge closed the door and went round his desk and sat down.

'So, Falco, you have done with the PD and now started pissing off the fire department, I just had a call from the chief.'

'Captain, I explained to them I needed to evacuate the building and that was the fastest way, I even got permission from the owner.'

'The owner, and who was that?'

'Me, it's one of mine.'

'Of course it is, I should have known.'

'I called Nick and he said to do what I thought was best, and with that many floors, what else could I do?'

'OK I will pass on that you had the owner's permission, but Falco would it really hurt you to play nice with others on a shout, just one day I would like not to get a call about you.'

'That's what Sundays are for, Captain.'

'Very funny Falco, but I am serious, now get back to work because I believe you have to catch up with your training records.'

'Yes, Captain.'

Will went back into his office and sat behind his desk, drinking his coffee. Just then Kathy came in, she went through to the captain's office and dropped off some paperwork, she then went into Will's office.

'How's the training records going?'

'I literally just got back in, and guess who I saw on the call?' he said, as he got up and sat on the edge of his desk.

'No idea.'

'Tony.'

'What was he doing there?'

'Looking at fire houses in New York to move here with your parents apparently.'

'Seriously? Well, they kept that quiet.'

'Yeah, but that may change now he knows about the baby.'

'You told him?'

'Yeah, it's not a secret, I'm not sure why it would be a problem.'

'This is all I need, Will, my mom is going to go crazy, but you and your ego you couldn't help yourself.'

'Wow.' He got up and moved behind his desk. 'OK well if you will excuse me, I have work to do. I will see you later at home.'

Kathy was going to say something but left and went back to her office.

***

It was late when Will got back home. Kathy went over to him as soon as he got through the door. He didn't kiss her, just put his helmet down and looked at her.

'You're late.'

'I was finishing training records.'

'Oh, I didn't think it would take you so long.'

'Well add that to another two call-outs and it did, I'm going for a shower.'

Will walked off into the bedroom, Kathy stood for a moment and then followed. She sat on the bed and waited for him to finish in the shower. He came out with just a towel around him, he saw Kathy sat on the bed so headed into the walk-in closet for something to put on.

'Can we talk?' Kathy said loudly.

'What about?' he said coming back out into the bedroom.

'Earlier today.'

'Is there any point in that?'

'I would like to know why you are so mad at me.'

'You're kidding, right?'

Kathy looked at him, he folded his arms.

'I am so happy we are having this baby, Kathy, and I know it took a while for it to sink in, but I wish I could tell the world, but you just don't seem to be that happy.'

'Of course I am.'

'So what was the issue in me telling Tony then?'

'Because like I thought that's all I have heard since I got home tonight.'

'And what did you say?'

'Nothing what could I say?'

"You don't get it do you, Kathy?'

'Get what?'

'I feel like you are ashamed of me, like you aren't proud to be having this baby with me.'

'You know with my mom it's complicated.'

'It's only as complicated as you make it.'

'And how about you? I don't see you taking me to all those fancy parties you took all those women too.'

Will went into the closet and brought an envelope back out, he handed it to her.

'This was going to be part of your Christmas gift.'

She opened it and inside were two tickets to the New Year's ball, one of the most exclusive events in the city.

'I was intending to show you off to everyone, and I know it's taken a while to do so but I wanted it to be special.'

'Will, I don't know what to say.'

"You know all through my life, school, work and in my social and even love life, where my mom came from and what I look like, especially the colour of my skin was not once an issue and I am struggling with the fact that it is now. Like no matter what I have or what I do, I'm still not good enough.'

'You know that doesn't matter to me, I love you.' She stood and moved towards him. 'And I think you are hot. I was actually hoping that our baby gets your Latin look, because that is a part of you, and your mom. I can't ever be ashamed of being with you because I love you too much.'

She wrapped her arms around him and laid her head on his chest.

'You really want our baby to look like me?'

'Absolutely.'

He kissed her and they moved back over to the bed, they sat and the kisses became passionate and intense. She laid back and he followed, he started to lift her top when there was a knock at the door. They sat up quickly and looked at each other and smiled. Will went and put something on, and Kathy opened the door.

'Kathleen, will we be eating soon, it's getting quite late.'

'Yeah, we will order something now'

They came out of the bedroom, Will was wearing just a pair of shorts, Debbie looked at him disapprovingly. Will went to the kitchen, made a drink then ordered some food. He then sat on the sofa next to Kathy, he put his arm around her, and she leaned on him. Debbie and Frank sat in the chairs.

'So, Will, I hear you saw Tony today,' Debbie said.

'Yeah, he was at a call.'

'And you told him about the baby.'

'Yeah, so.'

'A little insensitive really.'

'Why?'

'Well, he still loves Kathleen, and he was still holding on to some hope she would go back to him.'

'That's not my problem.'

'You could have at least allowed us or Kathleen to tell him, make it easier.'

'He asked me where she was, I told him. And exactly why should I lie or hide the fact, because I am so proud we are having this baby, and don't care who knows it.'

Debbie scowled.

'You still could have allowed us to tell him.'

'And you could have told us he was looking at moving here with you, but you didn't.'

'It wasn't decided yet, we were looking at possibilities.'

'Look, I don't really care about how you or Tony feel about this baby, Kathy and I are the only two that matter. You see, you may not like the fact I'm not white but I am past caring, and for the record, if you visit again, I will book you into a hotel, because I am tired of the way you speak to me and Kathy in our home.'

Debbie got up and walked down the corridor, Frank got up and smiled at them and followed. Kathy turned and kissed Will.

'I can't believe you just did that.'

'Well, it felt good, and I don't like the way she speaks to you.'

'I love you.'

'Love you too.'

Chapter 20

The next morning Kathy was up early, she had needed the toilet. She went out into the living room. Will was already dressed and ready for work, drinking coffee.

'What are you doing awake, you don't have to be up for another forty minutes?'

'Baby was laying on my bladder.'

'OK, I will start your breakfast.'

'You're in your uniform?'

'Yeah, got to stop by Park's office on the way in so it's easier.'

'Park's office, what for? You never said.'

'He said he has some info on Ashborne and Sutton.'

'Did he say what?'

'No, so maybe it's not good news.'

Will cooked her breakfast and made her tea, she watched him the whole time. He put them in front of her and she smiled.

'What?'

'Nothing, I'm just happy.'

'Good.' He kissed her. 'So what time are your parents going, the flight is at one.'

'Don't know, do you want me to let Jimmy know when I go out?'

'If you could, then he will have a car ready for them to take them to the airport.'

'That's not a problem, can't wait till it's just you and me again.'

'Well for a few weeks at least, who knows what the new year will bring and come summer we won't be alone again.'

'That's why I want to make the most of it.'

***

Will arrived at Park's office early. Park was there waiting for him, he knew Will started early.

'Hey Falco, how's Kathy?'

'She's good.'

'And the baby?'

'Good from what she tells me.'

'Well, I got a call yesterday from Detroit, I called them for an update. Anyway, they called me back, they both took a plea deal.'

'That's good, right?'

'Sutton got ten years and Ashborne got three.'

'Is that all?'

'Yeah, sadly, a woman lost her life, but even with the evidence, murder was tough to prove.'

'They had the body.'

'But no proof that Sutton killed her or that Ashborne told him too. He denied the murder the whole time, and the other two officers got suspended sentences because they were just following orders.'

'The great legal system at work.'

'At least they are locked up for now, and off the force.'

'Yeah, that's true, I have to go so let me know if you hear more.'

***

Will arrived at the office just after the team, he grabbed a coffee and went into his office. He was sat doing some paperwork when the first call of the day came in, it was only for alpha team, so they headed out to the truck. They arrived at a store and got ready. Will got the information from the officers there.

'OK, guys, just one suspect in the store, he won't talk to anyone, so we go straight in.'

'Are there any hostages?' Stanson asked.

'Just four, they think, so the plan is me, Stanson, Palmer and Bennett go in and Harvey stay with Turner by the door. We go in low and steady.'

They went to the door, Will looked in through the windows, he could see the back of the suspect. Should be an easy entrance. He opened the door slowly and they went in. Will sent Palmer and Bennett to the right, he and Stanson went straight down to the suspect.

'NYPD, put your weapon down and place your hands on your head.'

He turned round and looked at Will, his gun was pointing at them. He didn't say anything.

'You need to lower your weapon now.'

He just stared at Will not moving or saying anything.

'Does he understand us, Sergeant?' Stanson said.

'Yeah, I understand you,' the suspect said. 'I just don't want to do it.'

'Well, see, you have a choice, put your weapon down, or we fire.'

'But will you hit me? I quite fancy my chances.'

'Four against one, really?'

'Yeah, why not?'

Will looked at Stanson, they were both very confused.

'OK I'm bored now.' Will fired and hit him in the shoulder.

He fell to the floor, and as he did so, fired in Will's direction but missed by just inches. Stanson went over and took his weapon. He kept aimed at him, Bennett checked him for another.

'Control, this is alpha team we are all clear, we need EMTs and PD for escort.'

'Received, alpha team.'

Bennett and Palmer stayed with the suspect and Stanson went over to Will.

'Well, that was weird.'

'Yeah, it was, but be prepared because we do get them and quite often.'

'It was like he wanted us to kill him or something.'

'Well, the PD will question him so I am sure they will get some answers.'

The EMTs and PD arrived and so they left. Stanson had walked round the corner to speak to an officer he knew, the others were at the truck packing up their gear. A man stood behind Will and fired three shots into his back. Will fell to the floor. The team drew their handguns.

'Sergeant, are you OK?' Bennett shouted.

Will didn't move or speak for a moment, just laid face down on the floor.

'Sergeant!' Bennett shouted.

'Yeah, I'm OK, shit that hurt.' Harvey helped him up off the floor.

Stanson stood behind the man and put his gun to the back of his head.

'Drop your weapon, put your hands on your head.'

'Damn I should have counted,' he said lowering his gun.

Will turned round to see Dune standing there with Stanson behind him. Will drew his handgun and pointed it at Dune.

'Give me one good reason not to pull the trigger, Dune.'

'Go for it, you took everything else from me why not my life.'

'What?'

'You took my job, my pension, my wife left me, and I lost my home.'

'You did that to yourself, it is all on you. So did shooting me make you feel better?'

'Not really, because you didn't do what you should have done. You are so well known for killing anyone that dare shoot you, but you haven't. So, go on, Falco, pull the trigger.'

'So you shot me so I would kill you? If you are so desperate why not do it yourself?'

'Because taking you down for doing it just seemed better somehow.'

Will put his gun away.

'Sorry Dune, not today.'

Stanson cuffed Dune and handed him to the PD that were still around. Will took his vest off and sat on the back of the truck.

'You, OK, Sergeant?'

'That bloody hurt.'

'He was pretty close to you, do you want me to call for an EMT, just check you over.'

'Could be a good idea, it hurts when I breathe in, I don't think that's a good thing.'

'Control, this is alpha orange, can we have an EMT to our location.'

'Received, we will send them to you now.'

Stanson got Will a bottle of water, the rest of the team were stood by the front of the truck chatting. It took ten minutes for the EMTs to arrive, they got out and Stanson went and spoke to them. Will stood and went over.

'Lift your shirt, Sergeant, let's have a look.'

Will took his shirt off, the EMT had a look, to see if there were just bruises. She touched them and Will flinched, especially with the top one. It was really painful.

'OK, I think you may have fractured a rib, we need an X-ray to confirm though.'

'Really? Damn thought it hurt.'

'Well, it's a good thing you still had your vest on, or you wouldn't be breathing.'

'Yeah, he didn't want to kill me, just get my attention.'

'So are you coming for that X-ray.'

'Yeah, best had I guess, just give me a minute.' He walked over to Stanson 'They want me to go for an X-ray, so till I get back you have alpha, and don't tell Kathy what happened just tell her I'm OK.'

'OK sure thing, see you soon.'

***

Will got back to the office, the team were sat at their desks, he got a coffee and went to speak to Stanson.

'What they say, Sergeant?'

'I have a partial fracture on a rib but it's not serious.'

'Captain said he wanted to see you when you got back.'

'Great just what I needed.'

Will went into the captain's office and closed the door.

'Falco, what did the hospital say?'

'I have a partial fracture to my rib.'

'You OK to work?'

'Yeah, not an issue.'

'Good, so it was Dune.'

'Yeah.'

'Do you want to pursue charges?'

'Captain, he needs help not locking up, maybe they can make a deal, so he gets that.'

'OK I will pass that on to the DA, now go and see Sergeant Hill because she is going crazy in dispatch.'

Will left and went through to the dispatch office. She met him at the door.

'Will, what happened, are you OK? No one would tell me what happened, I couldn't reach you on your phone.' She threw her arms round him.

He moved with pain, she looked at him and then took his hand and led him into her office and shut the door.

'Let me see.'

He looked at her.

'I'm serious, let me see.'

He took his shirt off and turned round.

'Holy shit, Will, what happened?'

Will turned back to face her.

'Dune, he shot me three times in the back of my vest, he was stood really close too, fractured part of my rib.'

'What? Do you know how lucky you are that you still had your vest on?'

'I know but he didn't want to kill me, he wanted me to kill him.'

'Seriously, why?'

'Because he lost everything, and he blames me.'

'You didn't though, right?'

'No, I nearly did though.'

Will sat on her desk, she walked round so she could get a better look at the bruises. She ran her hand gently over them.

'You going to kiss me better?'

'Tonight, I will, but not here, so put your shirt back on.'

He put it back on and stood up, he was about to kiss her when his beeper went off.

'Later it is then.' He smiled as he left.

Chapter 21

The next morning, Will was still in pain. He was cooking Kathy's breakfast, he hadn't put his shirt on yet. Kathy came out of the bedroom, she walked up to him and ran her hands over his back.

'Still looks really sore, are you sure you should be working today?'

'Yeah, it's just a fractured rib, it will heal.'

'Does it hurt?'

'A bit, but nothing I can't handle.'

He finished making her breakfast, and turned round and put his arms around her.

'You don't have to worry about me so much.'

'Really, you have been shot three times in the last six months and one almost killed you.'

'Can you really count the last two, one barely hit me and yesterday were all in the vest.'

'But you were still injured Will.'

'Yeah, I know, but I have a job to do and I won't stop doing it, and I know I have to think about the baby, but my work is such a big part of who I am.'

'Yeah, I know, just like me, SWAT is in your blood and I would never ask you to stop but maybe just watch out a little more.'

'OK I promise, now I need to get to work and I will see you soon.'

***

Will was sat doing reports when the first call of the day came in, he had barely managed to drink his first coffee before their beepers went. Will had a feeling it was going to be one of those days.

The call was at Grand Central Station. When the team arrived, it was a bit chaotic, so many people outside. The building was always busy, but at this time of the morning it was even busier. Will went and got the information from the lieutenant in charge and went back to the teams.

'OK, we have two teenagers firing randomly, at people and in general, we don't know where they are, so we go in and check every inch of the place. The main hall is open, as we all know, so we have to be careful and vigilant. We go through the main area and then we will check the platforms if needed. We will go in through the entrance on Lexington to keep cover till we get to the main hall, there will be PD at the left and right entrance. We will go down the centre, trains have been stopped outside of the station and they are getting backed up so let's get this done.'

The teams paired up and went through the doors. They made their way down towards the main hall, when they got to it, they stopped. Will looked around as best he could without breaking cover.

'Tom, take bravo down the right side, we will go down the left.'

Will adjusted his vest.

'You OK, Sergeant?' Stanson asked.

'Yeah, just sore from yesterday is all, but we need to get this done.'

They moved forwards and down the main hall checking areas as they went. They worked steadily and thoroughly, they could hear voices coming from near the station master's office, so they kept moving. They went past four victims, all dead, and Will knew that there were more injured, outside. The victims were of various ages, from mid-twenties upwards. Will got eyes on the two suspects, one was taller with brown hair swept forwards, the other was shorter and had dark hair, nearly black. They were teenagers and seemed overly excited bouncing around like they were having fun. They both had handguns. Will got in the best possible position before announcing.

'NYPD put your weapons down on the ground and your hands on your head.'

They spun round and smiled.

'Woah, police officers, what did we do?' the taller one said.

'Well, you killed four people, that we have seen, and injured a few more so put the guns down.'

'Yeah, right, they are just blanks, that's what the guy said.'

'What guy?'

'Who we bought them off.'

'Well, they aren't blanks, four people are dead, so you need to put the guns down.'

'What, really?' the shorter one said.

'Yes, really.'

The two kids looked at each other and then back at Will.

'How do we know you are telling the truth?' the taller one said.

'OK, here is how it is going to go. You can put the weapons down or we will fire, and I can assure you we do have real bullets.'

'You can't shoot us if we only have blanks.'

Stanson looked at Will.

'Sergeant, these guys are giving me a headache, can I just shoot one of them.'

'Yeah, OK.'

Stanson fired and hit the taller one in the shoulder, he dropped to the floor, screaming in pain. The other pointed his gun at Stanson.

'Do you want one too?'

He shook his head and put his gun on the floor.

'Good choice,' Stanson said. He secured one and Bennett cuffed the other.

'Control, this is alpha team, we need EMTs and PD for the suspects and we have four fatalities.'

'Received, alpha team.'

Will sat down on a bench nearby and took off his helmet and vest. Tom came over and sat next to him.

'We cleared the rest of the building, there were no more victims, are you OK?'

'I just hate it when young people do shit like this, half of them don't even understand what the hell they are doing.'

'They could be done for murder too, last time I checked stupidity wasn't a defence in court. Thinking they were blanks could see them spend their lives in prison, or a good few years of it.'

'Something needs to be done to educate kids that guns aren't the answer or a joke.'

'True story, but what can we do.'

'I may have an idea actually, it's time we became more proactive and not just responsive to these things.'

PD came in with the EMTs and gave the teams the all clear to go. They headed back to the truck. Will watched as the coroner arrived, something had to be done to end the senseless loss of life.

***

Will went straight into the captain's office when he got back. He knocked on the door and went in.

'Falco, what can I do for you?'

'I've been thinking about some recent call-outs and the fact that a lot of them are young people.'

'OK, so what are you thinking?'

'That maybe we should be more proactive and not just reacting.'

'How do you mean?'

'Education, going into schools and teaching teenagers exactly what happens when they choose to pick up a gun.'

'The PD usually handle that.'

'But we have to deal with it, and gun crime is not going down, so shouldn't we do more?'

'I will speak to the chief and some schools and see what they say, but who would do it, you?'

'No, because we both know that would be a PR disaster, I was actually thinking Kathy while she is on desk duty, accompanied by someone from alpha, Stanson or Harvey.'

'OK, let's speak to Sergeant Hill see what she thinks.'

'Right now, because I haven't actually mentioned it yet?'

'Well, no time like the present.'

He phoned through to Kathy and asked her to come through, Will went to the door and was about to leave.

'Falco, where are you going?'

'Back to work.'

'This is your idea, stay where you are.'

Will leaned against a filing cabinet and folded his arms. Kathy knocked on the door and came in, she looked at Will, then at the captain wondering what was going on. Will didn't look at her.

'Sergeant Hill, Falco here has had a wonderful idea, about going into the city schools and educating on gun crime and thinks you would be the perfect person for the job, at least for the next few months.'

'Really! Did he?' She turned and looked at Will.

'He is even going to lend you one of his team to accompany you.'

'OK, and when is this going to happen?'

'As soon as I get the go ahead from the chief and I have arranged it with some schools, though it will probably be after the Christmas break.'

'And I am guessing it's decided, and I don't get a say.'

'Sergeant Hill, you are perfect for it and as you are off active duty it means I will only be one officer down when you are doing them and not two, which at this time of year is a definite plus.'

'OK then.'

'Right, well back to work you two and I will start sorting things.'

Kathy and Will left, and she walked off back to her office without speaking. Will followed her and closed the door. She turned round and looked at him.

'You're mad at me,' he said, moving closer.

'Not really mad, but would have appreciated a heads up.'

'I was going to, but the captain wanted to run with it straight away.'

'But you didn't even check with me, that I would actually want to do it.'

'Yeah, sorry about that.' He moved close and put his arms around her. 'Forgive me?' he asked and then kissed her.

'Maybe.'

He kissed her again and she reacted this time. He moved to her neck gently kissing it. She moved away.

'OK, you're forgiven.' She went behind her desk and sat down. 'Don't you have work to do?'

Just then the door opened, it was the captain.

'Sergeant Hill, get yourself ready, I have a school wanting you there in the next half an hour.'

'What? I haven't even got anything prepared.'

'They have some troubled teens and want you to go and speak to them.'

'OK, as long as Falco comes with me.'

'Hey, wait a minute I said Stanson or Harvey, they are much more suited.'

'But as it's short notice and it was all your idea, maybe you should do the first one.'

'Agreed, Falco, you're going.'

'Don't I get a say?'

'Not really, grab what you need and go.'

The captain left. Will turned to Kathy.

'Well thanks for that.'

'What?'
'You really think this is a good idea?'
'Maybe not, but payback is a bitch.'

Chapter 22

Will and Kathy arrived at the school. Will put his vest on and got his weapons sorted and then put his shades on.

'Do you need all those?' Kathy asked, gesturing at his weapons.

'Yeah, I want these kids to know what they face if we are called.'

'So it's a scare tactic then?'

'Something like that.'

Kathy shook her head and grabbed some stuff and went inside, Will followed. They went to the main office and asked for the principal, she came out and looked at Will very suspiciously.

'Sergeants Hill and Falco I presume.'

'Yeah, I'm Sergeant Hill, I believe you have some students you want us to speak with.'

'Yes, I do, they are the trouble causers in this place, so I think it will be a good place to start.'

'Good place to start?'

'Yes, if this goes well, I would like you to speak to all the seniors.'

They followed her down a corridor to a classroom at the end. She looked in through a window in the door, the students were all over the room sat on desks, talking, and joking around. The principal opened the door.

'OK, everyone, take your seats, we have two people here today to talk to you. I would like to introduce Sergeant Hill and Sergeant Falco from our own NYPD SWAT unit.'

Will and Kathy looked around the classroom, not one student looked interested or as if they wanted to be there. Will looked at Kathy, the principal left. Will sat on the desk and put his two rifles behind him. Kathy stood near him and took a deep breath before she started.

'So does anyone know what SWAT do?'

'You shoot people,' one young male said.

'Sometimes we do,' Kathy replied. 'What else?'

They all stayed quiet.

'So you all think we just shoot people?'

Most nodded in agreement. Kathy looked at Will, she wasn't sure what to say to that.

'How many of you know someone that has been involved in some sort of shooting?' Will asked.

Six people put their hands up.

'We attend hostage situations, school shootings, arrest warrants and search warrants if they are high risk and weapons are thought to be involved. We will always try to negotiate with suspects, directly or not,' he continued.

Will stood up and looked around him, they seemed to be listening, so he continued.

'Does anyone know what SWAT stands for?'

They all shook their heads.

'It means Special Weapons and Tactics. We are better trained than any other department in the force, we have to train every week and that's more than once too. We have to be in the best physical condition, and we work on our tactics every day.'

'Does anyone have any questions at this time?' Kathy asked.

'How many women are in SWAT?' a young teenage girl asked.

'Just two at the moment,' Kathy replied. 'But we do have some women in our dispatch, and other units have women too.'

'But why is it so few?'

'It is the toughest department to get into for any officer, and the number of officers that get to join, it's an exceedingly small percentage,' Kathy replied.

'Fact is SWAT have to be the best,' Will said as he held up a target from alpha team. 'Pass this round and have a good look.'

He passed it to the front row, and they all had a look and passed it on, a few were amazed by it and some were impressed.

'This is how good someone has to be to get on alpha team.'

'So who is the best shot?' a young male asked.

'Sergeant Falco is, he is the alpha team leader, they are the best team in the unit, they are all trained snipers too,' Kathy answered.

'How do you join SWAT?'

'You have to join the force first and then with hard work and training, any officer can try and qualify.'

'OK, what you can do now is two at a time come forwards and you can have a look at two of the weapons we use on alpha team. We carry a few others but these and our handguns are what we use the most.'

The first two students stood up when Will put his hand up to stop them, he heard something. It was gunfire. He went over to the door and looked to see if he could see anything.

'Oh no, he's here,' a female student said, with a terrified look.

'Who's here?' Kathy asked.

'My ex, he said he was going to come here and kill me and all my friends.'

'OK, listen up, all stay where you are. Kathy you might need this.' He handed her one of his handguns. 'In case he has company.'

Kathy crouched behind the desk out of sight. Will stood behind the door ready and called it in.

'Control, this is alpha red, we have armed suspects at our location, we need alpha team down here now.'

'Received, alpha red.'

He could hear more shots and screams but he knew he couldn't go out there alone, he had to wait for alpha and he hated that. He heard footsteps and the door opened. He waited until the suspect had walked all the way into the room.

'There you are baby, I said I would come for you.'

'Drop your weapon,' Will said behind him.

'I would but I brought a friend.'

Will felt a gun in his back, he should have checked, but he still had the advantage.

'So did I,' Will said.

Kathy stood and aimed at the second suspect. Will side-stepped, and Kathy came forwards and stood next to him. They put their hands up. Will took their guns, and handcuffed them to each other and made them sit at the front with their backs to the wall. Kathy stood next to them.

'You have any more friends out there?'

They didn't answer. Will went back to the door, and glanced out. He could see another one coming, so he stepped back and waited. The suspect opened the door and came in.

'Look out,' one of the suspects shouted.

He spun round and fired. Will fired back and he fell to the floor, fatally wounded. They heard more shots outside, Will pushed the door closed and got ready, then he heard Stanson.

'Sergeant, are you OK? We are all clear out here.'

Will opened the door and Stanson came in, he looked at the suspects and smiled.

'Nice work, Sergeant.' He looked at Kathy holding her arm. 'Are you OK, Sergeant Hill?'

Will spun round, he put his handgun away and went to her.

'You OK?'

'Yes, he just caught my arm.'

'What? Why didn't you say?'

'You can't kill him twice, can you?'

'Funny, let me see,' She moved her hand, 'Doesn't look too bad, but I want an EMT to look at it.'

'OK.'

PD came in and to take the two into custody, and to take the students out. The young female came over to Will and Kathy.

'Thank you so much.'

'You're welcome,' Will replied. 'Maybe look at getting some better friends from now on.'

She nodded and left with the others. Will grabbed his weapons, giving one to Stanson and taking Kathy by the arm and they left the classroom. The principal was in the corridor.

'Thank you both for what you have done today, and I would like you both to come back after the Christmas break to continue these talks. The students need to hear this now more than ever.'

'No problem, we would be happy to come back,' Kathy replied.

The principal walked off and Will and Kathy headed for the exit.

'Looks like we are coming back then.' She smiled at him.

'Can't I send Stanson?'

'No, you were fab in there with them, I think you may have started getting through.'

'But you know what to say now.'

'Yes, but I also want the best with me.'

'I will do some, but I need to be out in the field you know that, but no getting shot next time and you really need to carry.'

'OK, I will.'

She got her arm dressed by the EMT — it was just a graze. They went back to the office, Will grabbed two coffees, and followed Kathy into her office. He put them on the desk and shut the door. He walked over to her and wrapped his arms round her, she leaned on his chest, he held her tight. He was so happy she came out of that room OK. It was the first time he had ever been scared and that worried him.

Chapter 23

Christmas was a quiet one, Tom and Lynne had come round, and they had spent the entire day watching movies, eating, and laughing. Will spoilt Kathy and she had the best Christmas she had had in a long time, but now it was time for the New Year's ball and she was so nervous. It was the first time she had attended an event with Will and she didn't know what to expect or how she would be welcomed.

'Sweetheart, are you ready, the car is here?' Will called.

Kathy came out of the bedroom, she looked amazing in a beautiful purple gown. Will had got it for her as part of her Christmas presents, her small bump was being shown off. She had a diamond necklace on, also a gift from Will.

'Wow you look breathtaking.' He moved towards her.

'Really, I don't feel it.'

'Are you kidding? I am blown away.'

She smiled a big smile, and took his arm, they went down in the elevator. Will just kept looking at her and smiling, they went through the lobby and got in the waiting car.

***

They arrived at the Four Seasons and went through to the hall where they were holding the ball. It was very exclusive, and it was only a small number, around 200, that were there. Kathy gripped Will's arm as she looked around, when suddenly a tall beautiful woman came rushing over to them. She hugged and air kissed Will in a loving manner. Kathy recognised her from her movies and magazine covers.

'Will, you made it, and this stunning lady on your arm must be Kathy who I have heard so much about.'

'Kathy this is Ashleigh.'

'Nice to meet you, Ashleigh.'

'Oh, you can call me Ash, I mean we are practically sisters now.'

'OK.' Kathy was taken back by her.

'Will, be a sweetie and go and get some drinks, while I chat to Kathy.' Will looked at her questioningly then headed to the bar. Ashleigh guided Kathy over to some seats.

'Firstly, let me apologise that it has taken till now to meet you. I have been so busy with work, but I am going to take some time off really soon so we will have plenty of time to get to know each other.'

'That would be great, Will hasn't told me that much.'

'Really, well there will be time for that. So do we know if it's a niece or nephew yet?' Ash asked putting a hand on Kathy's bump, gently.

'No, not yet.'

'I really hope it's a girl, but it's OK if it's a boy, too.'

Just then another woman approached.

'Ashleigh, how are you?'

Ashleigh stood and air kissed the woman.

'I'm good Felicity how are you?'

'Very good, and who's this?'

'This is Kathy, Will's fiancée.'

'Will Falco is engaged?'

'Yeah, and having a baby.'

'Really, well that's unexpected news. I knew he hadn't been on the scene for a while, but I wasn't expecting this, and what a way to tie him down, my dear.'

'I'm sorry.'

'Oh, sweetheart, Will Falco is, how can I say it politely, doesn't stay with one woman long, been like that since Carla. Most of the women here have bedded him, but a baby, well I am sure he will toe the line for a while, but a leopard doesn't change its spots.'

Kathy sat in silence not knowing how to respond, Ash looked shocked by her response. Felicity smiled and walked off. Ash sat back down.

'You know she is jealous right? She's not always so harsh, but Will was the most eligible bachelor see, he's worth more than anyone in here and most single women hoped they would get him to settle down.'

'He's worth the most?'

'Oh yeah, most of these lot are millionaires or married to them or were married to them, but Will is well above that. I will be worth nearly as much when my parents die though.'

'Wow, really?'

'Yeah, I suppose it's weird for you, me going on about it like that, but I grew up in this world. Like Will, it's normal to us, even though Will is a cop. One conversation about money and it is obvious he has plenty, that's why he tends not to talk about it.'

Kathy looked over to Will, he was stood talking to a woman she recognised.

'Ash who's that with Will?'

'Oh shit, that's Carla, let's go and rescue him.'

They walked over to Will, he was still at the bar. Ash grabbed her drink off the bar, Will passed Kathy her orange juice.

'Ashleigh darling how are you?'

'Oh, I'm great, you?'

'My evening has improved,' she said smiling at Will. 'Who's your friend?'

'You remember my fiancée, Kathy, don't you? You met at the hospital when I was in after I got shot,' Will answered.

'Yes, you look lovely, dear, I didn't know you were still together.'

'Yeah, and they are having a baby, isn't that great,' Ash added.

'Pregnant, I see. Well, if you will excuse me.'

She walked away with a rather sour look on her face. Ash was smiling.

'Now that was fun, I love messing with her after what she did.'

'Couldn't tell at all,' Will replied.

'What did she want anyway?'

'Same as last time, but I think she may not try again after that.'

Will wrapped his arm around Kathy. She wished she could have a strong drink, this was perhaps a bit much for her. She excused herself, and went to the ladies' room. Ash followed.

'Are you OK, Kathy?'

'Yeah, I just needed a minute.'

'You're wondering, aren't you?'

'What?'

'Who Will has slept with in there?'

'Yeah, is that weird?'

'No, it's natural, especially with pregnancy hormones.'

'OK how do you know that?'

'Half my friends have had babies, I know a lot and some of it I didn't want to know.'

'OK, so how many is it?'

'You really want to know that?'

'It's more of a need, so I know what I'm dealing with.'

'OK, but know he loves you and that baby, and it won't change that, and he will never let you go for anyone in that room.'

'OK.'

'It's around forty or fifty, over five years.'

'Really? That's a lot.'

'But in the last eight months it's just one.'

Kathy started to breathe really fast, she couldn't catch her breath.

'You, OK?'

Kathy shook her head, Ash took her arm.

'Let's go and get some air.'

She guided Kathy out into the hall and towards the doors, but Kathy felt dizzy and needed to sit down.

'I'm going to get Will.'

Ashleigh ran off as quickly as she could, while holding her dress, and in high heels. Will came rushing over and crouched in front of her.

'Kathy, listen to me, breathe in through your nose and out through your mouth, deep breaths, that's it, slow them down.'

She did what he said, and she started to feel better. Will stood up.

'What the fuck happened?'

'I don't know we were talking and then she had a panic attack.'

'What were you talking about?'

'You, mostly and your exes.'

'Ash, what the hell?'

'Don't be mad at her, Will, I asked the questions.'

He crouched back down.

'I don't understand.'

'A woman made a comment earlier about you sleeping with most women here, I wanted to know how many, so I could be prepared for any more comments. So I asked Ash because I knew you wouldn't tell me.'

'And with good reason, I don't want that in your head, look what happened when you were told.'

'I didn't realise how many it was.'

'Sixty-two women in five years isn't that many and they aren't all here.'

'Sixty-two.' Her breathing started to quicken. 'Ash said it was forty to fifty.'

'Shit, OK you need to take deep breaths, focus on each one and slow them down.'

Ash went and got her a drink and as she took deep breaths and had a drink of juice, she began to feel better. Will sat down next to her.

'You know that number doesn't matter right, because the only one I want for the rest of my life is you.'

She took his hand and held it for a few moments and leaned on his shoulder.

'You OK or do you want to go home?'

'I'm good now, I have you by my side and that's how I want to spend my new year. That and in front of all these women that will never get to sleep with you again anyway.'

Will laughed and kissed her on the head.

'You are definitely feeling better.'

The three of them had an amazing night. Ash told Kathy some funny stories about Will when he was younger. He showed her off proudly, and although most of the people there were happy for him, there were a few women that were obviously jealous. Kathy had been so unsure about the night, but by the end she had such a good time she knew she could enjoy that life even if she couldn't wrap her head around the money.

Chapter 24

January was a busy month for Kathy. The talks in the schools had been more popular than she could ever have imagined and in most part the teenagers seemed to be paying attention. Will had done a few with her but mostly it had been Harvey and Stanson helping. Since she had been grazed by a bullet at the school, Will had been different even more so since her panic attack at new year. They had barely been intimate, and he had been far too protective of her and the baby. She was well into her second trimester, but she wasn't excessively big and was enjoying her pregnancy. But Will was driving her crazy, and she was so sexually frustrated that she was losing her temper with everyone and everything. It hadn't helped that Stanson had been so nice, especially when they had worked together and had even called her beautiful. She walked into her office and Gina came in.

'Hey, how was your weekend?'

'OK, I guess.'

'Will still being a pain in the ass?'

'Yeah, he wouldn't even let me take the plates into the kitchen yesterday.'

'Wow, that is insane.'

'I know, and I really need, you know.'

'What, sex?'

'Yeah, but he won't even touch me.'

'You need to talk to him about this.'

'I know but I don't know how to.'

'I don't think it matters how you do it, but you need to.'

'Maybe he isn't attracted to me any more, now I'm getting bigger.'

'Have you heard yourself? Will adores you and that baby, my guess when you were clipped at the school it scared him, and you and I both know scared is not an emotion Will is used to feeling. He has overreacted to this is all, now get that nonsense out of your head and go and speak to him.'

***

It had been a quiet morning and Will was in his office doing some training plans. He assessed his team so often and every month he slightly altered their training to suit how they were performing. He considered it a very important part of his work, even the slightest issue on a call could result in someone being killed or injured. Kathy came to the door and watched him for a moment before she spoke.

'Hey, I have some details missing on Stanson's training.'

'When from?'

'Beginning of the month, I have all the others but not his.'

'OK, I will see if I can track it down.'

She stood there for a moment.

'You need something else?'

'I was wondering if we could talk, maybe later or this evening.'

'Yeah, of course.' Will got up and walked round the desk to her 'Are you and the baby OK?'

'Yeah, of course.'

'OK, well I have to go down to the range with Turner and do some one-on-one training, she was a little off last week.'

'Oh, OK I will see you later then.'

Will passed Kathy with a smile and a kiss on the cheek. She watched him leave with Turner. She had seen Turner flirting with him in the office and wondered if she could be part of the reason he had gone cold. She knew that he loved her, but she also knew Will and if he wasn't sexually interested in her, was it because he was having sex with someone else? Had the women at new year been right and a leopard didn't change its spots? She walked over to her old office, Tom was sat at his desk, he saw her hovering at the doorway.

'Hey Kathy, what brings you to our side?'

She walked in and closed the door.

'I was wanting to speak to Will, but he is busy with Turner and I have some training missing for Stanson.'

'Well, I'm not busy, if you want to talk to me.'

Kathy sat down and smiled.

'Thanks, Tom, but this is kind of personal.'

'How about I get you a coffee and then we can talk, I may be able to help.'

Tom went and got two coffees, then came back in, closed the door. He put the coffees on his desk and then sat in front of her on the edge of the desk.

'You know Will better than anyone and I really want to speak to him about something but don't know how.'

'What about?'

'Well since the school shooting and me getting grazed, Will has been rather overprotective and we haven't,' she paused, 'been intimate at all.'

'Oh, not at all?'

'He's barely kissed me.'

'That's not like him, he generally can't keep his hands off you.'

'I know, I feel like he doesn't want me any more, then I see him with Turner, and they flirt with each other.'

'What? You can't think him and Turner, he wouldn't do that to you.'

'There was a woman at the party, Felicity, she said Will would never stay with just one woman.'

'Felicity, I know her.'

'You do?'

'Yeah.'

'Will had a relationship with her, didn't he?'

'Yeah, but that was years ago, she was the first after Carla, it lasted about a month, so I would honestly say she is jealous. She couldn't get him to settle down and neither could anyone else till you.'

'But have I? I'm just not sure any more.'

She suddenly moved her hands to her bump.

'You OK?'

'Yeah,' she smiled. 'The baby just kicked for the first time.'

'Really?' Tom put his hand on her bump, and he smiled as he felt the baby kicking.

He got out his phone and sent a text to Will, who appeared just minutes later.

'What's going on?'

'The baby kicked.' Kathy smiled.

'Seriously?'

Will knelt down in front of her, and put his hands on her bump. He waited for a moment, then the biggest smile appeared on his face as he felt the baby move and kick.

'That's so amazing,' he said.

He stayed there for a moment, then he stood up, bent down and kissed Kathy on the head and went back to the door.

'I best get back,' he disappeared.

Kathy looked at Tom and then got her coffee from the desk.

'OK, I am starting to see what you mean, that was not like him at all.'

'Glad it's not just me imagining it, thought I was going mad, pregnancy hormones or something.'

She finished her coffee and stood up.

'I need to get back to work, I'm going to borrow Stanson to go over his training as Will is busy with Turner.'

'No, worries, and Kathy you need to speak to Will.'

'I know, thanks Tom.'

Kathy left and gestured to Stanson to follow her to her office. They went in and she closed the door.

'Stanson, I seem to be missing your training info from the fifth of this month, so I need to know what training you did or didn't do.'

'The fifth? I was at work and did all the training that the others did, Sergeant.'

'Then I don't know where the records are, and I can't ask Sergeant Falco because he is on the range with Turner.'

'Are you OK, Sergeant?'

'Yeah, why?'

'You seem a bit stressed.'

Kathy started crying. Stanson moved round the desk and crouched in front of her, he handed her a handkerchief.

'Thanks, I'm sorry.'

'Are you sure you're OK?'

'I don't know, I'm so confused and these pregnancy hormones aren't helping at all, turning me into an emotional mess.'

Stanson put his hand on hers to comfort her, he hated seeing her like this. She looked at him and smiled, he smiled back. Then Kathy leaned forwards and kissed him. He responded, and it turned passionate quickly, she was about to lift his shirt when he suddenly stood up and she realised what she had just done.

'Shit, I shouldn't have done that.'

'I need to go,' he said and left quickly.

Gina appeared at her door, Kathy was sobbing in her chair.

'Hey, what happened?' She walked round to Kathy and hugged her.

'I just made a huge mistake.' She paused. 'I just kissed Stanson.'

Chapter 25

'Holy shit you did what?' she asked stepping back.

'I kissed Stanson.'

Gina hugged her again and held her for a few moments.

'I didn't mean to, he was being so nice, and it just happened.'

'Oh, Honey.'

Kathy could feel her breathing quicken and her chest get tighter, she could hardly breathe. She was having a panic attack.

'Kathy, you need to breathe in through your nose and out through your mouth, nice deep breaths.'

Kathy did, and after a few minutes, was feeling better. She had a drink of water and looked at Gina.

'What the hell do I do now?'

***

Stanson went into Tom's office and shut the door. Tom looked up from his paperwork and looked at him questioningly.

'Tom, I have a huge problem.'

'OK, should you not speak to Sergeant Falco?'

'Not about this.'

'Why, what's the problem?'

'Kathy just kissed me.'

'What?'

'She kissed me, Sergeant Falco is going to kill me, isn't he?'

Tom got up and walked round his desk and sat on it. Stanson was pacing up and down.

'OK, walk me through what happened.'

'I went to sort out some training records, I asked if she was OK because she looked stressed. She started crying, I comforted her, I gave her a handkerchief and then she kissed me.'

'Did you kiss her back?'

'Yeah, for a moment anyway, then I got out of there.'

'OK, we need to talk to Falco and explain.'

'Do we have to do that? I don't want to get her in trouble or cause an issue with them, she is pregnant.'

'I know, but she will probably tell him and then he may just kill you.'

'Shit, this is not good, is it?'

Tom heard Will and Turner come back in the office, he went over to the door and opened it.

'Sergeant, can we speak with you for a moment please?'

Will went in and Tom shut the door and went and stood next to Stanson, opposite Will.

'What's going on?'

'OK, before we tell you something, you need to stay calm, OK,' Tom said.

'OK, I will try.'

'Kathy kissed me,' Stanson said tentatively.

'Are you kidding me?' Will replied angrily.

'No, Sergeant.'

'What the fuck when?' he shouted.

'About ten minutes ago in her office, she wanted to speak to me about some training, confirm that I did it with the rest of the team.'

'Did you kiss her?'

'I reacted when she kissed me, but only for a moment and I stopped and left.'

Will moved right in front of Stanson, he was furious and could have punched him right there.

'Will, he came straight to me with this,' Tom interjected.

Will turned round, and moved back to where he was standing. He didn't look at Stanson.

'Why did you tell me?'

'Because you are my sergeant, and I value my place on alpha, especially as your number two.'

'OK, you can go back to work.'

Stanson looked at Tom and left quickly.

'Will.'

He turned round and looked at Tom.

'Why would she do this?'

'I think you need to ask Kathy that.'

'She spoke to you earlier, before this happened?'

'Yeah, she did, but there is no way I am getting in the middle of this Will, you need to speak to her.'

'I'm going to the gym.'

Just then Will's beeper went off.

'Great that is just what I need.'

***

Will and his team arrived at a house out of the city. There were two detectives waiting for them and several squad cars on the street. Will went to the detectives and then back to the team with the details.

'OK, we have three armed suspects in the house, and they are required for questioning about a number of armed robberies.'

'Any hostages?' Bennett asked.

'No, so Stanson, you and Turner take the back door, Harvey and I will go through the front with the detectives. Palmer and Bennett, you take the street in case they get out.'

They all got into position, the two detectives went with Will and Harvey to the front door. One of the detectives knocked.

'NYPD open the door,' he shouted.

Suddenly the suspects started firing at the door. One of the detectives got hit, Will and Harvey took cover and the second one helped his partner to safety.

'Red, this is orange we have one in custody he tried to escape through the back,' Stanson radioed.

'Received, we are taking fire at the front. White, have you got anything?'

'We have a suspect on the roof, shall we take him?'

'Yes, white, take him.'

Bennett fired and the suspect fell. Will turned to Harvey.

'OK we need this last one, are you ready?'

'Let's get him.'

Will moved back to the door, the firing had stopped. He kicked the door open and saw the suspect running through the house, he fired and hit him in the back of the leg. The suspect fell. Will and Harvey secured him and cleared the house.

'Control, this is alpha team we are all clear, we need EMTs and PD to take these guys into custody and we may need the fire department to get one off the roof.'

'Received, alpha team, they are en route.'

When they had handed over the suspects and the scene, Will and his team went back to the truck. The team were packing away their gear when an officer shouted to Will.

'Hey, Sergeant, is it not you that is meant to get shot at?'

Will handed his weapon to Stanson and walked over to him. Harvey watched, as Will walked over.

'Excuse me?'

'Well, I see the detective got shot but you didn't, how's that work?'

Will got up close to him.

'Least we have the balls to go in, as do the detectives, not like you stood here hiding behind your car.'

'You trying to say I'm scared? I was fired at three times last week.'

'I get fired at more than that, in a day.'

Will turned round and was about to go back to the truck when the officer said something else.

'So, are you sure that baby is yours? I hear your girlfriend gets about a bit in SWAT.'

Will turned round went straight to him, grabbed him, and pinned him up against the squad car. He was ready to punch him, but Harvey spotted him and got there just in time to stop him.

'Sergeant, don't do it.'

Will let him go and walked away. Harvey turned to the officer.

'Really, what the fuck? That's low bringing his baby into it, you're lucky he didn't shoot you.'

Harvey walked back to the truck and they went back to the office.

***

Captain Bridge was at his door when they walked back in.

'Falco, a word,' he said sternly.

Will followed him over to his office, they went in and Will shut the door. He stood opposite the captain.

'Good shout, Falco, right until you nearly punched an officer.'

Will stood there quietly. Captain Bridge sat on his desk in front of Will and sighed.

'How many times are we going to do this Falco? You in here after a shout, you have just about upset every precinct in this city with your attitude, but today you very nearly crossed a line that there would be no coming back from.'

'Yes, Captain.'

'Do you want to tell me why?'

'He was mouthing off like some of them do, about the detective being hit. I was walking away and then he made a comment about Kathy and the baby, that it might not be mine.'

'Well, that's low, but I can't ignore this, Sergeant. You're at your desk for the rest of the day.'

'Captain, come on.'

'Falco, if it weren't for Harvey, you would be up on charges.'

'Stanson isn't ready to lead alpha yet.'

'You let him lead when Dune shot you and bravo can attend any calls with them for the rest of the shift. Hargreaves can work with Stanson.'

'Is it just today?'

'Depends what mood you walk in here in tomorrow, but you are one step away from suspension after today, Falco.'

'Suspension, what for?'

'One more incident Falco and I won't have a choice, now I suggest you do something to keep your anger in check, you are about to become a father and you need to sort yourself out.'

Will stood looking at the captain and sighed.

'Yes, Captain.'

'OK you can go, and I suggest you spend some time down in the gym, work out some of that anger you have.'

'Yes, Captain.'

Will left and walked across to Stanson.

'Alpha is yours for the rest of the day, don't mess it up.'

'Yes, Sergeant.'

Will walked into Tom's office and shut the door.

'I'm at my desk for the rest of the shift.'

'What happened on that call?'

'I nearly hit an officer.'

'What? Will, you are lucky he didn't send you home.'

'Yeah, I know, I am on warning, one more and I am suspended.'

'You need to sort this out with Kathy.'

'No, I need to go to the gym, I'm not ready to talk to her yet.'

Chapter 26

Kathy decided to speak with Will about what happened. She found him in the gym. He was lifting weights when she walked over. He looked and saw her, he stopped and stood up and went over to the punch bag. He had a drink and looked at her.

'Hey, I looked for you in the office, Tom said you were down here.'

'Sure you weren't looking for Stanson?'

'He told you.'

'Yeah, about two hours ago.'

'I didn't know what to say to you.'

'And you do now?'

'Not really.'

'Then maybe we should talk when you do.'

Kathy was shocked, she thought he would want to talk, but he just seemed angry, not that she could blame him for that. She left and went back to her office.

***

Kathy had decided to go to Gina's after work as she couldn't face going home. She sat having a drink of tea, Gina was in the kitchen.

'So what now?'

'I don't know, wait till he will talk to me I guess.'

'Do you want to stay here for a few days?'

'That would be great.'

Kathy started crying.

'I just can't believe I messed this up so badly. I don't know what I was thinking, and of all the people why did I have to kiss Stanson? With our history, I'm not surprised Will is so mad.'

'He will calm down honey, he just needs time.'

'What if he can't forgive me, then what?'

'You can't think like that. Will loves you and that baby.'

Kathy couldn't stop crying. Gina tried to find more tissues, she left the room. Kathy started to have a panic attack, she could hardly breathe. She got up to get Gina but passed out, Gina came running in.

'Kathy,' Gina shouted. She got out her phone and called for an ambulance.

When paramedics arrived, they started to take care of Kathy. She came round.

'What happened?'

'You passed out, you wouldn't wake up, so I called 9-1-1'

'We are going to take you in, get you checked out,' the EMT said.

'Do you want me to call Will?'

Kathy nodded, they put her on a stretcher and took her out to the ambulance. Gina called Will then followed in Kathy's car.

***

Kathy was being checked over and Gina was pacing up and down when Will arrived at the hospital. He saw Gina and went straight to her.

'What happened? Are they OK?'

'She had a panic attack and passed out, the doctor is in there now'

Will sat down and Gina sat next to him, neither of them spoke until the doctor came out. Will stood up.

'How is she?'

'She is better now, and so is the baby. She said she has been having panic attacks since being pregnant, these are causing her oxygen levels to go up and down, and her blood pressure keeps dropping too, though it's not related. She needs to avoid stress and get plenty of rest and I will be making her doctor aware of what is going on so she can monitor the rest of the pregnancy closely.'

'Thanks doctor.'

He walked off. Will sighed, and grabbed his stuff to leave, Gina stopped him.

'Where are you going?'

'Home.'

'You're not even going to speak to her?'

'Not tonight.'

'Wow, I always had you down as a better man than that, Will.'

'Excuse me?'

'Your fiancée is laying in there, the woman carrying your baby and you are just going to leave.'

'This is nothing to do with you.'

'Like hell it isn't. I know what she did, Will, and I have told her off for it and believe me when I say she is devastated about this. Did you even bother to consider why this happened? No, of course you didn't, you were too busy treating her like a fragile object, and thinking of your ego. If you had paid more attention and not been so worried about her getting hurt it wouldn't have happened.'

'So it's my fault?'

'No, but you haven't helped, ever since the school you have been different and not even had sex with her or even been intimate.'

Will looked at her.

'She is my best friend and I know everything Will, but right now I'm not the one she needs, she needs to know you still love her and that baby.'

'Of course I still love her, but I'm angry, she kissed another man, who she has had sex with, I can't just ignore that, Gina.'

'How many women have you slept with Will?'

'That's nothing to do with this, because I haven't been near another woman since I have been with Kathy.

Yeah, she slept with Stanson when we were split up, but today she kissed him, and we were very much still together.'

'Were? Are you splitting up with her?'

Will walked off and left without saying anything else to her. Gina went into Kathy's room.

'Hey, you're looking better.'

'Feeling better too, did I see Will before?'

'Yeah, but he's gone home, sorry honey.'

'It's OK, I expected that, but at least he came, right?'

'Yeah,' Gina held her hand. 'So when they let you go, we will stop by yours and grab some stuff for you for a couple of days, you can stay at mine till you two can sort this out.'

'If we can sort this out.'

'He's just angry, but that will pass.'

'Will it? Thing is, I can't blame him for being this angry, after what I did.'

Gina held her hand for a moment.

'Can you get my stuff for me, so I don't have to see him.'

'No, but I will be with you. You are going to have to see him so it's probably better at home.'

'OK, maybe a few girly days is what I need.'

Chapter 27

Kathy opened the door, Gina followed her inside. It was quiet. Kathy looked around for Will, but he didn't seem to be there.

'Maybe he went out or hasn't come home yet.'

'Maybe, he could have gone for a drink or to Tom's I guess.'

'Well hurry up go and get your stuff and if he comes back, I will stall him.'

Kathy went into the bedroom, she went into the walk-in closet and started to look through her stuff. She got a bag and put a few things in it. She walked back into the bedroom. Will was stood there in his towel after coming out of the shower.

'Hi, I was just grabbing some clothes, I am going to stay with Gina for a few days.'

'You're OK now?'

'The doctor said I just need to take it easy, we are fine, physically anyway.'

Kathy moved towards the door and stopped.

'For what it's worth, Will, I am really sorry, and I wish I could change what happened today, but I can't. So when you are ready to talk, I will be at my place.'

'Talk right, because that will make this OK.'

Kathy looked at him, he didn't seem angry any more, he looked sad. She stepped towards him, but he put up his hand to stop her.

'You want to talk, OK. Today, I felt like you had ripped out my heart, I have never loved anyone like I love you, not Carla, nor anyone, and you kiss a man who you had sex with.'

'It was just a kiss, Will.'

'If he hadn't stopped though, then would it have been more?'

'No, of course not.'

'How can I be sure of that?'

Kathy walked over to the bed and sat down, a tear rolled down her cheek, she wiped it away. Will handed her some tissues. She took them and looked up at him, tears filling her eyes.

'I think we should talk about this another time, the doctor said no stress,' Will said.

'No, please Will.'

Will walked towards the door and turned round to face her.

'Why did it have to be Stanson of all people?'

'You don't want to go there Will.'

'I need to know because it can't be worse than what's in my head right now.'

She paused and looked at him for a moment.

'OK, he is an attractive guy and there is a spark between us, always has been. He was being so nice, and

I have been somewhat sexually frustrated. I was upset, he comforted me, and it just happened.'

'A spark?'

'Yeah, it's not love, it's not even close to what we have.'

'So it's a sexual thing?'

'No, that's not what I said.'

'So what then?'

'I don't know, maybe it is because I slept with him, maybe it's because you haven't touched me since before Christmas, I don't know.'

'So, because we haven't had sex, you kiss another man?'

'Not just that.'

'Then what, Kathy, I have a right to know?'

He moved towards her, she looked up at him.

'I thought there was something between you and Turner.'

'Turner, why the hell would you think that?'

'I have seen her flirting with you so many times and you always flirt back.'

'I flirt with Turner?'

'OK maybe you don't realise you do it, but believe me she notices, and the thought of you two down on the range together…'

'Kathy, we were training.'

'I know, but I know how close you get when you train.'

'So I am sleeping with all the guys, too?'

'You think I'm crazy and maybe I am, my hormones are all over the place, but I am telling you, she has the hots for you.'

Will came and sat next to her on the bed.

'I never told you this, but I fancied you from the moment I met you in the captain's office.'

'Why did you never tell me that before?'

'You were on my team and I had to be professional. The first time I kissed you, I had wanted to do that for so long but I knew I couldn't and shouldn't. I had it in my head it was what was best for you.'

'So you pushed me away, till that day.'

'Yeah.'

'And that's what you have been doing since I got grazed at the school.'

'It made sense in my head, to protect you I can't be too close to you, but I should have realised.'

'Will, it's not your fault, I was wanting to say something but I didn't know how and then all this happened. I am so sorry for what I did, I know it will take a lot for you to trust me again, but I am willing to work hard to do that.'

Will looked at her and sighed.

'I want to, I really do, but it's going to take some time to work through all this.'

'I get that, so do you want some time to yourself or do you want me to stay?'

'Stay, we can talk some more over dinner.'

Kathy smiled and put her hand to his face. He put his hand on hers, she leaned forwards and kissed him, it was gentle, but he didn't respond. She moved back and looked at him.

'Right, you aren't ready, maybe I should go.'

'No, don't go.'

She looked at him, near to tears again, and he kissed her, it was tender and loving. It then turned passionate and intense, she laid back on the bed and he followed. His hands were all over her and she was about to remove his towel and stopped. She sat up.

'I best go and let Gina know what's going on.'

'Yeah, OK, I will get dressed and order some food, we can talk some more.'

Kathy went out of the bedroom. Gina was sat on the sofa, she stood when she heard Kathy.

'About time, what have you been doing?'

'Will was in the bathroom and he came out as I was leaving.'

'Oh and? Don't tell me you have been having sex in there while I was waiting.'

'No, we have been talking, and he wants to talk some more, so that's a start, right?'

'Yeah, so you are staying?'

'Yeah, I mean I need to.'

'OK, but if it all goes wrong, which I am sure it won't, just call me, and I will come and get you, OK?'

'Thanks, come on I will take you down.'

Kathy took Gina down in the elevator and asked Charles to call her a cab. She waited till it arrived and gave her a hug. She went back upstairs, and Will was in the kitchen on the phone.

'OK see you at work tomorrow,' he said as he finished the call.

Kathy walked over. Will had made her a tea, and had a beer open for himself.

'I have ordered some food if you want to grab a quick shower before it gets here.'

'Yeah, OK.'

She went and got a shower, and came back out in her robe. Will had got the dinner set up at the table. They sat and ate and talked some more. Will was still feeling unsure but he knew that he had to try and trust her.

'How many school talks do you have left?' he asked, taking the plates into the kitchen.

'Just three.'

'I was thinking that Harvey could do those with you.'

'You don't trust me with Stanson.'

'I just think after what happened it would be more appropriate to take Harvey.'

'OK sure.'

She stood and moved over to the living room. She sat on the rug by the fireplace, he came over and sat next to her. She leaned on him and he put his arm around her. She relaxed in his arms, but she could still feel a tension between them. Will moved his hand.

'You're not wearing anything under there are you?'
'No.'

She turned round to face him, and she kissed him. Will untied her robe, and she kissed him again. They made love right there by the fire.

Chapter 28

An hour later they were relaxing on the sofa when the front door opened, and Ashleigh walked through. She didn't speak and went straight into her bedroom. Kathy looked at Will, he got up and went to her bedroom door.

'Ash, what are you doing here?'

'Well, I was supposed to be staying at my parents' tonight, but Mom and I fell out and I walked out.'

'What about this time?'

'She is trying to set me up with some guy who is a right bore, so I said no. Then she went on about my future, marriage, kids, so I said I would date who I wanted, same old story really.'

'Still, you should have called or texted.'

'Why? I never usually do.'

'You haven't shown up since Kathy moved in and if you had showed up about twenty minutes ago…'

'Eeeewww Will, you were having sex in the living room, I don't need to know that.'

'Maybe not, but you nearly saw it.'

'OK, I will text next time, and even wait for an answer if we can stop talking about this now.'

Will laughed.

'You want a drink?'

'I would love one after tonight.'

They walked through to the living room. Kathy was just coming out of their bedroom with her pyjamas on.

'Why did you put those on, preferred how you were before?' he said teasingly as he put his arms around her.

'Seriously Will, stop doing that.'

He laughed as he went to pour them both a strong drink. Ashleigh sat in the chair and Will sat on the sofa next to Kathy. She leaned on him and he put his arm around her resting his hand on her bump.

'So Ash how long are you staying?'

'Just tonight but I will be back at the weekend if that's OK. Now Kathy is twenty weeks, we should start looking at baby stuff, of course that would be easier if we knew the sex.'

'It's a girl,' Kathy smiled.

'Oh, my goodness, really? That's fab I have seen so many cute outfits.'

'I'm not sure it's a good idea this weekend,' Will said.

'Why not, you need to get started.'

'Kathy needs to rest, she was in hospital earlier.'

'What? Why? Are you and the baby OK?'

'I had a panic attack and passed out, but I am fine and would love to go shopping on Sunday.'

Will was going to object.

'Will, I will be fine, I won't be on my own and she's right, we need to start looking.'

'OK, I'm at the gym with Stanson anyway, but if you need me to pick you up, you call me.'

'OK, and maybe we will pop in the gym when we are done,' Kathy joked.

'That's not funny.' He got up. 'Do you want some tea before bed?'

'Yes, please.'

Will went over to the kitchen, Ashleigh got up and sat next to Kathy.

'You want to explain that.'

'When Will and I weren't together last year I slept with Stanson and today I made the big mistake of kissing him, but I don't want to get into that while Will is here.'

'You kissed another guy today?'

'Sssshhhh, not so loud, I nearly stayed at my old place tonight because of it all and the way he reacted says I'm not completely forgiven yet.'

'OK, you can explain on Sunday, but I need to know, is he cute, this Stanson?'

'Yeah, and is really fit too like Will.'

'Really, is he good in bed?'

'I can't believe you just asked me that after what I just said.'

'I'm curious now.'

'Yeah, he is, but Will is better.'

'What is it with you two? I didn't need to know that.'

'Sorry, I will try not to do that again.'

They were laughing as Will brought Kathy's tea over.

'What's going on?'

'Nothing just girls' talk.'

He sat and they all chatted while having their drinks, then they went to bed. Kathy slept better than she had in weeks, but she had a feeling that Will was still mad about today even if he wasn't saying so.

***

Will was in his office the next morning as his team arrived. He had got in slightly earlier than normal to speak with the captain, he had explained the whole situation and for now was back on active duty. He got up and stood at his door as they sat down.

'Morning everyone, after your coffees, it is training time. I want you all down on the range in thirty minutes.'

Stanson went over to Will and stepped inside his office as Will sat back down behind his desk.

'We good after yesterday, Sergeant?'

'Yes, we are, Stanson.'

'I hope things are OK with you and Sergeant Hill.'

'They will be I am sure, but we still have some things to sort out.'

Stanson went back to his desk and sat, wondering what he meant. Will went to see Kathy before they started. He took her a coffee, he went in and closed the door, she looked up.

'Thanks, what did I do to deserve that?'

'Well, I was just coming to speak to you so thought you would like one.'

'OK, so what did you need?'

'Just wanted to let you know we are training this morning so if you need me, you will have to text as we are on the range first.'

'Oh OK, are you all down there?'

'All of alpha, so I will see you later.'

Will left and went down to the range and got set up. He knew his team wouldn't be down there too long, but he liked them to stay sharp.

All the team arrived bang on time, they all got ready and fired their first clip. Will collected the targets. Turner was slightly off.

'Turner, you need to work on this, or you won't be shooting on a call.'

'Maybe another one-to-one, Sergeant.'

'Stanson.' Stanson came over. 'Take Turner to the end booth, she needs extra help'

'You want me to do that, Sergeant?'

'Yeah, you're my number two.'

'But Sergeant, you have more experience to help me,' Turner objected.

'Maybe so, Turner, but I have three others to train and Stanson is more than good enough to help you, so off you go.'

She walked off, visibly annoyed. the other three laughed.

'Got another admirer, Sergeant,' Harvey said.

'What, Turner?'

'Yeah, she has the hots for you.'

'You think?'

'Sergeant, to say you have been out with a lot of women, you don't know much about them, do you?' Bennett laughed.

'It seems not.' He looked at Turner. 'Don't tell Kathy though she will kill her.'

'We won't, Sergeant.'

***

It had been an extremely busy day, full of training and call-outs, Will was looking forward to getting home. The team were walking across the parking lot. Turner wasn't there, she had disappeared pretty quickly. Just then, a man around six feet tall approached them, and stopped in front of Will.

'Are you Sergeant Falco?'

'Yeah, who are you?'

The man punched Will on the left side of his face, he had something in between his fingers and Will's face was bleeding. Stanson, Bennett and Harvey all drew their handguns on him and stopped him leaving. He stopped and turned back to Will.

'OK who the fuck are you and why did you just hit me?'

'My girlfriend told me all about your touching approach to training.'

'Who the fuck is your girlfriend?'

'Claire Turner.'

'And what exactly did Turner tell you?'

'That when you were training your hands were all over her.'

'Did she also tell you I train all my team the same, that she requested I train her again or that I have a pregnant fiancée waiting for me at home?' Will shouted.

'No.'

'Didn't think so, now get out of here before I let my team use you for target practice.'

He left very quickly. Will touched his face. It was still bleeding as he turned to Stanson.

'It's not deep, is it?'

'Can't tell in this light, might need a stitch or two and a good clean.'

'Shit, really, Kathy will be furious with this, she said she had a crush on me.'

'I definitely wouldn't want to be Turner tomorrow, if Sergeant Hill gets hold of her,' Bennett said.

***

Will got home about an hour later, he had gone to the ER and had needed stitches. Kathy was on the sofa, Ashleigh was sat next to her.

'Hey, you're late.' Kathy stood up and approached him, then saw his face. 'What the hell happened? Is this why you are late?'

'Yeah, Turner's boyfriend punched me, and he had something in his hand to cut my face.'

'What? Why?'

'Turner told him I was overly touchy in training.'

'I will kill her.'

Will put his arms round her and kissed the top of her head.

'No, stress remember.'

'So is this guy still in one piece?' Ashleigh asked.

'Yeah, he is.'

'Really?'

'I'm on a suspension warning for nearly hitting a cop yesterday, I wasn't going to give this guy the satisfaction of getting me suspended or up on charges.'

'I think it would be self-defence.'

'Well, I think the fact that Stanson, Bennett and Harvey all drew their own handguns on him, made him think twice about doing it again.'

'Wow, loyal team there, Will.'

'Yeah, they are, and what do we owe this pleasure Ash?'

'Things ran late so I texted Kathy, she said I could stay.'

'Well, I can't argue with that then.'

'No, you can't.'

'While you are here, make yourself useful, and order some food while I have a shower.'

'OK, will do.'

Will went into his bathroom and looked in the mirror, he wasn't sure how to handle this one.

Chapter 29

The next morning, the team arrived. Captain Bridge was standing at his door as they walked in.

'Officer Turner, can I have a word please?'

'Yes, Captain.'

She walked over and followed him into his office. Will was standing just inside. Captain Bridge walked round his desk and sat down.

'So, Turner, do you want to explain why Sergeant Falco here, needed three stitches in his face after your boyfriend hit him.'

'I wasn't aware he had, Captain.'

'So why do you think he would?'

'I don't know.'

'Well maybe it's because you told him I was overly touchy with you on the range,' Will stated.

Turner stood in silence for a moment.

'So, Turner, did you say anything of that nature to your boyfriend?' Captain Bridge asked.

'I may have said that I was uncomfortable with how Sergeant Falco was touching me in training.'

'Excuse me,' Will shouted.

'Sergeant, let me deal with this.'

Will folded his arms and leaned against a filing cabinet, clearly frustrated.

'What made you uncomfortable Turner?' the captain continued.

'Do I have to discuss this in front of Sergeant Falco?'

'Yes, you do, now go on.'

'His closeness and how he did it, like in a flirtatious way.'

'Sergeant Falco, do you train all your officers in the same way?'

'Yes, Captain, every single one of them.'

'And would they all agree to that.'

'Feel free to ask them, Captain.'

'And Turner asked for further tuition?'

'Yes, she did.'

'And you got Stanson to do that.'

'Yes, I did, as I was training the others in my team.'

'OK, now Turner, did Stanson train you in the same manner?'

'Similar, yes.'

'But your boyfriend didn't hit him?'

Turner went quiet again.

'Now I will say this only once, Turner, if you have a problem with any of my sergeants or officers, you tell me and not your boyfriend. From now on, Stanson will do all your training, so we avoid any further issues. Tell your boyfriend if he touches another one of my officers he will be arrested.'

'Yes, Captain.'

'Off you go Turner get back to work.'

Turner left and Will closed the door behind her.

'Well, I have to say, Falco, I am impressed that you kept your cool last night, well done.'

'I do pay attention sometimes, Captain, and I wasn't going to let him get me suspended.'

'Good call, now get back to work because you have plenty of paperwork not in yet.'

Will went back to his office, but before he could sit down, his beeper went off.

***

The call was at an apartment block. Detective Park met Will as he got out of the truck.

'Falco, just the man.'

'Park, what can we do for you today?'

'I have two suspects in number 301, they are armed and wanted on five charges.'

'Sounds fun, so what's the set-up?'

'We have only one entry point, no fire escape on that window at all, we checked.'

'OK, are you coming in too?'

'If that's OK with you.'

'If you stay back, you want them alive?'

'However it works out.'

'Good stuff.'

Will turned.

'What happened to your face?'

'Turner, my female rookie, her boyfriend happened.'

'Really is he in a body bag?'

'No, not yet anyway.'

Will went and got suited up and the team followed him and Park to the correct floor. They moved down to the door. Park knocked on the door.

'NYPD open the door.'

There was a lot of noise from inside, Park signalled to Will to go in. Will kicked the door open, he went in followed by Stanson, Harvey and Bennett. Palmer and Turner stayed outside. They found two suspects in the bedroom, they were armed and pointing their guns at Will and Stanson.

'NYPD drop your weapons.'

'We didn't do anything.'

'Then put the guns down and we can sort this out.'

'What so you can lock us up for something we didn't do.'

'No, so I don't have to shoot you.'

They looked at each other and then lowered their weapons.

'Park, you are safe to come in.'

Park entered, and looked at the two men stood there. He turned to Will.

'The ones we want aren't here.'

'What? This isn't them?'

'No.'

'Who are you after?'

Park took out his phone and showed Will two pictures, Will recognised one of them. The team headed back out of the building and Will went straight to Turner.

'Where is your boyfriend?'

'At home probably.'

'Which is?'

'Why?'

'Just give me the address, Turner.'

Turner wrote it down and passed it to Will, he showed it to Park.

'Let's go.'

The team took off in the truck followed by Park, they pulled up at a building about ten blocks away. They jumped out still ready. Will turned to Turner.

'You stay here. Palmer, stay with her and don't let her use her phone.'

'Yes, Sergeant,' Palmer replied.

Will went in followed by the rest of the team and Park. They stopped outside apartment 11. Park knocked.

'NYPD, open the door.'

There was nothing. Will kicked the door and went in, shots were fired towards them. Stanson followed Will through the apartment and stopped at a doorway leading to the bedroom.

'NYPD drop your weapons,' Will shouted.

There was no response. Will took a look, they were trying to unlock the window. He moved through into the bedroom.

'Stop what you are doing, put your hands on your heads, and turn around.'

The two suspects did what he said without any resistance.

'Park, you can come in we are clear.'

Park walked in and looked at them.

'Yeah, these are the two I want, thanks Falco.'

'You're welcome.'

Stanson and Park cuffed them and took them out, they got to the squad car. Turner didn't even look at her boyfriend. Before Park opened the door, Will spoke to the suspect.

'Bad luck for you, if you hadn't come and hit me, I would never have known it was you that they wanted.'

Park put him in the car.

'Thanks Falco, so it was him that hit you?'

'Yeah.'

'Then an added charge of assaulting a police officer it is, see you soon.'

'Yeah, I am sure you will.'

The team packed the gear away and jumped in the truck. Turner didn't speak all the way back to the office. Turner went straight into the ladies' toilet. Kathy was just washing her hands.

'Turner.'

'Sergeant Hill.'

Kathy moved towards the door and stopped, she turned to Turner who was at the sinks washing her face.

'Turner, you ever tell anyone that Sergeant Falco is overly touchy in training again and I won't be responsible for my actions. That kind of allegation can ruin careers and it doesn't go away for the rest of someone's life. Sergeant Falco is the most professional man you will ever meet in this unit, when it comes to women, especially those on his team. Now I suggest you are thankful you have such a man you can learn from.'

'Yes, Sergeant.'

Kathy left and went through to see Tom, she wanted to ask him something.

'Tom.' She went in and closed the door. 'Do you know what happened the other day, and why Will is on notice for suspension?'

'He didn't tell you?'

'No, and with how things are, which I know you will know about, I don't want to ask and cause another argument.'

'Kathy.' He sat back in his chair and looked at her. 'As much as I consider you two family, I can't keep getting in the middle of your fall-outs, I have problems of my own you know.'

Kathy was surprised by his response. Tom was the man who knew Will best and had always been there for advice before.

'I'm sorry, I shouldn't have asked.' She paused and looked down. 'I will go and speak to Will.'

She left and went over to Will's office. She didn't look at Stanson or the others as she passed. She went in and closed the door.

'Hey.'

'Hey, are you OK?'

'Yeah, I'm fine, just wanted to ask you something.'

'OK.' He stopped typing and looked up.

'Last night when you got home, you said you nearly hit an officer.'

'You want to know what happened?'

'Yeah.'

Will got up and walked round the desk, he sat on the edge just in front of her.

'I made a mistake, I let him wind me up. Harvey jumped in just in time, luckily for me.'

'But why? I know you lose your cool sometimes but going to hit someone is not you Will.'

'He mouthed off. I had just been told about you kissing Stanson, he asked if I was sure the baby was mine because you get around in the unit.'

'What?'

'If it had been any other day, it wouldn't have bothered me so much, but at that moment I lost it.'

'OK, well I best get back to work.'

'Kathy, it's not your fault, I should have ignored him. Captain benched me for the rest of the day and now I am back on duty, no big deal.'

She stepped forwards and put her arms round him. He hugged her and then she looked at him. He smiled, and she smiled back. She went to kiss him, but he moved.

'I need to go,' she said and left.

Will sighed heavily as he watched her leave.

Chapter 30

Sunday soon came around. Ashleigh and Kathy were in the lounge planning their shopping trip. Kathy had found it strange but wonderful that she had been able to talk to Ash about all the problems she was having with Will. She knew Will so well, and not just that, she didn't stay out of it like Tom always tried to. She knew Tom knew about the kiss, so he was obviously not as understanding as Ash had been.

'So have you two talked any more?'

'No, not really, he is really distant.'

'OK, that's not good, I thought he would be at least talking now.'

Kathy looked at Ash, she looked sad.

'Look, have you had sex since that night?'

'No.'

'OK, I will talk to him and see what's going on.'

'You shouldn't Ash, I don't want him to be mad at you too.'

'He won't be, don't worry.'

They stopped talking when the elevator buzzer went. Will appeared with a bag. There was a knock at the door, Will opened it and Stanson stepped in. Ashleigh nudged Kathy.

'Hi Stanson,' Kathy said.

'Hi.'

'Will, can I speak to you in the kitchen please?'

Will looked at Kathy curiously, but started to follow.

'Stanson, this is Ashleigh, won't be a moment.'

She walked through to the kitchen with Will, she leaned on the counter so she could see them.

'What's going on?'

'Nothing. Ash just wanted to meet Stanson is all.'

'Why?'

'Curious, I guess.'

'Why would she be curious?' Will asked, as he looked at Kathy. 'You know what don't answer that because I don't think I want to know and we need to go, you take it easy today, don't overdo it and if you need me to come and get you just call me.'

'I will be fine, stop worrying.'

'You haven't seen Ash when she gets shopping.'

Kathy put her arms around him, he held her tight and kissed her on the head.

'I just want you two to be safe.'

'I know, now get going.'

Will kissed her and went over to the front door.

'Come on Stanson, let's leave these two to go shopping.'

***

After three hours of looking at baby furniture and clothes, Kathy and Ash went for a drink at an exclusive café on 5th.

'So which one was your favourite? Mine was definitely the solid oak,' Ash said after ordering the drinks.

'Yeah, it was gorgeous, but a bit expensive.'

'For that kind of quality, you pay top prices, no expense was spared when I got my place and it will be the same when I find an apartment in the city.'

Kathy had a drink of her iced tea and sighed.

'What's wrong?'

'I sometimes struggle getting my head round the whole money doesn't matter thing, I grew up in a relatively nice neighbourhood, but my parents had to work hard for everything.'

'Oh, that must have been tough.'

'Sometimes, but it was normal life for me.'

They sat for a few minutes in silence, Ash didn't know what to say. The manager came over to them.

'Miss Ashleigh, I thought you should know, there are some photographers and fans outside, someone saw you come in.'

'Oh shit, OK thanks, can you make the rear exit available please?'

'Yes, of course.'

'OK, we are going to need a ride out of here.' She got out her phone and called Will.

'Ash, is Kathy OK?'

'Of course she's OK, but we are in a cafe on 5th and there are some photographers and fans out front, can't get Kathy out without her being knocked over. I have arranged for the back entrance to be used to leave.'

'OK, we will come and get you.'

***

Will and Stanson picked them up in Kathy's car, they sat in quiet at first before Will spoke.

'You two have fun?'

'Yeah, it was great, brought a catalogue home for you to look at, so you can help Kathy choose everything.'

'So you didn't buy any yet?'

'No, she is only twenty weeks, but we will have to order it all soon.'

'OK, we can have a look later then.'

Will pulled up outside an apartment block, it was quite run down. Ash looked out of the window.

'Did we take a wrong turn Will?'

'No, this is where Stanson lives.'

'Oh.'

'See you tomorrow, Sergeant, thanks for today.'

'Yeah, see you in the morning.'

Stanson got out and Kathy got in the front next to Will. She was really quiet.

'You OK?' Will asked.

'Yeah, just a bit tired.'

'OK, let's get home then.'

They drove home in relative quiet, when they got upstairs, Kathy went to have a lay down. Will followed Ash out onto the roof terrace, he got them both a drink and they stood overlooking the park.

'Well, something happened today,' Will stated.

'How do you mean?'

'Kathy being so quiet.'

'How would you know?'

'What?'

'Will if you were any more distant you would be out of state.'

'Just what have you and Kathy been talking about today?'

'I have been talking to her most of the week, since you know.'

'Ash, I love you, but this is none of your business.'

'Your happiness is none of my business now, Will? Of course it is, you two have so much going on right now and a baby coming, are you really going to let a kiss ruin everything you have?'

'Was it just a kiss though, she said there is a spark between them.'

'A spark?'

'Yeah, you know chemistry as in she likes him.'

'And she loves you, Will she doesn't want to be with him.'

'How can I be sure of that?'

'My advice, ignore what happened just for a few days and be like you were, make love to her, hold her, kiss her and see how she responds to that and talk to her.'

'OK I will give it a go, but I can't promise.'

Will had a drink of his beer and looked at Ash.

'So is that all that's wrong?'

'No, she may have a slight issue with the price of the baby stuff.'

'Issue why? The price doesn't matter.'

'That's the issue.'

Will had another drink and turned round and then sat down on a chair.

'I don't understand, how is that the issue?'

Ash sat down next to him.

'It's not for us, we are used to this life Will. Kathy had a hard life growing up and it was bred into her to watch her spending, not everyone is as lucky as us. Take Tom for example. I mean it's not like your parents didn't provide you with a healthy bank balance even before they died.'

'Yeah, I guess, I have just got so used to living here now and not thinking about money, I never thought it would be a problem. Once she was living here, I just thought she would get used to it, like when we went Christmas shopping, and Tom I guess our friendship is built on trust not money so we don't talk about it.'

'Well, I know what we can do with the baby stuff.'

'What's that?'

'Cross the prices out.'
'OK we can do that, are you sure it will work?'
'It's worth a try.'
'OK let's do it before she wakes up'

***

Kathy got up about an hour later. Ash and Will were sat on the sofa chatting, Kathy went into the kitchen and made some tea. Will followed her.

'You have a good rest?'

'Yeah, feel much better now.'

'You want to look at some baby catalogues with me?'

'OK.'

They went and sat on the sofa and Kathy opened the first one. She looked at Will confused.

'Why are all the prices crossed out?'

'Because I want us to decide what we want based on practical things not how much they cost.'

'And I suppose this has nothing to do with what I said to Ash earlier.'

'A little, but I don't want you to worry about the cost of this, I want you and our baby girl to have what you want.'

Kathy looked at Will and smiled. She knew their intentions were good, but she was not used to this way of life, and although she was trying hard to fit in, the way he was brought up was always going to make her different.

Chapter 31

The next morning, Kathy was sat eating breakfast, Will had just left and Ashleigh came through into the kitchen and poured a coffee.

'Kathy I was wondering if I could go with you to work this morning.'

'Did you ask Will?'

'No, because he would say no and in fifteen years I have never seen where he works, he's so scared I will let it slip who he is, which I won't. I also wanted to speak to your Captain, I want to officially support your initiative in schools.'

'And Stanson will be there.'

'OK, that too, but that's a bonus.'

'OK, you can come but I'm not taking the grief from Will.'

***

Will was sat in his office when Kathy and Ashleigh walked in, he watched them walk past and into and Captain's office. Tom appeared at his door.

'What's Ash doing here?' Tom asked.

'No clue.'

The teams were sat talking and it was obvious they had recognised Ashleigh.

'How does Sergeant Hill know Ashleigh? Did you see her last movie, wow she was so good?' Bennett asked.

'Yeah, I did, but she is much hotter in real life,' Webb replied.

'Come on guys, show some respect,' Stanson interrupted. 'She is friends with Sergeant Falco, and he will not be happy if he hears you talking like that.'

Will and Tom heard, and they looked at each other.

'Wow, that's interesting.'

'Yeah, they only met yesterday, briefly.'

'I think he has a soft spot for her.'

'You think so?'

Just then Kathy and Ashleigh came out of the captain's office. Tom walked off and Will went to his door. Ashleigh avoided him and went straight over to Stanson, she sat on his desk. Kathy stopped at Will's door and he gestured for her to go in. He closed the door and she turned round to face him, he had his back to the door.

'You want to explain?'

'She wanted to come.'

'Why, she never did before?'

'She has spoken to the captain about supporting our work in schools.'

'And that's the only reason?'

'She may have wanted to see Stanson again as well.'

'Really? Why?'

'He is a good-looking, single guy, who she thinks is worth getting to know.'

'What is it with everyone going after him?'

'Are you jealous now you aren't the only handsome one on the team?'

'Jealous? No.'

'Sure sounds like you are.'

He stepped forwards and wrapped his arms around her, kissed her on the head and then put a hand on her bump.

'Why would I be jealous when I have you and our baby girl, I don't need anyone else. Stanson is welcome to all other women but not you.'

Kathy smiled. Will kissed her, she felt a rush of relief and then she reacted and took hold of him. Her bump was starting to get in the way a little now, but right then she didn't care. She stepped back.

'I best go and get Ashleigh, she wants to look round while she is here.'

Will opened the door. Kathy walked out and looked around, but Ashleigh wasn't there.

'Where's Ashleigh gone?'

'Down the range with Stanson.'

Kathy turned to Will.

'Well, I can't go down there and get her, I'm not allowed.'

'OK, I will go and get her.'

Will walked down to the range. He opened the door and went in, Ashleigh was there with her arms around Stanson, kissing him.

'Ash!' Will shouted.

She stopped and looked at him.

'Hey Will, I asked Ryan to show me how to shoot.' She smiled.

'Yeah, looks like it, can you wait outside a minute.'

She disappeared out the door. Will folded his arms and looked at Stanson.

'Look, I'm sorry, Sergeant, it just happened.'

'Seems to be happening a lot lately, especially with women I care about.'

Stanson looked very worried at that moment.

'Don't look so worried, I know what Ash is like. You like her I take it.'

'Yeah, I do, a lot.'

'OK, do you like her because she is famous?'

'I haven't actually seen her movies.'

'OK, so why do you like her?'

'She's sweet, beautiful, quite funny and so kind, she is different to women I usually meet.'

'You only met her yesterday.'

'I know, but she asked me to dinner right before she kissed me, and I would like to date her.'

'She is an incredibly special woman, and like a sister to me. You ever hurt her, and I will literally rip your head off your shoulders.'

'Yes, Sergeant, I understand. I intend to look after her and treat her good as long as she wants me to.'

'Good, because you are really good, and I would hate to lose you off my team.'

'I won't hurt her, I promise, Sergeant. I also want to stay on alpha, so I have two reasons to make this work.'

Just then their beepers went off, they ran upstairs. Tom was coming out of his office and both teams were ready to leave.

'What we got?'

'Armed suspect at the Staten Island ferry port.'

'OK let's go.'

'Will, can I come?' Ashleigh caught him leaving.

'No, you're a civilian.'

'Oh, come on, I will stay in the car.'

'OK, but you get out and I will arrest you, understand?'

'OK.' She followed the teams, smiling.

Chapter 32

They arrived at the scene. There were a few squad cars and a lot of people. Will got out and started to head over to the officer in charge. Ashleigh was about to follow.

'Palmer, stay here with our guest, if she tries to leave the vehicle, you have my permission to arrest her.'

'Will,' she said, almost offended.

'I don't need you anywhere near this, at best you're a distraction.'

'OK fine.'

The teams got ready and Will went and got the details from to officer in charge. 'Sergeant Falco, we are glad to see you, we have five armed suspects, a lot of hostages and we are holding all ferries so they can't escape.'

'You know where they are?'

'At the departure point.'

'There's no ferry in?'

'No, we don't know what they want.'

'Well, we will try and find out.'

Will went back to the truck and explained the situation to the teams.

'Five suspects and a lot of hostages, they are at the departure point. Tom, take bravo to the right, we will go to the left, I will get as close as I can before I announce. Stay low on approach, it's all glass but if we move quickly, they may not see us coming.

The teams made their way to the door, they did as ordered, and stayed low and moved quickly. Will opened the door. Will took his team to the left, Tom took bravo team to the right, they got as close as they could before Will announced. All was going to plan, and the suspects were taken by surprise.

'NYPD, put your weapons down on the ground and your hands on your heads.'

The suspects turned round startled. They were well outnumbered, but were not wanting to give up.

'Not just yet we are waiting for the next ferry.'

'No, ferries are coming in while you are in here armed.'

'You can't do that.'

'Yeah, we can, and they did, so why not drop your weapons.'

'If that next ferry doesn't arrive, we will start shooting.'

'Fire one shot and you are all dead men, you are outnumbered, and you know it, so why not get out of this without a bullet.'

'You don't understand.'

'Then explain to me, so I can.'

'My daughter is on that ferry and my ex-wife is planning on flying to California with her for good.'

'This isn't the way to stop her, all this does is land you in trouble.'

'What choice do I have? I don't have the money to take her to court, so she can do whatever the hell she wants, and I can't stop her.'

'OK, put the weapons down, come with us and I can help you, I promise.'

'How can you help me?'

'If you trust me, I can help you.'

He paused for a moment and looked at Will. He put his weapon down and all the others did the same. Will went over to him and then ordered bravo to collect the weapons.

'What time is that flight?'

'In four hours.'

'OK, that should be workable.'

He took out his phone and phoned his lawyers' office. He told them what he needed and how much time they had. He was on the phone for around twenty minutes, all the time not calling in the all clear. When they had done, Will walked towards the exit with the suspects, his team each escorting one.

'Control, we are all clear and heading out.'

'Received, alpha team.'

They went to the waiting squad cars. He put the men in the back but crouched by the last one before he closed the door.

'Now a lawyer will meet you and your friends at the station and the other matter will be sorted, here's my card if you need anything just let me know'

'Thank you so much and I'm sorry.'

'Don't worry, I'm just glad we could help.'

He shut the car door and they drove the suspects away. Tom was next to him.

'Will, how do you know he was telling the truth?'

'What makes you think he wasn't, Tom? He gave up easy enough.'

'He knew they were outnumbered most would give up at that point.'

'You think he was lying.'

'No, I just want to be sure.'

'Tom, my lawyers will work it out, either way, we got everyone out alive — that's what counts.'

'I guess so.'

Tom walked off and got in the cars with the rest of bravo. Will got in the truck and they all headed back to the office. Will got a coffee when they got back. Tom was sat at his desk, Will went in, and closed the door.

'Tom, we have worked together on alpha for nine years and known each other for about twenty-five, and today was the first time you ever questioned my judgement on a call.'

'Yeah, I know, and I'm sorry, but today when he mentioned a daughter you changed.'

'What do you mean, I changed?'

'I don't know, if he hadn't said it, you would have put one in his shoulder, and you know it.'

'You think I was too soft, because he has a daughter?'

'Yes, and I think it's because of the baby.'

'Wow, I never expected you of all people to say something like that.'

'Will I…'

Will left, slamming the door, before he had time to finish. He went down to the gym, he didn't do anything he just sat. Stanson appeared after about ten minutes.

'You OK, Sergeant?'

'Tell me honestly, Stanson, do you think I made the right call on that last shout?'

'I would say so, Sergeant, peaceful resolution is always best, you told me that.'

'Did you believe his story?'

'Yeah, he gave me no reason not to.'

'OK then, thanks Stanson.'

***

Tom went into Kathy's office, she looked up when he did. He closed the door.

'What's up, Tom?'

'I think I just screwed up.'

'How?'

'I know I wasn't exactly helpful the other day and I'm sorry.'

'Tom, it doesn't matter. Now, what just happened?'

'I just accused Will of making a bad call on the last shout.'

Kathy gestured for him to sit down.

'OK, why?'

'I don't know, it was questionable I guess but I said he did it because of the baby.'

'And how did he take it?'

'He stormed out.'

'Well do you want me to speak to him?'

'I thought we both could.'

'OK, but can I ask why you said it?'

'Honestly, Lynne and I have wanted a baby for so long and it happened for you guys so easily. I can't help feeling a bit jealous. Thing is, a couple of week ago we thought she was pregnant, last week she started bleeding.'

'Why did you not talk to us?'

'Because I'm so happy for you two, Lynne and I are so used to this now but still every time it happens it's bad and I don't know how much more Lynne can take.'

'Why don't you take up Will's offer to pay for IVF?'

'I guess because I hate feeling like a charity.'

'Did you at least talk to Lynne about the offer?'

'No, I just turned him down.'

'You men really need to find a way to talk about stuff.'

'Yeah, I know, between Will and me, you must feel like an emotional punchbag.'

Just then Will walked in, he saw Tom and was about to leave.

'Will, can we speak with you?' Kathy asked.

'If it's about earlier, no.'

'Why not?'

'Because I made a good call and I don't appreciate being challenged on it, but shit happens.'

'Is that it?'

'Yeah, pretty much.' Will's beeper went. 'OK, are we done? I will see you later.'

He left without speaking to Tom.

Chapter 33

The following weeks were tense, Will was only communicating with Tom for work purposes. Will and Stanson had become close friends, this was helped by his relationship with Ashleigh. Kathy could see what was going on but didn't know how to step in. As the pregnancy went on, she was nervous, and she needed Will so didn't want to upset that. Saturday night, Kathy and Will were relaxing on the sofa.

'Can you believe in just four weeks our little girl will probably be here.'

'You don't have to remind me, I am getting bigger by the day.'

'You are beautiful,' he kissed her on the head.

Just then Ashleigh opened the door and ran through, upset. Stanson walked in but stopped when he saw them. Will looked at Kathy.

'You go, I can't move as fast,' Kathy said as she sat up so he could follow her.

Will went down the corridor and onto the roof terrace. Ashleigh was standing looking at the view, she was obviously upset and had been crying.

'Do I need to go and punch someone?' he joked as he walked over.

'Not unless you want to hit my parents,' she replied, turning to face him.

'What happened?'

'I introduced them to Ryan and to say it didn't go well would be an understatement.'

'They didn't like him?'

'Oh no they liked him, but a police officer isn't good enough for me apparently.'

'What?'

'They said he isn't from the right family and being a police officer means he won't amount to anything.'

'I'm a cop.'

'I told them he worked with you, but they want someone better for me and I don't know what to do. I never felt like this before, he's different to all the others I've dated.'

'So you have two choices then, do what they want or what you want.'

'Easier said than done. I wanted him to stay with me at my parents' till my place was ready and now I can't do that.'

'He will be moving in with you then.'

'Yeah, I tried staying at his once and that is not something I want to do again, and I would like to get to know him better more intimately.'

'So you want to stay somewhere with him so you two can have plenty of sex.'

'Something like that.'

'OK, stay here, you have a room, and my walls mean I won't have to hear it, at least.'

'Really, we can stay here?'

'Why not?'

'I didn't think that would be an option with Ryan and Kathy really.'

'Ash, you two have spent time with us and she didn't kiss or jump on him, so I think we are safe.'

'Joking about it, that's a good thing, but he may walk round half naked and things if he is staying here and they may spend some time alone.'

'Do you want me to change my mind?'

'No, thanks Will, I really appreciate this.'

'Not a problem, you would do the same for me.'

'My parents won't be happy though.'

'Ash you are thirty-six now, I reckon you can decide who you date and sleep with, and he knows what will happen if he hurts you.'

'You are right, and the fact you didn't scare him off makes him even sexier.'

She hugged him and then they went back inside. Kathy and Stanson were sat talking, he stood when Ash walked over and then they all sat down.

'Guess what?' Ash said to Ryan.

'What?'

'Will says we can stay here till my new place is ready.'

'Really, thanks Sergeant.'

'You can call me Will at home, but don't do it at work because the team will go mental about it, I have strict rules on that.'

'No, worries.'

Will went over to the kitchen to make everyone a drink, Kathy got up and followed him.

'You asked them to stay here?'

'Yeah, why not? Ash needed somewhere to stay, she has a room here so why not use it, it's not a problem is it?'

'No, I was just surprised is all.'

'Because of Ryan staying too?'

'Yeah.'

'Well, they kind of come together now, and besides he is so in love with Ash he only has eyes for her now.'

Will took the drinks over, Kathy followed and sat quietly thinking about what Will had said. He trusted Ryan to be there, but not because he trusted her, he trusted Ryan.

'I wouldn't worry Ryan, Kathy's parents don't think I'm good enough for her,' Will said when he had sat down.

'What? Why the hell not?' Ash exclaimed.

Will looked at Kathy and she nodded to indicate he could tell them.

'Because my mom was from Brazil.'

'Your mom was one of the nicest people I have ever met.'

'Yeah, well, my Latin heritage is not what they wanted for Kathy.'

'I don't get it, you're handsome because of your mom's family.'

'So I'm told.' He smiled at Kathy.

'Well, they best not come near me.'

'It's not my dad just my mom,' Kathy said.

'Well, she best stay away from me then, because I won't be able to keep my mouth shut.'

'Really, you don't say?' Will joked.

'Hey, I'm sticking up for you here.'

'Yeah, I know, you always do.'

They chattered and had a few drinks. Will and Kathy went to bed early, Kathy hadn't been sleeping great.

***

At around four in the morning, Will's phone rang. It took a few moments for him to wake and answer it. He took it outside the bedroom because he didn't want to wake Kathy. It was Detective Park.

'Hey what's up?'

'Falco, so sorry to call you at this time, but this is serious.'

'Why, what's going on?'

'I don't know how to tell you this.'

'OK.' Will was waking up fast.

'I'm down an alley off 8th Avenue, we have found one of your team.'

'What do you mean, found?'

'He's been murdered.'

Will froze, the words not really going in, as though it was a dream. He went and sat on the sofa.

'Falco, are you there?'

'Yeah, who is it?' he held his breath waiting for an answer.

'It's Palmer, I'm so sorry.'

'OK, I'm on my way.'

He hung up. He put his head in his hands for a moment, he could feel a lump in his throat and tears starting to form. One ran down his cheek, he wiped it away quickly. He went into the bedroom and put his uniform on very quietly, he stopped by the bedroom door and looked at Kathy laying there fast asleep. He really wished this was some bad dream. He took a deep breath, grabbed his helmet and left.

Chapter 34

Will stopped his motorcycle just outside the police cordon, he flashed his badge and they let him through, and started walking down the alley. Park saw him and met him halfway.

'Falco, you don't want to go down there, you shouldn't see him like that.'

'No, but I need to, he's my team and I need to see for myself.'

As Will got to where the coroner was, with a body, he saw the blood on the floor and all over the back of his shirt, as they rolled him over. Will closed his eyes. It was Palmer — his heart sank.

'What happened?' Will asked.

'Four stab wounds to the back, he bled out very quickly I would say,' the coroner said.

Will turned to Park.

'Was he robbed?'

'Not that we can work out.'

'It doesn't make sense, Palmer wouldn't hurt anyone, he has always been so shy and quiet, never even carried a gun outside work.'

'Look, we will find out who did this, but it may take some time.'

'OK, what can I do?'

'Let's grab a coffee and work out how to go at this, we need a starting point or at least a few theories.'

'Sounds good. I will need to tell the teams too, as soon as possible, Bennett was close to him, he might know something.'

'Good that may help, let's get that coffee.'

They walked down the block to a diner, it was always open. Will and Park sat down, and the waitress walked over.

'Just two coffees please,' Park said.

She went to the counter and came back a few minutes later with the coffees. Will looked at Park.

'There has to be more to this, I don't think Palmer got on the wrong side of anyone in his life, so this was random or there is more to the story.'

'What do you know of him outside of work?'

'He has been to mine a couple of times, but he didn't talk about himself much. I know he has a younger sister, he lives near Bennett and his parents live just outside the city, he was single mainly because he was shy. He was damn good at his job, never questioned an order, was a bloody good shot but he didn't carry a gun except in work, he didn't feel the need.'

'Did he ever fall out with anyone on the job?'

'No, not in all his time on the unit.'

'Honestly, I don't think this is random, nothing was missing, there was still money, his bank cards and his ID in his wallet. I think he was targeted, maybe they knew he didn't carry. But my concern now is why, it could very well be because of working on alpha team.'

'That had crossed my mind, I have pissed off plenty of people on the force and otherwise, this could be payback on me, or the unit.'

'I think we need to work out a timeline of where he was, but short of going round all the bars nearby, and asking for surveillance footage, we need a starting point.'

'Bennett would probably know if anyone, I don't know if they were out together last night or not but it's a possible. Palmer was so shy I can't see him going out alone.'

'Well, if we head over to the ME's office and speak to them and see if we have a time of death and anything else they can give us.'

'Thanks for taking this one, Park, I reckon your work on homicide in Miami and all those murderers you hunted down is going to pay off for us big time.'

'I took this case because of who it was, I would rather not deal with murder cases now, that's why I moved to the major case team here.'

'So are you going to tell me why you moved when you did?'

'Not tonight but I will, but let's just say the last serial killer I went after made it very personal, after that I needed a change, and that is why I understand how personal this is for you Will and I will help catch whoever did this, I promise you that.'

***

It was seven in the morning when Will called the rest of alpha team, he phoned Tom to get bravo team in too and then he phoned Kathy. She woke up, and looked at her phone shocked to see Will's name on the screen.

'Hey, where are you?'

'I'm at the office.'

'It's only seven o'clock, Will, and it's Sunday, what's going on?'

'I need you to come into the office.'

'Why? What's happened?'

'I will tell you when you get here, Stanson is already up, come in with him, OK.'

'OK, see you soon.'

She got up and headed out into the living room. Stanson was in the kitchen making coffee, he poured her a cup. She took it and went and sat on the sofa, the breakfast bar stools were uncomfortable now she was so far along. Stanson came over and sat on the chair. He had his jeans on, but not his shirt, but now he was with Ashleigh, Kathy didn't look at him the same as she used to.

'Will phoned you too?'

'Yeah, told me to go in with you.'

'No, problem, got a feeling something's wrong.'

'Me too but I can't think what.'

***

The teams were all in the office by eight, Will was there with Park, he was waiting for everyone. Kathy stood by Tom at his office door, Will got her a chair.

'You're going to need to sit for this one,' he said.

She knew at that moment that it was extremely serious.

'OK, everyone, I know it's early and I know it's Sunday, but this couldn't wait.'

'Sergeant, Palmer isn't here,' Bennett interrupted.

Will looked at Park for a moment who put a reassuring hand on his shoulder.

'I have some really bad news.' He paused for a moment. 'In the early hours of this morning Palmer was found murdered just off 8th Avenue.'

There were gasps of shock and then silence, complete disbelief etched on each of their faces. Kathy was fighting back tears, she couldn't believe what Will had just said.

'I know this is a shock and it hurts us all, some more than others. Now if anyone knows anything about where he was last night, we need to know. I know it's our day off, but I will be staying in today and helping Detective Park, we need to track his last movements, then we may just have a chance of finding who did this.'

'Sergeant.' Bennett stood up. 'I was with him last night till about midnight.' He was obviously devastated, Palmer was his closest friend in and out of work, Will could only imagine how he was feeling. He knew what it would do to him if anything happened to Tom.

'OK come in my office and we will start there. Everyone else if you're staying get your uniforms on and get your gear.'

Will went into his office with Bennett and Park. The teams went off and got changed. Kathy got up and started making coffee, they were all going to need it. As the teams came back through, all of them in uniform, Kathy got a pain right across her bump. She put one hand on her bump and one on the countertop to steady herself. Stanson noticed.

'Sergeant, are you OK?' he asked as he took her to sit down at his desk.

Tom came over when he saw what was happening.

'I'm OK, just Braxton Hicks, the doctor said this could happen.'

'Do you want me to get Will?' Stanson asked.

'No, I'm fine, don't worry him, not now.'

'OK, let me get you a drink.'

Will came out of his office with Bennett and he was relieved to see them ready in their uniforms.

'OK then, bravo team, you will take the first three bars that Bennett and Palmer went in.' He handed Tom a list. 'Get the surveillance tapes so we can see if anyone was following them. Stanson, you take alpha and go to the club he said he was going to and two bars that are close by.' He handed Stanson a list. 'Park and I will head to the bar where Bennett last saw Palmer, and will go from there.'

The teams finished their coffees, and started to move to leave. Tom approached Will and spoke to him quietly.

'I think Kathy needs to go home.'

'I don't follow.'

'She was having pains before, called them Braxton Hicks, but with her panic attacks and blood pressure issues, maybe she should be resting.'

'That sounds like a good idea Tom, good call, I will take her home, Ash can sit with her.'

'Ash is staying with you?'

'Yeah, as of last night, her parents don't approve of Ryan and her new place isn't ready yet.'

'Ryan?'

'Yeah, sorry, Stanson, you know they are dating right?'

'Yeah, it had been mentioned between the teams. You two are pretty close then, to call him Ryan.'

'It felt weird calling him Stanson if he is going to be sleeping at my place, but he isn't you, Tom. Plus, when Ash's place is ready, I won't see them so much.'

'OK, well I will get over to those bars and see what we can come up with there.'

Tom left with bravo. Just then, Captain Bridge walked in, he signalled to Will to follow him, they went into his office. Will shut the door.

'Sergeant, I can presume you have informed the teams.'

'Yes, Captain, they are all willing to put the leg work in on this one.'

'OK, I will put the overtime in, that isn't an issue.'

'I am sure they would be staying anyway.'

'Someone has to do the notification to his parents, I just had a meeting with the chief, he said if you want to do it that's fine or I will.'

'No, Captain, I want to do it, he was a good officer and I want to tell them that.'

'Yeah, he was, have you got anything to go on?'

'Not much but we have a starting place.'

'Good, and tell Park thanks for stepping in for this one, apparently homicide called him to take the case when they knew who it was.'

'Why?'

'Park has an exceptional reputation, they wanted him on their division, but he turned it down, with it being a cop they wanted the best detective in the city on it and apparently that is Park.'

'Really? He doesn't talk much about his past in Miami.'

'Well, I will not discuss that, it's up to him.'

'OK, I would never ask a confidence to be broken Captain, you know that.'

'Good, now get back to work, we have a killer to find.'

Will walked out of the captain's office and went over to Kathy. The rest had left, and Park was ready to go.

'Come on I'm taking you home.'

'Why? I can help from the office.'

'Kathy, you should be resting, you don't need the extra stress and you can stay with Ash.'

'And the doctor's later?'

'Ash can take you, she can drive. I don't know what time we will be done here.'

'All right I will go home, but you need to keep me up to date, OK?'

'I promise if I get any info, I will tell you.'

Chapter 35

Will had never done a notification to family before, but he felt that he needed to do this one. Park pulled up outside the house, they looked at each and got out. They walked up the path and steps and knocked on the door. It was a quiet street and Will wondered what had made Palmer want to leave this and join the force in the city. A man answered the door, he was in his fifties, tall and slim like Palmer.

'Mr Palmer?' Park asked.

'Yes, is something wrong?'

'I'm Detective Park and this is Sergeant Falco, may we come in?'

'What is this about?'

'It's about your son.'

He must have read their faces, he knew something was wrong and let them in. He showed them through to the living room, his wife was there, and she stood when they entered.

'What's going on?' she asked.

'They have some news about Michael,' he answered.

He gestured for them to sit down and he then sat opposite on the sofa next to his wife. He held her hand tightly.

'I am so sorry to tell you, we found your son this morning, he has been killed,' Park said.

His mom started sobbing and his dad held her tight and reached for some tissues.

'How did he die?'

'He was murdered, we are so sorry.'

'Our Michael, but who would do that? Everyone loved him.'

'We are investigating what happened, we have to ask was he having any problems at all?'

'No, not that he told us, he loved his job, it was his life.'

'I was Michael's team leader,' Will said. 'He was one of the best I have ever worked with, he was an important member of alpha team and the unit.'

'Sergeant Falco, you said, yes he talked of you often, wanted to be just like you.'

Will was taken back, he never realised that, and he was starting to regret not getting to know him sooner.

'We are doing everything we can to find the person responsible for this.'

'Thank you, please will you keep us informed of any developments and we will call if we think of anything.'

Park and Will stood and moved towards the door, Palmer's dad followed.

'Again, we are so sorry for your loss.'

He opened the door and they left. They slowly walked back to the car, they got in and sat for a moment Will hoped he never had to do another one of those, he hated that he had no answers at all for them, as to why he had been killed, it was the worst feeling to Will, feeling useless. He had hoped what he had said about Palmer and how he had been a vital role on alpha and the unit had given them something to be proud of, but now he had to find the killer to help them grieve properly and get justice, which was going to be the hardest part. Palmer had no enemies, not like he had, and he was struggling to work out what he had done to deserve what had happened.

Will and Park drove back into the city and to the bar where Bennett had last seen Palmer. He had said a woman had come over to them asking questions, she had been more interested in Palmer, so Bennett had left them to it. Will wanted to see if she was on any surveillance recordings so they could track her down and see if she had spoken to anyone else in the bar. They pulled up outside. They walked into the bar, some customers stared at Will, in uniform and wearing his vest and handguns.

'Hi, I'm Detective Park.' He showed his ID and badge. 'And this is Sergeant Falco, we need to look at your surveillance from last night.'

'What for?'

'It's in connection with a homicide.'

'Then no I don't think so.'

'Why not?'

'Because I don't want you scaring my regulars by asking questions.'

Will looked around and moved towards the bar.

'Makes me think you're connected,' he said.

'No, way and you can't pin nothing on me.'

'Tell you what I am going to do, I will count to three and if I don't see you move to get the surveillance footage from last night, I am going to shoot those bottles one by one,' he said signalling to the bottles on the back.

'You can't do that, you're a cop.'

'I'm not known for playing by the rules.'

Will took one of his handguns and placed it on the bar, he kept his hand on it.

'One... two... three...'

He picked it up and shot the first bottle, it was a full bottle of whisky, he then aimed at the next.

'Wait, OK I will get it.'

He went through a door at the end of the bar.

'We could have got a warrant.'

'He could have deleted it all.'

'He could do that anyway.'

Will smiled at Park.

'Would you do that if I were waiting for it?'

'Fair point.'

The owner came back out and handed Will a memory stick.

'It's all on there.'

'I will be back if it's not.' He took $100 from his pocket and put it on the bar. 'That's for the whisky.'

They left the bar and Will handed Park the surveillance.

'Let's go back and have a look, shall we.'

***

Back at the office Will and Park went through the footage slowly. They found the point where Bennett and Palmer went into the bar, Park wrote down the time. They watched and saw a woman enter, a man followed her and he sat at the bar, the woman then spoke to another man sat at a table, then went over to Bennett and Palmer.

'That must be her,' Park said, writing the time down.

They watched some more and saw Bennett leave, a little while later Palmer left with the woman and one of the men followed. Park wrote the times down again, so he knew where to go back to.

'OK, I need to get the lab to clean this up so we can see their faces, but it looks like we have three suspects here.'

'And I have three bullets waiting for them.'

'Falco, you know we will find them, but you can't shoot them unless they give you reason to.'

'The second they killed Palmer, they gave me a reason.'

'You know it doesn't work like that, I hope they give you a reason when we find them, I really do but it would help the case if we knew why too, and that may give his parents closure.'

'OK, you can ask why, then they are mine.'

***

Stanson and Will got home pretty late, and they still didn't have anything back on the images sent to the lab, though they had found other footage that had helped piece Palmer's night together. Kathy was relaxing on the sofa with her headphones in, she didn't hear them come in. Ash was making a drink, Stanson went into the kitchen and held her tight for a few minutes. Will crouched down by Kathy and put his hands gently on her shoulder and her bump. She opened her eyes and smiled.

'Hey, did you find anything?' she said taking out her earphones.

'Yeah, we have three possible suspects just waiting for the lab to clean up the images of them.'

'That's good.'

'Yeah, how did it go at the doctor's?'

'Yeah, good, everything is as it should be.'

'That's great, I'm going to grab a shower, then we can get some food.'

'OK,' she smiled.

Will and Stanson went to their respective rooms, and Ash went over to Kathy and sat down.

'Why didn't you tell him?'

'Because he has enough going on, right now.'

'He should know, Kathy.'

'He needs to focus on catching the ones that killed Palmer, not fussing and worrying about me.'

'But the doctor said…'

'The doctor said it could be days if not weeks, and I will call her if things change, slow labour is no reason to worry him right now.'

'OK, but if it gets worse, call me straight away.'

'Ash, don't worry, I will be fine.'

Chapter 36

The next morning, Will was in his office. He was sat, coffee in his hand, looking over some reports, there had been no word yet on the surveillance and he was trying to keep his mind busy. The teams were in and writing out tactics, Tom had allowed Will to lead most of bravo's training while Kathy had been off, even when they hadn't been speaking Will had kept his word on that. The tense atmosphere in the office and the unit was obvious, they were all keen to find the people that killed Palmer. The rest of the PD had also shown an unusual amount of support, even though they didn't like Will, they still hated when a cop was killed, and Palmer had always got on with everyone. Park walked in and headed straight towards Will.

'Falco, I got the pictures back, I need to know if any of them seem familiar, maybe they have been watching the team.'

'Let me see.'

Park handed them over and Will looked at them. He took a few moments looking at each, searching his mind to see if they were familiar. When he got to the last one he stopped and looked at Park.

'I know this guy.'

'You know him?'

'Yeah, he was part of the alpha team from Detroit.'

'What? Thought that was finished last year, Ashborne is in prison and so is Sutton.'

'Yeah, they are so what is his connection to Palmer's death, if they killed him,' he said pointing to the other two. 'How the hell does he know them?'

'This could be an incredibly significant lead, but we are going to need to ID these two to establish a connection. I will run them through the facial recognition, if they have a record, we will have their names soon enough.'

'I would say they do, or they have never been caught, this is the not the first time they have done this.'

'I agree, you don't kill someone like this without having priors or it being personal.'

Just then, Will saw a man walk into the office, he looked at the photos then at the man, he got up, passed Park and out into the main office. He grabbed the man by his shirt and pinned him up against the wall by the door.

'Give me one good reason why I don't put a bullet through your head right now.'

'Sergeant, I didn't know what they were planning, I swear.'

'Falco, what's going on?' Park asked.

'He looks familiar, Park. He's the one on the photo.'

Bennett got up from his desk and came over.

'He killed Palmer, Sergeant?'

'I didn't kill anyone.'

'But you were there, weren't you?'

Will's other hand was on his handgun, the teams were all stood around, they wanted to know if this guy was involved. Stanson saw Will's hand move to pull his gun. He stepped forward and put his hand on Will's arm.

'Sergeant, you don't want to do that, not here, not like this.'

Will looked at Stanson, he knew he was right and stopped. Captain Bridge stepped out of his office.

'Falco, let him go.'

'Captain, he's connected to Palmer's death.'

'Let him go!' he shouted.

Will let him go but didn't move, the officer actually looked scared surrounded by both teams, all angry and wanting an explanation. The captain walked over.

'I presume you have a death wish or a damn good reason to come here.'

'I have information about what happened, but I didn't kill your officer.'

'Join me in my office. Falco, Detective Park, you too.'

Will moved and let him pass, then he and Park followed them into the captain's office. The captain sat behind his desk, Officer Partridge sat opposite, Will stood by the door and Park stood by the captain's desk.

'So what information do you have?' Park asked.

'I was told to follow the two officers and when the others arrived to point them out, that's all. After I left, I went back to my hotel, which you can check with the reception desk, I am sure they have cameras.'

'So you showed the other two who Bennett and Palmer were?'

'Yes, I didn't know they were going to kill one of them and if I had I would have warned someone or something.'

'Who told you to do it?' Will asked.

'Captain Ashborne.'

'She's in prison,' Park stated.

'Yeah, but she has a lot of contacts and said if I didn't show them who the officers were, she would hurt my little girl. I didn't think she would be capable of doing this to another cop.'

'This was revenge, she wanted to get back at the unit because she didn't get what she wanted when she was here,' Will said.

'Yeah, and she isn't done.'

'What do you mean she isn't done?' Park asked 'What else does she have planned? You must know.'

'I called her when I heard about your officer, I said I wasn't happy at being involved in such a thing, she said I was part of her alpha team and would do as she told me and then she said she was going to bring down the whole unit. She targeted those two officers to hurt Sergeant Falco, they let the other walk away because they discovered he carried outside of work, but the original plan was to kill them both. She said next she will attack the heart of the unit and hurt Sergeant Hill and I doubt it will stop there.'

'The heart of the unit?' Park asked. 'What does she mean by that?'

'I don't know.'

'Shit, she's after Gina,' Will shouted and left and ran through to dispatch.

Gina wasn't there, so he went into Kathy's office.

'Where is Gina?'

'She just left, she has a photo shoot and interview about her work on the force, she was quite excited about it.'

'Where did she go?'

'She texted me the address.' She got her phone out. 'What's this about?'

'The people who killed Palmer may be after Gina, so I need to find her, can you send me that address?'

'What? Will you have to get to her.' She sent the address to him.

'We will, I promise.'

Will kissed her and left, he got both teams and they all headed out. Kathy sat at her desk looking out at where Gina sat, she couldn't bare anything happening to her best friend. She felt pain right across her bump, it was a contraction.

'Not now,' she thought.

She managed to breathe through it and got up and went to her door.

'Kim, can you go and get the captain for me.'

The young woman left, and moment later, Captain Bridge appeared with her.

'Hill, are you OK?'

'Not really, I think the baby is coming.'

'You want me to call Falco?'

'No, he's looking for Gina, can you call Ashleigh, her number is in my phone.'

'OK.' He turned to Kim. 'Can you phone for an EMT unit.'

'Yes, Captain.'

'OK Hill, let's get you sat down.'

Chapter 37

Will and the teams arrived at a warehouse, Gina's car was parked outside so Will knew he was in the right place. They approached quietly, they got out and ready without much noise. They had no idea how many were inside, they headed to the door. Will opened it, and looked inside, there were a lot of crates everywhere and he could hear voices coming from the far end.

'OK, alpha team, we go down the right, bravo the left, eyes and ears open at all times.'

Inside at the other end, Gina was tied to a chair, the couple that had killed Palmer were in front of her, both armed and Gina had noticed he was carrying a knife in his belt too.

'So are you going to kill me, like you did Palmer?'

'We need you to answer a few questions, we asked the officer, he wouldn't answer them, so he died, you answer, and you get to live.'

'Why do I doubt that? You will kill me whether I answer or not.'

'That's what he said, and look where is he now.'

'Really, well you can ask but I don't know if I will be able to help.'

'You need to tell us about Sergeant Falco.'

'What makes you think I know anything about him?'

'You dated him, you are best friends with his fiancée, and you work with him so I would say you know pretty much everything.'

'Well, I do know one thing about him, you will pay for what you did.'

'I doubt that, how will he even find us, he doesn't know where you are, or who we are, he won't connect it all together to save you.'

'You sure about that?'

'What do you mean?'

'I told my best friend where I was coming to.'

'But that doesn't link to us.' He got awfully close. 'Now, tell me about Sergeant Falco.'

'He's a perfect shot you know and is probably here right now.'

The female looked uneasy and started to move away and went between some crates. She returned and shook her head but disappeared again.

'You're scared aren't you,' Gina stated.

'Of a cop, never, I have done this job for years.'

'But Falco is no ordinary cop, he makes shots that others can only dream of, he has the highest kill rate on SWAT and has never missed, whoever hired you knows that, but I am guessing they didn't tell you.'

He stood back and looked at her, a concerned look came across his face. Then he heard a noise behind him, and he moved quickly behind Gina. Will and Stanson were stood aimed right at him, he had a gun on them and one on Gina.

'Please try something, I will take great pleasure putting a bullet in your head.'

'Sergeant Falco, we were just talking about you.'

'Really, where's your partner?'

'She's around.'

Will heard a noise to his left, he glanced then fired to his left without turning at all. The female suspect fell to the floor fatally wounded.

'You will regret that, Sergeant.'

'No, I really won't, now, did Ashbourne send you?'

'What does it matter, Sergeant? You think she won't send more if you kill me.'

'Why Palmer?'

'He was an easy mark, unarmed and she told us which were the younger ones. You see she knew that the others wouldn't fall for the plan and that you all carried outside the office.'

'So she went for what she considered the weak links?'

'Yes, and he was weak, and too loyal to you.'

'Too loyal?'

'Yes, and now you will regret turning her offer down.'

'No, but you will regret killing his best friend,' Will said indicating to the suspect's left.

He turned to see Bennett, who fired, and the suspect dropped to the floor. Will walked over to Gina.

'Was there just two of them?'

'Yeah.'

'What did they want from you? Why didn't they just kill you?' he asked, untying her.

'They wanted to know about you.'

'Me? Why?'

'They didn't say, just said they wanted to know all about you.'

'But why does Ashborne want to know about me, it makes no sense.'

'Ashborne, that captain from last year?'

'Yeah, apparently she arranged Palmer's murder, but we can't connect the dots, and it may take some time to do it, we doubt she openly left links between her and these two.'

Gina got up and hugged Will. He smiled and then radioed it in.

'Control, this is alpha team, we are all clear, we need PD to secure the scene, a coroner and CSIs down here.'

'Received, alpha team, we have them en route to your location.'

Will's phone rang, it was Captain Bridge.

'Captain, we got them.'

'Falco that's great but you need to get to the hospital, Kathy has gone into labour, happened as soon as you left.'

'What? She isn't due for another four weeks.'

'I know, I called Ashleigh and she is with her, hand over the scene and get down there quick as you can.'

Will hung up and looked for Ryan.

'Stanson,' he called. 'The scene is yours, I have to go Kathy is at the hospital, the baby is coming.'

'What? She isn't due yet, but don't worry you go, I got this.'

Will headed for the door as quickly as he could. He got to the truck.

'Hargreaves, I need you outside at the truck,' he radioed.

Will took off his vest and put his weapons in the truck, Tom appeared.

'I need the keys to a car.'

Tom handed them over without question.

'What's going on?'

'Kathy is having the baby.'

'She isn't due yet.'

'No, she is four weeks early, and I need to go, all my gear is in the truck, can you check it back in?'

'Of course, go. Kathy needs you.'

Will drove to the hospital as quickly as possible, sirens and lights on, he had never driven so fast in all his life. He parked up and ran inside and went straight up to the maternity unit. Ashleigh was sat in the waiting room, she stood when she saw him.

'Will, thank God you are here.'

'Where's Kathy?'

'They took her up to surgery.'

'What? When? Why?'

'Will, you need to sit down and take a breath.'

'Ash, just tell me.'

'OK, but don't get mad. Yesterday at the doctor's they said she was in slow labour, but the baby wasn't in the right position, so she wanted to see her tomorrow. They said they may have to turn the baby or book her in for a Caesarean. However, due to all that happened at work today labour progressed. She was being monitored when her blood pressure dropped and the baby went into distress, so they rushed her upstairs.'

Will sat down, he leaned back and looked up at Ash.

'Why didn't she tell me?'

'She didn't want to worry you, she wanted you to focus on catching Palmer's killers,' Ash replied as she sat down.

'Why didn't you tell me?'

'She made me promise not to, she didn't think it would be a problem, then with the stress of Gina being in trouble, she went into labour.'

Will sat for a few moments in silence, closing his eyes and taking deep breaths.

'I can't lose them, Ash.'

'You won't, Will, they will be OK.'

She put her arm around him, he just stared at the floor, he was so scared of losing one or even both of them. They sat in silence, it felt like an eternity. Other people came and went from the waiting room, everyone with smiles, this was a place of joy and new life but right now Will only felt fear. He looked at Ash, he wished he had known about what the doctor had said but he also knew Kathy, she was so strong and brave facing this alone, he just hoped that she would be all right. Sometime later the doctor came over. Will stood up.

'Are you Kathy Hill's fiancé?'

'Yeah, is she OK?'

'We had to perform an emergency Caesarean, but they are both doing fine, your daughter is very healthy and only slightly smaller than we would hope. We had a few issues with Kathy's blood pressure, so we will need to monitor her closely for a few hours and then through the night, but if all goes well, there is no reason she can't go home sometime tomorrow.'

'Can I see them?'

'When we get them settled in a room you can.'

'Thanks, doctor.'

'Excuse me,' Ash chipped in. 'Is that a VIP room?'

'No, I don't think so.'

'How do we arrange that?'

'Follow me.'

Ashleigh followed the doctor to the desk and arranged a VIP room for Kathy and the baby. Will sat down and breathed a sigh of relief that they were both OK.

Chapter 38

Will and Ash were sat in a private waiting room, it was quite a big room and it had a coffee machine in there. They had been shown through after Ash had sorted out the room being changed. Will had got them both a coffee, he stood looking out of the window and Ash was sat quietly. A nurse came in, Will turned around.

'Would you like to see them now?' she asked Will.

'Yeah.' He put his cup down and then followed the nurse through into Kathy's room.

Kathy was asleep, he went over and kissed her on the head.

'How is she?' he asked the nurse.

'She is doing OK, she will be asleep for a while and will be in some pain when she wakes, but her blood pressure is much better now.'

He went over to the crib. He looked at his little girl, he felt the love flow over him, and he smiled, she was so small but beautiful.

'Would you like to hold her?'

'Can I?'

'Of course you can.'

Will sat in the chair and the nurse brought his daughter and placed her in his arms. Will just sat smiling at her, she laid on just one of his arms, she was so small. Just then she started to cry, he looked the nurse.

'What do I do?'

'She's probably hungry, let me go and get you a bottle for her.'

She left, and moments later, came back and passed the bottle to Will. He looked at her with a blank expression, she showed him how and then left him to feed her. She came back after a while and showed him how to wind her and how to change her. She then fell asleep in his arms. Kathy was still fast asleep. The nurse left. Will went to the door and signalled to Ash, she came in.

'Oh, my goodness she is so beautiful, and so tiny.'

'Yeah, she is amazing,' he smiled. 'But we have a problem.'

'What?'

'The stuff for the nursery hasn't arrived yet and we don't have any clothes small enough for her.'

'And you want me to go and sort that.'

'Yes, please.'

'Consider it done, how's Kathy?'

'She hasn't woken up yet, but they say she's all right.'

'OK I will go and get everything sorted and will bring some clothes here for this little angel, see you all soon.' She kissed Will on the cheek and left.

Will sat back down and watched his daughter sleep.

***

A few hours later, Ash came back, she had a couple of bags with her.

'Hey, wait till you see what I bought.'

She took out some romper suits and showed him, they were covered in butterflies, flowers, and birds. Will smiled.

'Thanks Ash, really appreciate it.'

'Not a problem, not for my niece, I got her a bunch of stuff, but took most of it back to yours.'

'Thought you were taking your time, did you get the nursery stuff sorted?'

'Yes, they are delivering it tomorrow.'

'That's great thanks.'

They both looked at her, sleeping in the crib.

'She is so beautiful Will.'

'Just like her mom.'

'There is some of you in there too, that black hair and beautiful skin tone isn't from Kathy.'

Kathy started to wake up, Ash left the room, smiling as she went.

'Hey.'

'Hey, how are you?'

'In pain, and tired but OK.'

'Well, our girl is sleeping, she's beautiful, thank you so much.' He leaned forwards and kissed her.

'Thank you, she is half you too, Will, and there is no one else I would rather have done this with.'

'Well, she needs a name now.'
'Thought we had decided.'
'I wanted to be sure.'
'Did you call my mom and dad?'
'Shit, no I didn't.'
'Did you tell anyone?'
'Tom, and he said he would tell the teams and Gina.'
'Can you phone my parents please?'
'Yeah, I will do that now'

Will moved the crib closer to Kathy, so she could see her daughter, and left the room. Kathy laid looking at her daughter, she reached over and stroked her cheek gently. She heard voices outside the room, but she couldn't see who was there. She looked around the room, it was large with warm colours and lighting, the blinds were closed so she wasn't sure of the time. The bed was so comfortable, there was also a chair, a sofa, and another bed which she presumed was for Will. This was the nicest room she had ever seen in a hospital, it was better than some hotel rooms. Ash came in.

'Hey Kathy, how are you feeling?'
'OK, bit tired, thanks for being here today.'
'What are sisters for? I love you and that little princess.'
'So was it you or Will, that sorted this room?'
'That was me.'
'It's amazing but you didn't have to Ash.'

'Yes, I did, you need comfort and rest and being in a room with other women would not have done that.'

'Is Will still on the phone?'

'Yeah, and the team just arrived with Lynne, Selena and Gina.'

'Wow that is a lot of people.'

'Good job we have a private waiting room or there would be no space for anyone else's visitors.'

'Private waiting room?'

'Yeah, all VIP suites come with them, and a dedicated nurse too.'

Will came back in, he was obviously stressed.

'You OK?' Kathy asked.

'Well, my future mother-in-law just asked me who the baby looked like, before she asked how she was.'

'Seriously?'

'Yeah, but they are coming tomorrow, apparently.'

'Where are they staying?'

'I will find them somewhere, don't worry.'

'They can't stay with us?'

'Are you serious, Kathy?'

'Will, come on I'm sure it will be fine.'

'No, it won't, she just asked me if my daughter looks like me before she asked how you both were, and we all know why, and it worries me that it was her first priority after I told them you had surgery.'

'Yes, but…'

'But nothing, the answer's no, I'm going home to get changed. Ash, can you stay in here till I get back?'

'Yeah, sure.'

Will left, he was angry, and Kathy was upset, which was the opposite to how he saw the birth of their child being.

Chapter 39

Will took the car back to the office and got changed and collected his bike. He went home and showered, he got dressed and then he went and got a strong drink and sat on the sofa. He couldn't believe Kathy had asked if her parents could stay, after their last visit. He knew that she would want them here for support, he wished more than anything at that moment that his parents were still here, to see him become a father. He knew they would be so proud, and they would have loved their granddaughter so much. It was so difficult for him to keep Kathy's parents away in so many ways, they were the only grandparents she would ever know and that hurt him more than he would ever admit. He also knew though that he couldn't have them in his home not while he was there, it wouldn't be a good outcome for anyone. Just then his phone went.

'Hello.'

'Will, it's Debbie.'

'What can I do for you?'

'We have managed to get a really early flight and will be there at about eight in the morning.'

'OK, I will get a hotel room sorted for you.'

'We will be staying with you.'

'No, you won't.'

'I want to be with my daughter and granddaughter.'

'I will find you somewhere close by.'

'Will, I don't think you understand me.'

'No, I do, but you are not staying in my home, I thought I made that clear last time you came.'

'Well, it's different now, isn't it?'

'No, it isn't, not unless you have changed your opinion of my heritage anyway, and besides, we are a little bit full here, I need to get back to the hospital so I will be in touch with details of your hotel.'

'You're not at the hospital?'

'I needed to get changed and showered, not that it has anything to do with you.'

'Of course it does, she is my daughter.'

'When it suits you.'

'Excuse me?'

'I have to go I will organise you a car and a room for tomorrow.'

He hung up, he needed to get back to the hospital but he was so angry with Debbie and he needed to get rid of that anger before he headed back. The last thing he wanted to do was take his anger out on Kathy — he went in the gym. He took off his shirt and put on his gloves, he punched the bag so hard to begin with he needed to take a breath after a few punches, he paused then carried on. He was there for about an hour before Stanson appeared at the door.

'Not answering your phone?'

'Sorry, needed to get some stress out.'

'Ash told me to come and see what was keeping you.'

'Not Kathy then?'

'She was asleep when I left. What happened?'

'We had an argument about her mom and then her mom phoned me, and I lost my temper.'

'Her mom? I know she doesn't like you but what's the problem?'

'Kathy asked if she could stay here and her mom called to say she was going to be staying here.'

'But you said no.'

'Yeah, so they are both angry with me now. I don't care about Debbie, she has never really liked me, but Kathy, I thought she would understand.'

'What are you going to do?'

'I won't change my mind, there is no way that woman is staying in my home again not while I am here, but I do need to speak to Kathy.'

'The team are still waiting to meet your daughter too.'

'Yeah, I almost forgot about that, let me freshen up then we can head back.'

***

When he got back, he went into the waiting room, where alpha, were waiting. With one noticeable absence,

Palmer should have been there too, and Will couldn't help but feel the void that was there in his place.

'Hey, Sergeant, congratulations.'

'Thanks Bennett.'

Lynne hugged him and kissed him on the cheek and Tom shook his hand.

'Congratulations, something we never thought would ever happen. If I remember right, it was only two years ago you told me that settling down wasn't for you.'

'Yeah, well a good woman can change that,' he replied.

Selena got up and hugged him.

'Congratulations, how is Kathy?'

'She's doing OK, the surgery took it out of her.'

'I know that one, she will need plenty of rest.'

'Yeah, the doctor told me, she gave me all the information I need.'

That's good and if you need any help just shout, so where is the little angel?'

'I will go and get her now.'

Will went through to Kathy. Ash got up, she put her hand on his shoulder and left. Kathy was awake and holding the baby, feeding her. He walked over and kissed his daughter, he went to kiss Kathy, but she moved.

'You were gone a while.'

'Yeah, I took the car back, and went home to get changed and showered.'

'You go in the gym?'

He looked at her curiously.

'Well, did you?'

'Yeah, for a while.'

'You're that mad over this?'

'Honestly yeah.'

'My mom called me, she said she had spoken to you.'

'Yeah, she called.'

'And you told her she could stay in a hotel.'

'Yeah.'

'So it doesn't matter what I want or how I feel about it.'

'Kathy have you ever been told you aren't good enough?'

'No, but…'

'Your mom said I wasn't good enough for you, not because I was a cop, or because I came from a bad neighbourhood, but because my mom was from Brazil, because I am not white. When she first met me, she thought I was corrupt because I had money, would she have thought the same had I been white?'

He sat on the bed and took her hand.

'I will never stop your parents seeing you or our baby girl, but I can't be around someone who sees me as less because of what I look like, so if she stays at our home then I won't be.'

'What? Will, you are making me choose between you and my parents.'

'No, I'm just explaining how I feel, and I will always be with you and our baby, Kathy, I love you more than I have loved anyone before, but if you want your mom to stay, I can't be there.'

'So where would you stay?'

'At Tom's or a hotel.'

'And Ash and Ryan.'

'That's up to them, but knowing Ash they would get a hotel room.'

She put the bottle down and moved the baby to wind her. She was silent as she rubbed her daughter's back. When she had done, she laid her back in her arms and she looked at her, then at Will, he was looking toward the door.

'Can you put her back in the crib?'

Will stood and took her from Kathy and gently put her in the crib, he watched her for a moment and smiled. Kathy looked at Will as he watched her.

'OK, book them into a hotel,' Kathy said.

Will turned and looked at her, she looked sad.

'You're sure?'

She took his hand and he sat right next to her.

'Yeah, I'm sure, because we both need you right now'

'You need me?'

'And I want you.'

He leaned forwards and kissed her, she responded and then stopped.

'I can't do any more, till I'm healed.'

He smiled.

'That's OK, the doctor spoke to me about it all. Now I need to take this little one to meet her family before Selena kills me.'

'OK, I could do with a rest anyway.'

He kissed her on the head, picked up the baby and left the room. He went into the waiting room, he smiled with love and pride. Selena came straight over to him.

'She is beautiful, what's her name?'

'Rose Adriana, after Kathy's grandmother and my mom.'

'As gorgeous as she is, can I hold her?'

'Yeah, of course.'

Selena took Rose and went and sat down, Lynne moved next to them and sat gazing at her. Tom got up and went over to Will.

'Why don't you go and sit with Kathy, we got this.'

'We?'

'OK, they got this.'

'Selena, you are in charge of my angel.'

'Not a problem.'

Will went back into Kathy's room and sat on the bed next to her, she rested on him.

'What have you done with Rose?'

'Selena has her, so thought I would spend some time with you.'

Kathy relaxed a little, she was in pain, but she had never felt so happy, even after the issue with her parents.

'So what time do they arrive? My mom never actually told me.'

'Around eight in the morning.'

'So early.'

'Yeah, and I best sort a hotel.'

'Right now? I'm comfortable.'

Will took his phone out, then put his arm round Kathy. He texted Ash, after a few moments she stuck her head round the door, and smiled.

'What's up?'

'Do me a favour, book a hotel room for Kathy's parents.'

'Yeah, sure where?'

'Anywhere close by, here take my card, use that.' He threw his wallet to her.

'Names?'

'Frank and Debbie Hill.'

'OK I will be back in a few.'

Will held Kathy, she started falling asleep on him. He just sat and relaxed, enjoying the closeness, soon he drifted off to sleep too.

He woke a couple of hours later, Kathy was still asleep. He looked around, then eased off the bed, he left the room. The waiting room was empty, the team had gone home. He looked around, confused, and wondered where Rose was. He went to the desk, the nurse looked at him and smiled.

'She's in there with a nurse.' She pointed towards the office. 'We didn't want to wake you and she was hungry.'

'When did everyone leave?'

'About twenty minutes ago, we will bring her back in when she has finished.'

'Thanks.'

He went back into Kathy's room and watched her sleep, he was happy and relieved when he had seen that Rose looked like him. The doubt that had been there for months was now gone. He took out his phone, there was a message from Ash with the details of the hotel and that his wallet was in his jacket. He sat back in the chair and thought about the last couple of days and what a whirlwind it had been.

Chapter 40

Will woke the next morning. Kathy was already awake feeding Rose. Will got up and went and kissed them both on the head.

'Morning, sleep well?' Kathy asked.

'Surprisingly yeah, that bed is amazingly comfortable, did you?'

'Not too bad, Rose woke twice.'

'Really, I didn't hear her.'

'Yeah, you were fast asleep.'

'Sorry.'

'It's OK, you had a crazy day yesterday, and once back at work you will need to sleep so it's better that you get into the habit of not hearing her.'

'What time is it?'

'Eight a.m.'

'Really? I have to go.'

'You're going to work?'

'No, I have to help Ash, all the baby stuff arrives soon.'

'Oh OK, how long will you be?'

'Not long don't worry.'

'I'm not worried, I am waiting for my mom to call, they should have landed by now and she said she would phone when they did.'

'I can call if you like make sure it landed on time, they are probably just getting through the airport.'

'Thanks, now can you take her for a minute while I go to the toilet, she needs winding though.'

Will took Rose, he put a cloth over his shoulder, held her with one hand and rubbed her back with the other. Kathy sat on the edge of the bed and smiled.

'She looks so tiny when you hold her, but you are a natural.'

'Thanks, I couldn't be happier, doing this, never thought it would happen.'

'Why not?'

'Kathy, I'm nearly forty, and till I met you, I didn't think I would find anyone to settle down with.'

'Forty is not old, and it's not like you are in anything but perfect condition.'

'That may be, but I am glad it happened now before I got too much older.'

Kathy got up and went to the toilet, she was moving a little easier, but it was still slow going. When she was back in bed, Will headed out, kissing them both before he left. Kathy laid back on the bed, she was so happy but was not looking forward to her parents arriving. She had wanted them to stay, and she thought Will was being over the top, but she loved him, and she knew that things would be tense when they arrived. If only her mom could see Will for the man he was.

***

An hour later, Will was at home, he and Ash had finished the nursery and they were sorting the smaller crib in Will and Kathy's room, when the internal phone went.

'Hey Jimmy, what's up?'

'I have Kathy's parents here.'

'OK, I will come straight down.' He hung up and went to his bedroom door. 'Kathy's parents are downstairs, you OK with that?'

'Yeah, of course.'

Will went downstairs, Frank greeted him with a handshake, Debbie didn't even smile.

'Will, good to see you, we didn't know what hospital Kathy was in, so we came here instead.'

'Did you check in OK?'

'Yes, lovely place thanks for sorting it.'

'Not exactly close though, is it?' Debbie said annoyed.

'Best we could do at short notice.'

'Not better than here though is it.'

'It's the better option for everyone.'

'So, is she still in hospital?'

'Yeah.'

'And you are here?'

'Yeah, so?'

'My daughter needs someone with her right now.'

'She has someone with her, I was getting the nursery ready.'

'It wasn't ready?'

'My daughter arrived four weeks early, caught us all by surprise, but we are all sorted now and ready for them to come home.'

'So how are my girls?' Frank asked.

'They are great and beautiful.'

'I can't wait to meet my granddaughter.'

'Well, why don't you go back to the hotel and when the doctor decides if they are coming home or not, you can see her then.'

'We can't wait here?' Debbie asked.

'Well Ashleigh is here. She probably won't mind though.'

'Ashleigh?'

'Yeah, her and Ryan are staying with us at the moment, shall we go up?'

They went upstairs and Will gestured for them to sit on the sofa, he went to his bedroom.

'Kathy's parents are in the living room, can you play nice till I see whether Kathy is coming home.'

'I will try my best, but I can't promise.'

'That's all I ask, they didn't want to go back to the hotel and right now I don't have the energy to argue.'

'Rose keep you up?'

'No, I slept through her waking twice apparently. Well, I will be back soon — be nice.'

Will left and went back to the hospital. When Ash had finished, she went out into the living room and then to the kitchen, she was dressed in hot pants and a vest top, her hair in a messy bun.

'Do you know who that is?' Frank said to Debbie.

'Should I?'

'It's Ashleigh, the actress and model.'

'That may be, but she dresses like a prostitute.'

'Debbie, really?'

Ash walked over to them.

'Can I get you a drink or anything?'

'A coffee would be great,' Frank answered.

'I'm fine,' Debbie replied.

'OK, won't be a minute.'

Ash went back to the kitchen and made a coffee for Frank and herself and took them over, she sat in the chair and watched them carefully. Frank could feel the tension, so he decided to try and break the ice.

'So are you filming at the moment, Ashleigh?'

'No, I'm on a break, but I don't talk about work here, it's my personal space, if you don't mind.'

'OK, no problem.'

'So you are staying here?' Debbie said.

'Yeah, Ryan and me, just till my new place is ready.'

'And how long will that be?'

'I don't know, a few months maybe, it's a complete renovation.'

'Well, I don't think that's right with a new baby. Can't you stay elsewhere, it's not like you can't afford it.'

Ash moved forwards in her seat and looked at Debbie.

'Wow, aren't you a delight. Now I promised Will I would be nice, but I will say this, I have been staying here since I was a little girl, so you don't, and never will have a say in that. Will is my best friend, and I never want to hear a bad word about him come out of your mouth, and trust me when I say you better not hurt Kathy or their baby either. They are my family, and I will do anything to protect them.'

Ash got up and went into the kitchen leaving Debbie opened mouthed in shock. Ash stood and finished her coffee watching them, she could see why Will didn't want them to stay.

***

Will had put all the stuff in the car and took the baby seat up to Kathy's room. He went in, Kathy was sat on the bed holding Rose.

'You ready?'

'Yeah, can't wait to get home.'

'Have we got everything? Your painkillers and next appointment.'

'Yes, we have them in my bag.'

'OK, let's go and see if Ash has managed to not kill your mom.'

'I'm sure it's fine.'

'You do know Ash, right?'

'A little, but killing is not her style, saying something to her well that might be a different story.'

Will took Rose and fastened her into the car seat, then helped Kathy. They walked slowly out to the desk. Will thanked the staff before they went down to the car. Rose fell asleep on the way back. When they got home, Will took all the stuff into the lobby before helping Kathy out of the car and taking Rose in. They walked round very slowly, Kathy was struggling with the pain and was finding everything exhausting, but she knew it would pass soon and every time she looked at Rose, she knew it was worth it. Jimmy came from behind the desk and opened the door.

'Wow she is beautiful, would you like a hand with the bags?'

'Thanks, Jimmy that, would be great.'

They all went upstairs. Will opened the front door, Ash met them and took Rose from Will and took her straight into the bedroom. Jimmy dropped the bags inside the door. Frank got up and hugged Kathy.

'Hey, sweetheart, how are you?'

'Sore and tired, but happy. Thanks, Dad.'

Kathy walked round slowly and sat in the chair.

'So where is my granddaughter?' Debbie asked.

'Ash took her in the bedroom, she's fast asleep.'

'OK I will go and have a quick peek then.'

She stood up and was about to go to the bedroom.

'No, you can stay there and wait till she wakes up,' Will stated.

'But I just wanted to see her.'

'And you can later, there are very few people I allow in our room and you aren't one of them. Kathy, do you want a drink or do you want to go and lay down?'

'I think I will go and lay down.'

Will helped her up and walked her to their bedroom. Ash had got Rose in the crib, she was still asleep. She left with a smile. Kathy sat on the bed and Will sat next to her.

'You need anything, just shout OK.'

'Yeah, right now I just need sleep.'

'OK, and don't worry about anything.'

Kathy laid down and Will left the bedroom and closed the door.

Chapter 41

Will was in the nursery with Ash sorting all Rose's clothes. There was so many of them and they hadn't had time to do it all in the morning. He got a text from Kathy and he went through into their room.

'Hey what's up?'

'Rose is awake, I've fed her, can you take her so I can get up?'

'Of course.' Will went over and got Rose, she laid her head on his shoulder and he held her there. Kathy slowly got off the bed and stood.

'OK, let's introduce her to her grandparents.'

They went through to the living room, Kathy sat in the chair. Will took Rose to Frank first, who had the biggest smile on his face. Will placed her in his arms.

'Frank, meet your granddaughter, Rose Adriana.'

'Hey beautiful,' he smiled. 'She's so small, but so perfect.'

Will went and sat on the chair arm by Kathy and held her hand. She leaned on Will and watched her dad.

'Will, can you take a photo please, she looks so content with you, Dad.'

'Well, she is just like her mom, a little angel.'

He looked up, as Will took a picture of them.

'Do you want to hold her?' Frank said to Debbie.

'Of course I do,' she snapped.

He gently handed her over. Debbie took Rose, but she didn't smile, she just looked at her. Rose started to cry.

'You want me to take her, Mom?'

'I know how to settle a baby, Kathleen.'

Debbie stood up and started pacing up and down with her, but Rose wouldn't stop crying, and Debbie refused to hand her back to Kathy or Will. A few minutes later, Ryan walked in the door. He put his bag down and went into the kitchen, he kissed Ash and they had a brief whispered conversation. He looked at Will who looked frustrated, then at Debbie still trying to settle Rose. He walked straight over to her, took Rose without a word, and smiled at her.

'Hey, little one, did you miss your Uncle Ryan?' he said to her.

Rose stopped crying and just looked at him, he carried her through to the kitchen away from the tension. Debbie sat back down, extremely unhappy. There was a tense silence, then Will's phone rang.

'Hello Park, what can I do for you?'

'I need some extra eyes on these files, we have an ID on both shooters and they have files on them from multiple states and I need to find the connection to Ashborne, I know you guys just had a baby but…'

'You can come over, Ryan and I can help, not a problem.'

'OK, if you are sure. I will be there in thirty minutes.'

Will hung up and Kathy looked at him curiously.

'Park is on his way over, he needs some help with the files on the two who you know.'

'Oh, yeah that's fine with me.'

'Cool, we can set up on the table.'

Will headed to the kitchen to fill Ryan in.

'Mom, Dad would it be OK if we see you tomorrow?'

'What? Why? We have waited all day to see Rose and we have barely seen her.'

'I know, Mom, but someone from work is coming over to go over some files.'

'Well, we can look after Rose while you do that.'

'It's OK, Ash and I have that covered.'

'Right, well I guess we will see you tomorrow then,' she snapped.

'I will call you in the morning when we are up and ready, all right.'

'OK then, come on Frank let's go and see if we can find some food.'

They stood, Frank kissed Kathy on the cheek, and Will came over.

'Will, my parents are going can you take them downstairs, please?'

'Yeah, sure, Park will be here soon so I can wait for him.'

They left and Kathy sighed heavily. This would be a long, few days. Will had been right about them not staying, she couldn't have taken the hostility. She looked over at Ash and Ryan, they made a lovely couple and were so good with Rose, and Kathy was so grateful for the support right now.

***

About thirty minutes later Will came back in with Park. Kathy was holding Rose and was alone.

'Where are Ash and Ryan?'

'Shower.'

Kathy tried to get up with Rose.

'Let me take her.'

'Will I need to get used to doing stuff on my own, unless you are planning being off for a few months.'

'Kathy, you just got out of hospital and had surgery yesterday.'

'I know that because I can't do anything without pain shooting across my stomach, Will.'

Will crouched in front of her.

'I am here as long as you need me, Ryan has alpha till then.'

'Will, you and I both know you need to go back soon, there is still Palmer's murder to tie up, and the team need you.'

'Let me take Rose now and you can get up and go wherever you were going, and we can talk about this later.'

'I just need a drink.'

'You want me to get it?'

'No, you can take your daughter, but I can get my own drink.'

'OK.'

Will took Rose, Kathy got up and went to the kitchen. Will walked over to the table where Park was sorting out files that they had brought up.

'Wow, there's a lot.'

'Yeah, might take a while, listen sorry for intruding, you literally have your hands full.'

'This little angel is just that and we all want an end to this case, but maybe I should call Tom, he can help, and Lynne can cuddle this one.'

'She is beautiful Falco, you're a lucky man.'

'Yeah, just a bit.'

Just then Ryan and Ash walked over, smiling.

'So where do we start?' Ryan asked.

'Well first let's call Tom, then order food, and then we can start on this lot.'

'OK, I will take Rose, so you boys can get on.' Ash took Rose and went over and sat on the sofa.

Will took out his phone and called Tom, then ordered food. It was possibly going to be a long evening.

Chapter 42

An hour later, they had eaten, and the men were making their way through files. Lynne was holding Rose, and was stood with Kathy in the kitchen while she was making coffees. Ash walked over to the table.

'So we haven't been introduced, I'm Ashleigh,' she said to Park.

'Hi, I'm Sam.'

'You helped Will last year, right, when he got shot.'

'Yeah, that's me.'

'And now you are helping them catch the person responsible for killing Palmer.'

'Well, they are actually helping me, SWAT don't investigate murders usually.'

'Are you single?'

'Ash,' Will said.

'What?'

'A bit personal don't you think, and when Ryan is sat right there,' Will joked.

Ash hit Will on the arm.

'I don't mean for me, but I have a few single friends.'

'Yeah, I'm single, I have been in New York about a year, not had much time for dating.'

Ash sat down next to him.

'So where are you from?'

'Miami.'

'Nice city, did a movie there a couple of years ago, so why did you leave?'

'Ash why don't you go and help Kathy with the coffee,' Will suggested.

'OK, fine, I was just asking.'

She got up and went into the kitchen.

'Sorry about that, Park, she can get a bit too curious about people sometimes.'

'No, worries.'

Kathy brought the coffees over and kissed Will before leaving them to their files. The women went outside onto the roof terrace and sat down, Lynne still had Rose, who was wide awake.

'You're a natural, Lynne.'

'She's not hard work,' she smiled.

'So when are you and Tom having some?' Ash asked.

There was a tense silence and Ash realised there was something she didn't know.

'What am I missing?'

'Tom and I have been trying for three years,' Lynne said sadly.

'Have you had tests to find out why?'

'We can't afford them, we looked at a few places, but they are just too much.'

'Why did you not ask Will or me? We could have helped.'

'I would never expect that, it is something we have got used to, the chance we won't have any.'

'Will offered Tom the money a couple of years ago, but Tom turned it down,' Kathy interrupted.

'Why?' Ash asked.

'Knowing my Tom, it's probably pride, he has never wanted to be seen as Will's charity case or be made to feel that way.'

'Lynne, you know this is different, it's not charity. You will make a wonderful mother, let us help you have a chance of living that dream.'

Lynne smiled at Kathy and then looked at Rose.

'OK, I will speak to Tom.'

Kathy smiled at Lynne, she knew it would be a tough road for them, but she wanted to help and for once Will's money could do some real good for someone. They talked for a while until Rose had been fed and fallen asleep, then they headed back inside. Kathy put Rose down and went over to Will and the others.

'You find anything?'

'We have a couple of leads to chase up.'

'That's good.'

'Yeah, but we aren't sure it's enough yet, this could take a while.'

'Hang on', Ryan said. 'I may have something.'

'What?' Park asked.

'The guy who killed Palmer, he has a younger sister, and it appears that crime runs in the family because she is in the same prison as Ashborne, that can't be a coincidence.'

'No, it can't and that could be the link we need to get her. But I will need to make a few calls tomorrow, get some records on phone and visitors because we still need to tie them together,' Park answered.

'Does this mean you can call it a night?' Kathy asked.

'Yes, it does,' Will smiled.

After half an hour everyone had left, and Ash and Ryan had gone to bed. Kathy and Will sat on the sofa relaxing.

'So, you going back to work in the morning?'

'No, why do you ask?'

'Will, you can go back, it's OK. I realised tonight I can manage, and you have been off one day and are itching to get back.'

'I'm fine, I want to spend time with you and Rose.'

'OK, tell me what you talked about tonight.'

'The case.'

'And?'

'How today went.'

'I was right.'

'Just because I talked about work doesn't mean I want to go back.'

'Come on Will, alpha are down to four, and bravo are supporting every call-out, there is no sergeant on days, they need you back.'

'Charlie team has a sergeant and they can call someone in if they need to, are you sure you aren't trying to get rid of me?'

'Of course not, but my parents will be here all day tomorrow, and you are easier to live with when you are working.'

'I have been off one day.'

'Yeah, I know, but tomorrow won't be as busy, so you will be bored and you know it, and it may be better if you aren't here, the atmosphere was tense tonight which isn't good for Rose, so I think you should go back.'

'Are you sure?'

'Yeah, and besides, I have Ash for another couple of months, and Lynne and Selena will be coming round, you know that, and Lynne will need to get some practice in.'

Will looked at her questioningly.

'Turns out she never knew about your offer and she wants to accept, so is going to talk to Tom.'

'What did you say to her?'

'I said you had offered a couple of years ago, but Tom turned you down. She wasn't surprised, but Rose may have convinced her to accept.'

Will kissed her on the head, he knew she meant well but he wasn't sure Tom would see it that way.

Chapter 43

The next morning, Will was up and ready to go to work when Kathy got up with Rose. Will poured her a coffee and took it over to the sofa for her as she sat down.

'Good morning.'

'Morning, you sure you will be OK?'

'Yes.'

'Can I get you anything before I go?'

'No, I'm fine, now go to work.'

Will kissed her, then he took Rose for a moment giving her a kiss before passing her back to Kathy and heading for the door. Stanson appeared from his and Ash's bedroom, surprised Will was ready for work.

'You back in today?'

'Yeah, Kathy thinks I should go back in.'

'Good, because it was chaos yesterday.'

'That's not what you said last night.'

'I know, but I didn't want you to think I couldn't cope or that you had to come back so soon, it was Tom's idea.'

'Well do you want a lift?'

'On the bike? Yeah sure.'

'OK Kathy, see you later, love you both.'

They left, Kathy put Rose in her new baby chair then picked up her coffee that Will had got for her. The peace was amazing, which she knew wouldn't last long once her parents arrived.

***

Will got changed, he and Stanson chatted as they walked through to the office. They grabbed coffee, and Stanson sat at his desk, and Will went through to his office to be greeted with a pile of paperwork that needed doing. Captain Bridge saw Will cross the office and came to his doorway.

'You're back Falco.'

'Yeah, you know me, can't stay away.'

'More like Sergeant Hill is fed up with having you at home.'

'I think so, she is worried I will get bored.'

'Falco, you were off a day and a half.'

'I think she wanted some peace, a bit of time of just her and Rose.'

'Probably, my wife sent me straight back to work after ours were born, maybe it's a SWAT thing.'

Will laughed.

'Maybe so, Captain.'

Just then, the teams came in, Tom saw Will and went straight over and into his office, the captain went back to his office. Tom shut the door.

'Couldn't help yourself, could you?'

'What?'

'Telling Lynne, I had refused the money for the fertility tests.'

'How was that me when I was sat with you all night, it was Kathy.'

'Because you told her.'

'I didn't know she would tell Lynne.'

'But you knew how I felt about it all.'

'Yeah, which is why after you said no, I didn't offer again.'

'And now because your girlfriend can't keep quiet, I have Lynne asking to accept the offer and if I say no, it looks like I don't want kids, so I'm the bad guy.'

'Tom when I offered you the money, it was about nothing but caring about you and Lynne, after all the time you have had my back, been there for me, I owe you so much and this was one way I could help you guys. I also know you are a proud man and I understood when you said no. Kathy doesn't understand that, and I apologise for the fact she told Lynne.'

'I am not a charity, Will, that's why I said no, when we were growing up and even more so later with people who knew about your parents, they all thought like Carla did, that I was your charity case and I didn't want the most important thing in my life being defined by it too.'

'I know that Tom, just like when you wouldn't let me help with the wedding, I get it. I will never see you like that though, so what if I loaned you the money?'

'I'm listening.'

'Well, it would mean you can have all the tests you need, so you make Lynne happy, but you pay me back at a rate you can afford, that way no one can call it charity.'

Tom thought for a few moments.

'OK deal.'

Will stood up and shook his hand.

'Now let's get some coffee, I have had one but with all this paperwork to get through I am going to need a lot more.'

***

It was an hour later when the team's first call came in. Will was in his office when his beeper went.

'OK let's go we have a hostage situation,' he said as he walked across the office.

They got in the truck and bravo followed in the cars. They arrived at a small theatre and got out. There were a couple of squad cars, they had put up a cordon and there were many people around, watching. Will walked over to the officer in charge.

'OK, what we got?'

'We have a guy holding half a dozen hostages, the leading lady is his obsession and he wouldn't take no for an answer.'

'Where are they?'

'According to the stagehand who got out, they are on the stage.'

'OK.'

He walked back to the truck, radioing through the details as he went, so he could get the go ahead he needed. Will had attended quite a number of these, where someone had an obsession with someone of the opposite sex, they never usually ended well, and he knew he needed a few options on how to get the hostages out safe.

'Right, we have an armed man on the stage with up to twelve hostages. Harvey with me on the balcony, grab your sniper, Stanson, you Bennett and Turner go in at ground level, see if you can get him to give up, but wait till we are set up. Bravo, cover the back entrance and street in case he tries to run for it.'

They all got what they needed and got into position. Will and Harvey set up on the balcony near the back, so they were hidden, but still had a clear line of sight.

'Control, this is alpha team, we are in position, do we have a green light?'

'Alpha team you have a green light.'

'Received, orange you have a go.'

He heard them enter below.

'NYPD, put your weapon on the ground and your hands on your head,' Stanson announced as he and the others moved forwards, towards the stage.

'Stop where you are, or I will shoot her.'

He had the woman in front of him, Will watched and waited.

'OK, why don't you tell us what the problem is and maybe we can work this out.'

'She is nothing but a tease, she led me on and then won't even speak to me, so I came here to show her she can't treat me this way.'

'OK, but this isn't the answer, lower your weapon so we all can sit down and talk about this.'

'No, because she won't listen, so I have to make her listen.'

'If you don't, we have no choice but to fire.'

'You can't hit me from down there, so I think it's time we left.'

'You think we don't have the exits covered, come on you have nowhere to go.'

Will looked at Harvey then at the suspect. the suspect was right, Stanson would not be able to get a good angle on him, Will knew what he had to do.

'Control, we have a stand-off. Do we still have a green light?'

'Yes, alpha, you still have a green light.'

Will nodded at Harvey and then he fired. The suspect dropped to the ground, the woman screamed and dropped to her knees. Stanson went onto the stage and checked the suspect and made his weapon safe, then he looked up to the balcony.

'Control, this is alpha, we are all clear, we need PD and call a coroner.'

'Received, alpha team, they are on their way.'

Will and Harvey packed up and went down to the truck and the rest joined them when PD had taken over the scene. Stanson walked to the truck and didn't say a word as he packed his gear away and got in. Will and Harvey watched him, then looked at each other. As they got in the truck another call came in.

'Alpha team, we have an armed suspect in Central Park, near the entrance to the zoo, charlie team are en route, and are requesting alpha and bravo to attend.'

'Received, we are on our way.' Will turned to the team. 'You heard guys, let's go.'

Chapter 44

They arrived at Park Drive, and were met by PD. Will got out and went to find out what was going on. There were a number of squad cars, and people everywhere that the PD were trying to organise and get the area cordoned off. There was a group of zoo staff stood close to the entrance, looking worried.

'Sergeant Falco, we are glad to see you, we have an armed suspect, who is now in the zoo, he is irate and we have a bunch of kids in there, we think one of them maybe his, but we aren't sure, it's possible he just took them as hostages.'

'OK, any idea where he is now?'

'No clue, we lost sight of him when he was firing at us and we didn't want to hit a kid, that's why we called you.'

'OK, good move, are all your guys out?'

'No, but they can be.'

'Good, get them out and cover the perimeter, we will handle this.'

Will went back to the truck, grabbed his gear and weapon then briefed the teams.

'OK, we have one armed suspect, he is somewhere in the zoo. PD will cover the perimeter as we need to go through the whole place, they lost sight of him when he started shooting. Alpha team will follow me to the right and cover all exhibits that side, bravo you will go straight up and cover the left side exhibits. Charlie, you guys take the cafe, gift shop and restrooms, let's find this guy but be careful as he is believed to have children with him.'

'Children?' Tom asked.

'Yeah, there is a school group, he has them with him, they aren't sure if one of them is his or not.'

'So what do you want us to do when we find him?'

'Radio me, I will make the call.'

They all made their way to the entrance, they went in slowly, checking everywhere, charlie team veered off and checked the shop and cafe. Will took his team right past the sealions and then onto the penguins. Tom took bravo up to the tropic zone, they checked it all then they moved on, then Tom spotted the group over by the red panda exhibit. It had to be them as the rest of the place was empty.

'Alpha, this is bravo, we have a visual by the red panda exhibit.'

'Received, bravo, hold your position I am en route.'

Will moved quickly to where they were and stayed hidden till he could assess the situation. The alpha team got there, and they kept low.

'Bravo, you guys stay here, I don't want this guy to be overwhelmed. Stanson, with me, Harvey and Bennett go left, Turner, stay with bravo. Let's do this easy and steady.'

They slowly moved round before Will announced.

'NYPD, put your weapon down.'

The man looked either side and saw he was surrounded, he grabbed a child and put the gun to their head. Other children were screaming, some were crying, but they were all frozen to the spot, huddled together.

'Drop the weapon, there is no way out of here.'

'No, you lower yours, or this kid gets a bullet in the head.'

'Last warning, drop it.'

'No.'

Will fired, the suspect dropped to the floor, the child screamed and ran to a teacher. Stanson went over and secured the weapon, he looked at the suspect and then the kids. He sighed heavily.

'Control, this is alpha, suspect is down we are all clear, we need PD in here now to escort these children out,' Will radioed.

'Received, alpha team, they are on their way now.'

Will walked over to the teacher.

'Do you want to follow us and get these kids out of here?'

She nodded and they started leading the children away following Will. They got to where Tom was and were met by the PD.

'Those kids are going to need a whole lot of therapy.'

'Tough call, but better him than those kids,' Tom replied.

Will sighed as he took his helmet off, he stood watching the kids leave with the officers.

'Do you ever think about our kids, growing up in this kind of world, so much violence?'

'Not really, you know we are the good guys right.'

'Yeah, I know that, but all the people we come across in this job.'

'You think anyone will mess with Rose with parents like you and Kathy, I think she will be safe.'

Will smiled and they walked back to the truck and cars. They went back to the office. Will got coffee and was about to go in his office when the captain shouted.

'Falco, get in here.'

Will went in and shut the door.

'Well, Falco, I can tell you're back at work.'

'I'm sorry?'

'Two dead suspects and complaints coming in from four people so far.'

'They were good shoots, Captain, ask Harvey.'

'Stanson is your number two, so why should I ask Harvey?'

'He was with me on the balcony at the first call is all and he was there at the second too.'

'You didn't choose any other action though.'

'Captain, I followed the book both shouts, three warnings, I had a green light on the first anyway, Stanson tried to talk him down. Second one he had a gun to a child's head, did they want me to wait till he fired first?'

'Well, I had a call from the manager of the theatre, saying their leading lady was so distraught after you killed him, she can't perform and there is damage to the set. I also had a call from the school asking if you had to kill the man while the children were there, not to mention an irate zoo keeper because you scared the animals.'

'Sometimes it doesn't matter what we do, there is always someone that will find fault with it.'

'OK, write your reports, we may need to start recording your shouts, Falco, because I have IAB on my back about you again.'

'What for? I haven't had an issue for a while now,'

'I don't know, I am yet to be informed on that one, but I don't like them looking at my unit.'

'OK, I will let Tom know, make sure we have perfectly clean shouts.'

'Good, now go and write up and make sure everyone is on the same page.'

Will left and went straight to Tom's office, he went in and shut the door, sat down, and drank his coffee.

'So IAB are looking at us again.'

'What?' Why?'

'Captain doesn't know, but we have to keep our shouts perfect.'

'We always do.'

'I know but the captain is talking about cameras, we don't want that, so we need to get rid of IAB as quickly as possible, you know I don't like being kept an eye on.'

'I know, but maybe it wouldn't be a bad thing, would at least stop the allegations from precincts.'

'Yeah, but it would also mean they could hear what we say and then twist it to suit their needs.'

'Fair point but we don't say anything out of line, and we could turn them off when the all clear is given.'

'Call me paranoid, I don't like them, and why are we the only unit that isn't trusted on our word?'

There was a knock at the door. The door opened, it was Park.

'Falco, we've got her, I need you in the captain's office.'

Chapter 45

They both went over to the captain's office went in and Will closed the door and stood by it. Park sat down opposite the captain.

'So, we have evidence that links Ashborne to Palmer's death, so tomorrow I have to go and arrest her and bring her back for trial.'

'OK, that's great but what do you need from us?' Captain Bridge asked.

'An armed escort.'

'How many?'

'Three, I want it to stay pretty low key, so we all fit in one car, but I need to have people with me that are good at what they do, that's why I'm here.'

The captain sat back in his chair and thought for a moment.

'OK, you can have Falco, Hargreaves and Stanson.'

'Captain, who will be here for call-outs?'

'Harvey and Fremont can manage for a day or two, I will combine the teams and we have charlie and delta.'

'A day or two? Hang on I can't be away overnight.'

'Falco, you are my best officer and the most senior I have with that kind of experience, I need you to go, and Stanson and Hargreaves are next best two and I want this to go perfectly.'

'So I don't get a choice.'

'Falco, listen, I know Kathy just had the baby, but we just found out she has a prison officer on the take too, she is going to know about this transfer which means she will have something planned. I need you to ensure we get her back here for trial.'

'How is it going to happen?'

'I was thinking fly out and drive back is the best way, I have a route planned out.'

'I need to speak to the guys and to Kathy but if you need me that bad, I will do it, I don't want this woman to get away with what she did.'

'OK, good, now go and get Hargreaves and Stanson and we can go over everything in detail.'

***

That evening Will was just about to leave, the teams had gone but Tom was just finishing up too. Will went into his office and shut the door.

'Tom, we need a plan for tomorrow.'

'Thought we had one.'

'Yeah, well, call it gut instinct. I'm not happy with it.'

'Why, seems solid to me?'

'You don't think it leaves us open for Ashborne to try and have us taken out?'

'How will she know it's you going?'

'She isn't stupid, an armed escort, who else would it be?'

'OK, so what did you have in mind?'

'Well, I was looking at a map of the area and I figure she will have something set up between the prison and the freeway. Well, there is a road near the prison that cuts down to the other airport. I figure I have the company jet there waiting to fly us out. It's not a short route, but we will get enough of a head start before they realise what happened to get there before we hit trouble.'

'OK, sounds good, are you going to tell Park?'

'No, it's between us, Stanson and Park won't know.'

'Thought you trusted them.'

'I do, but the people around them not so much.'

'Stanson is staying at yours with Ash.'

'Yeah, but he has friends in the PD and I definitely don't trust everyone in Park's department.'

'But they both know about you.'

'Yeah, and if that gets out, they will be in serious shit, but this will be a reactive op and I don't like surprises.'

'Fair point.'

'I can't risk lives on this, and they don't know everything about me.'

'Does anyone?'

'You and Ash.'

'Not Kathy?'

'No, some things she doesn't need to know and others she wouldn't understand.'

'So how are you going to tell Kathy about tomorrow?'

'Don't know, she will hate it however I tell her.'

'Well let's go and tell our ladies we might not make it home tomorrow.'

'If we have each other's backs, we will always make it home.'

***

Will got home, there was no one around. He went into the bedroom and Kathy was there but Rose wasn't. Will walked over to Kathy and went to kiss her but she turned away. He stepped back and looked at her curiously, she looked mad.

'Stanson told you about tomorrow didn't he.'

'Yes.'

'Of course he did, and now you are mad because I agreed and didn't tell you.'

'Well look at that right again.'

'I wanted to speak to you properly and not over the phone.'

'You still agreed before talking to me.'

'I didn't have a choice, the captain told me I was going.'

She sat on the bed and looked at him.

'When I told you to go back to work, I didn't mean this, Will. You know this is not going to be easy and it will be more dangerous than any shout.'

'I know, but I have my best men with me, and this is my job, the captain said he needs me on this, I have more experience than anyone on the teams.'

'So the captain boosts your ego and you just jump at the chance to get killed.'

'Hang on a minute, that's not fair, Kathy, this is my job and I will not ask members of my team to risk their lives to do something that am not prepared to do myself, you of all people should understand that.'

'You're right, I'm sorry, I'm just worried is all, and you should be too. Ashborne will relish the chance to take you down.'

'I know and that's why they need me, so she doesn't take it out on any more of my team.'

'I'm sorry I am just really stressed about this and I had my parents here today.'

'How did that go?'

'They left as soon as Ryan got in, I think they thought you would be arriving pretty close behind.'

'Saves me having to be nice, I guess. So where is Rose anyway, I missed her today.'

'She is out on the terrace with Ash and Ryan.'

'Well, I will grab a shower and go and see her then it's been a long day.'

'Yeah, so I hear.'

'What did he say?'

'He mentioned the theatre is all.'

'Let me guess, he thinks I fired too early and he could have talked him down right.'

'Was he right?'

'What?'

'I was just asking if he was right.'

'The guy was never going to give up, I have seen it a hundred times before, these stalkers and people with such an obsession. Ryan didn't question my decision at all just accepted it even though he wasn't happy, and you question it when you weren't even there.'

'I was just asking Will.'

'Why because it was Ryan?'

'What's that supposed to mean?'

'Nothing, it doesn't matter, I'm going for a shower.'

'No, Will, what did you mean?'

Will looked at her for a moment.

'Would you have questioned it for anyone else? Because you never have before in all the time you have known and worked with me, but Ryan that's a whole other story.'

'What are you suggesting?'

'That you like him, are probably still attracted to him.'

'Will, are you kidding?'

'No, I see the way you look at him.'

'I literally just had our baby and you are accusing me of what exactly?'

'I'm not accusing you of anything, this is a man you slept with and kissed, I am just saying you have a biased view when it comes to him is all.'

'I am going out onto the terrace before I say something we will both regret.'

Kathy left, slamming the door. Will sat on the bed and wondered why he could not let go of this between Kathy and Ryan.

When Will had finished in the shower, he got dressed and went out onto the terrace, they all ate in relative silence. Will took Rose from her baby seat and sat down with her, just gazing at her, he barely spoke to anyone just lost in his own thoughts. When Ryan had taken the plates inside, Kathy took Rose to feed and change her for bed, Ash came and sat next to Will.

'Well, something's going on.'

'Not now, Ash.'

'Must be serious, it's about Kathy and Ryan, right?'

'It feels weird talking to you about this Ash, you're his girlfriend.'

'Yes, and as his girlfriend I can tell you he is only having sex with me.'

'Really Ash, I don't need to think about that.'

'Sorry, but my point is he hasn't been near Kathy not since she kissed him.'

Will sighed and looked at her.

'You see that's the problem right there, she kissed him, not the other way around, she looks at him in a way

I know that she is attracted to him. It's the same way Ryan looks at you.'

'Oh Will, there is always going to be men that she looks at, for whatever reason, whether it's because they are hot or because they respect them, or they are just close friends. Not many people who sleep together will find themselves living in an apartment with their respective others, all together. They will always have that connection, but it doesn't mean they will act on it again or that in fact they want to. You are reading far too much into this, maybe you should talk to Kathy, because tomorrow you can't afford to be distracted.'

Just then Ryan came back out.

'OK, we are going to bed, go talk to her.'

Will sat for a few minutes and thought what to say then went inside. Kathy was sat on the sofa with a cup of tea, Will poured a scotch and went and sat next to her.

'Ryan has gone to bed with Ash in case you were wondering.'

'I know.'

'Good.'

'Kathy, look let me explain please.'

'OK.'

Will had a drink, sat back, and took a deep breath.

'I know you aren't sleeping with Ryan, but I do know you have a different kind of friendship with him, maybe it's because you slept with him, but it's different.'

'And you have a problem with our friendship?'

'No, not really, I love you so much and I have not had the best relationships before, you've met Carla, I don't know why I feel like I do when I see you two together, smiling and laughing but I do.'

'You're jealous.'

'No, I didn't say that.'

'Will, it's OK, we all get jealous of someone and the way they are with our other half.'

'Really?'

'Yeah, I was jealous of women in your life, including Ash till I got to know her, because she knew so much about you that I didn't, that intimate side that you never let me see.'

'So we are OK?'

'I just have one question, did you ever doubt you were Rose's dad?'

Will didn't respond for a moment and his expression was very telling.

'You did?'

'For about thirty minutes when I first found out.'

'Wow, that's really great. Thanks.' She was holding back tears.

'Kathy, I was stupid, when I found out I was trying to work out how long before you had slept with Ryan and I soon realised that it didn't add up.'

'So it was only about the timing of it.'

'Of course, I know you didn't sleep with him when we were together.'

'OK, we really need to talk more, Will, not let things like this build up, I know that's hard for you but if we are going to stay together for life, you are going to have to try.'

'Yeah, I know, I'm sorry.'

Kathy curled up and laid on him, and wrapped her arm around him, he put his arm around her and kissed her on the head. They stayed there for a while in silence, both thinking about the future and what it would hold for them.

Chapter 46

The next morning Will was in the locker room getting ready, he hadn't really slept that well after his chat with Kathy and the thought of today. He knew his lying to Kathy was probably not the best idea, he had in fact suspected her and Ryan a couple of times when they were first together but he had never let on and he never would, right now though he needed to get his head in the game because if he didn't, they may not all come back alive. They had to be in early to get the flight. Stanson and Tom walked in a few minutes later, there was a tense atmosphere, they got ready and went down to the gun cage to get armed up and collect all the gear they needed. Park walked in, he had his vest on and his own issued weapon, he also had four coffees in his hands.

'Thought you guys would appreciate some coffee this morning.'

Will took his and smiled.

'You know us too well.'

'I have a question, how are they letting us fly with all this on?' Stanson asked.

'You've never given an escort before, have you?' Tom asked.

'No.'

'The airline gets a phone call to clear us to fly, they put us on a flight and organise it, so we are at the back, plus we aren't on the flight with Ashborne, so they tend not to mind.'

'Why do they put us at the back?'

'So we can be separated, and so the public can't try and take our weapons. They will even stop people using the restrooms behind us.'

'Oh, OK, that makes sense.'

'OK, are we ready,' Park asked.

'I think we are.'

***

When they boarded, they got some very curious and strange looks from some of the passengers. They all sat and put their gear by the window, they kept hold of their weapons.

'Do you think they feel safer with us on board?' Tom said to Will.

'They are probably just wondering why the hell we are on their flight.'

'Is everything set?' Tom asked quietly.

'Yeah, the jet will be there just after we land so they are refuelled and ready to leave, just hope this works.'

'You don't think it will?'

'I reckon it's the best option, but we still have to be on our guard at all times.'

'So did you tell Kathy the new plan?'

'No, I didn't have chance, we had a massive fight last night.'

'What about?'

'Ryan.'

'He's with Ash though, you can't think they are cheating.'

'No, he is besotted with Ash, it's more about Kathy's feelings than his, but I am working on my jealousy with it.'

'OK well if you need to talk about it, you know where I live.'

'I do and thanks, can't really talk to Ash about this one.'

'I get that, now let's try and relax shall we before the shit starts.'

The two hours seemed so much longer, they were all on edge even Will. The flight crew were nice but were very uneasy about their presence and it made the whole situation more uncomfortable. When the flight landed, all four of them were relieved to get off, they got off first and headed straight to where they had a car waiting. They had a special escort to get them through the airport as quickly as possible. They got to the car, it was a plain black SUV with plenty of room for what would soon be the five of them.

'OK, Tom drives, I will go in the front, Park and Stanson in the back.'

'Is it not better if I go in the front, so you are next to Ashborne when we get her.'

'No, I know how to spot an ambush and other problems, do you?'

'Fair point, I am in the back then.'

They drove the half hour in relative quiet, the prison was not exactly a welcome sight to Will because he knew this was where the trouble started. They went through the gates in the car, Park and Will got out. A guard brought Ashborne out, she was handcuffed, Park signed the relative paperwork. Ashborne stood looking at Will the whole time.

'Sergeant Falco, I can't tell you what a pleasure it is having you escort me.'

'Yeah, I bet, because I won't hesitate to put a bullet in your head.'

Will opened the door and she got in and moved over next to Stanson, Park got in next to her. Will walked back around and got in the front. They set off and started driving. About ten minutes down the road, Will signalled to Tom and he turned off. Will turned round, Park gave him a curious look and Ashborne looked worried. Will knew at that moment his gut instinct was right. Stanson continued to look out of the window. The roads were quiet and so Tom could drive at a reasonable speed. It was a very tense journey, no one spoke, they were all focussed on what they were there to do.

As they were getting close to the airport, Tom saw two vehicles in his mirrors, they were coming up fast.

'We got company,' Tom said.

Ashborne smiled.

'Can you lose them?' Will asked.

'Not really, but we aren't far off now so I can speed up and hope for the best.'

'Do it.'

Tom accelerated, he started to pull away. They were coming to the turn off, he turned off slowing slightly. They were on a part of an airport, Park noticed. As they got close to the jet Tom slammed on the brakes.

'You two get her on that plane, we will sort these guys out.'

Stanson and Park paused.

'Come on get out, *go*,' Will shouted.

They got out and dragged Ashborne with them and headed for the jet. She was smiling as they heard the cars coming closer, although she was trying to go slowly across to the jet, so Park was literally dragging her, while Stanson was watching out for shooters. Tom turned the car round, Will opened his window took his seat belt off, he leaned out of the window and he shot out the front tyres on the first car. He sat back in the car as it spun, the other car was close behind it and just avoided it but it was too close for Tom to avoid and they went head-on into it. There was an enormous bang. Stanson turned round.

'Get her on that plane,' he said to Park.

He started running over to the wreck, hoping Will and Tom were all right.

Chapter 47

Two men emerged from the car that had spun. Stanson shot them both and moved closer to the car, he couldn't see any movement at all. His heart was pounding, he moved slower as he approached, scared of what he might find.

Tom looked at Will.

'You all right?'

'Depends what you mean by all right, that fucking hurt.'

'Yeah, sorry, couldn't avoid it.'

'We need to move and get on the jet.'

Will glanced in his mirror, he saw Stanson approaching, there was a man behind him.

'Ryan, look out!' Will shouted.

Stanson spun round, the man stabbed him in his left shoulder. Will opened his door and shot him before he could stab him again. Stanson was on the floor, Will got out slowly, then helped him up. Tom got out and checked the men in the other car, they were unconscious. They grabbed all their stuff and headed for the jet. They got on and the co-pilot closed the door. Ashborne was sat near the back, she was surprised to see them and disappointed her plan hadn't worked. Park stood.

'You guys OK?'

'Will be, but one of those bastards stabbed Stanson, so he's dead as are two others.'

The plane started to move so they all sat while it took off. Will got up as soon as he could and grabbed the first aid kit that was kept on board. He passed it to Tom, he took out some dressings and put pressure on Stanson's shoulder.

'Shit, that hurts.'

'We need to keep pressure on it till we land, just hope we can slow the bleeding enough.'

Will looked at Ashbourne she was smiling, obviously enjoying their pain. Will grabbed something from the kit and went over to her.

'You can smile now, but we will be in New York in two hours and you won't be smiling when you get life for murder.'

'Good luck proving that.'

'We already did.'

'That's impossible,' she said defiantly.

'Really, because you aren't that good and you picked the wrong unit to go after, your two friends that killed my officer are dead, we connected them to you. So tell me exactly what have we missed?'

Ashbourne looked more worried than she had before, she knew they had got her. Will smiled, then stuck a needle in her shoulder. She was soon out cold, Park looked at Will.

'Don't panic it's just a sedative, I didn't go through all that for it to be anything else.'

He went to the front and grabbed the phone and sat down.

'Captain, it's Falco, meet us at Newark in two hours, we need an ambulance for Stanson and transport for Ashborne. You may want to call Detroit too because we left quite a mess at the airport as we left. I will explain when we get back.'

'OK, Falco see you soon.'

Will sat back in his chair, Park stood and went over to him.

'Good back-up plan, Falco, but only you and Hargreaves knew about it.'

'And my pilots.'

'You didn't trust me and Stanson.'

'I trust you both, but you have a leak in your office, and I don't risk my life like that.'

'What do you mean a leak?'

'Someone in your office leaks information for the right price, I don't know who, but I just couldn't risk it.'

Park looked at Will, then went back to his seat. He knew Will was serious, but that was an issue for another day.

***

When they landed the co-pilot opened the door, Captain Bridge was waiting. Tom got Stanson into the waiting ambulance, he had lost a fair amount of blood, so they got him on a stretcher. Park and Will got Ashborne into the waiting squad car, she was still quite drowsy. Park shook Will's hand, then got in with them. The captain walked over to Will.

'What happened over there?'

'We hit trouble in more ways than one, she had cars waiting for us, I am guessing they were supposed to take us out and free her, but when we took a different road, it delayed them enough for us to get to the airport.'

'You had this planned last night?'

'Yeah, I arranged for my jet to be there to get us.'

'Good plan as it turned out. Falco, well done.'

'Thanks, Captain, but just doing my job.'

'You and Hargreaves look pretty beat up though.'

'Our car went head on into one of theirs, just a bit bruised is all.'

'You were in a head-on collision, then both of you get in that ambulance and go and get checked out.'

'Captain, I have to get all the gear back.'

'I can do that, now go to the hospital.'

'OK, just let me speak to my pilots.'

Will went on the jet for a few minutes, got all the gear together then got in the ambulance as ordered.

***

Stanson had started to lose consciousness on the way and so they had lights and sirens all the way in. Will and Tom got out after they had taken Ryan in, they were all taken to separate rooms to be treated. Will was on the bed when the doctor came in.

'OK,' he said as he entered. 'What happened, Sergeant?'

'Was in a head-on collision, don't know what speed, Tom had started to brake but it all happened really fast.'

'How long ago?'

'Two and a half hours give or take.'

'And you only just came in now.'

'Yeah, it happened in Detroit, we just landed.'

'OK, any loss of consciousness or any dizziness?'

'Not really, but I have felt tired and aching all over since it happened.'

'Were you wearing a seat belt?'

'No, I had taken it off before it happened.'

'You took off your seat belt?'

'Yeah, it's hard to shoot out someone's tyres with it on.'

The doctor looked at him not sure if he was serious.

'Well, I want a full set of X-rays and a CT.'

'Is all that really needed?'

'Yeah, I need to assess the full extent of your injuries, so sit tight and we will get them done as soon as we can.'

Will sat back and pulled his phone out, deciding whether to call Kathy, but he put it away. He didn't want to worry her.

After all the tests and X-rays results were in, the doctor came back in.

'OK the CT is clear no concerning head injuries, but the X-rays are showing a few fractured ribs and a partial fracture of your collar bone. You have a lot of bruising and I would say you have internal bruising too judging by your injuries and the fact you weren't wearing a seat belt. You are an incredibly lucky man, Sergeant.'

'Thanks doctor, good job we had our gear on really.'

'I would say so, probably helped cushion the impact, now I will get the nurse to bring you some painkillers, a long soak in a warm bath will help and plenty of rest.'

'Am I clear for work tomorrow?'

'Yes, but I would prefer light duties for a couple of days, these maybe minor injuries, Sergeant, but I want you to take them seriously.'

'I promise I won't overdo it.'

'Good, now any questions?'

'How are the other two?'

'Hargreaves is OK, a bit of bruising and a few fractured ribs, he had his belt on so the impact was less than yours. Stanson, his wound wasn't deep, but due to the flight lost a fair bit of blood, but he will be all right.

He is on some blood now, we would prefer him to stay in tonight but he refused so he will be clear to go in about an hour when we can be sure he is OK. You and Hargreaves can go as soon as you get your painkillers.'

'OK, thanks.'

Will waited for his painkillers then left the room, Tom had done the same. They both stood outside Stanson's room watching, they had sewn the wound and he was on a blood transfusion, and a nurse was monitoring him. Will decided it was time to call Kathy to tell her what had happened.

Chapter 48

They got back to Will's late, Stanson was monitored for a couple of hours before he was cleared to go. Will opened the door, Kathy was by the door waiting. She wrapped her arms tightly around him.

'Not so hard, fractured ribs remember.'

'Oh, I'm sorry,' she let go and then kissed him.

Lynne walked over to Tom and held him for a moment. Ash ran over to Stanson and kissed him, then she turned and hit Will on the arm.

'What was that for?'

'You were meant to keep him safe, Will.'

'Ash, honey, if it wasn't for Will, I may have come back in a body bag.'

'What, really?'

'Yeah.'

'OK I forgive you, Will, and I will kill that woman if I ever get my hands on her.'

Tom and Lynne moved towards the door.

'We are going to get home, I would say it has been fun, but it really hasn't, but I will see you tomorrow.'

'Night, Tom.'

Kathy and Will headed for the sofa and sat down. Stanson and Ash started to head for the bedroom.

'Ryan, I know you are technically off with your shoulder and all, but if you could come in and get your report done first thing, Park will need it.'

'No, worries, I can do that.'

They headed for bed and Will and Kathy were alone.

'Is Rose asleep?'

'Yeah, she went down about half an hour ago.'

'I won't disturb her then.'

'Did it all go to plan then?'

'Except the car wreck, yeah.'

'So you were right about her trying to escape.'

'Yeah, and I reckon had we gone down the planned route those two cars would have had taken us out for sure, luckily we confused them enough to get such a head start.'

'Well at least she will stand trial now.'

'Yeah, and I reckon Park will ensure some more charges will be added after today.'

'Good, I hope she gets life.'

Will kissed her on the head and sat back, Kathy curled up next to him leaning on his chest. They were both very aware of how lucky he was to have made it home at all.

'You see your parents today?'

'No, not today I just couldn't face them while waiting for you to get home.'

'When do they go home?'

'They haven't decided, they are looking for places to move here, again, their house hunt has intensified now Rose is here, apparently.'

'Great, and will Tony be joining them.'

'I daren't ask right now.'

'Well, I am going to lay in the bath for a while as per doctor's orders, then we can head to bed if you want.'

'Sounds good to me.'

***

The next morning Will arrived at the office, Stanson had gone in with him. They had got a car because Will's bike was still at the office and Ryan couldn't have held on anyway. Tom arrived just after them, they were chatting with a coffee when Park walked in.

'Falco, I need to speak to you.'

'OK, my office?'

'No, the captain's.'

Will took his coffee and followed Park, they went in and Will closed the door behind them. He sat down.

'I had a phone call from the prison this morning. Ashborne is dead.'

'What?'

'Apparently another prisoner stabbed her.'

'Who? Why?'

'A lifer in for a double homicide, she said Ashborne looked at her funny.'

Captain Bridge leaned forward on his desk.

'So that's it, Palmer's case is now closed.'

'Yeah, with the exception of the paperwork, so I still need the reports on yesterday. I wanted to let you guys know in person.'

Will stood up and walked towards the filing cabinets, he didn't say anything at all, he didn't know how to feel. Now no one would be held accountable for Palmer's death and he felt empty and sad. Even his parents' killer was now in prison.

'I have to get back and sort all this out, I will catch you up when I hear more from the prison,' Park said and left.

There was silence for a moment.

'You OK, Falco?'

'I'm not sure, Captain, I guess she got what she deserved, but justice for Palmer would have been better.'

'Do you want to let the teams know?'

'Yeah, I will speak to them as soon as they get in.'

'I will also be arranging both alpha and bravo to speak with a counsellor.'

'Bennett and a couple of others would definitely benefit from that, Captain.'

'And you?'

'Me? You know me, Captain, I'm good.'

'Falco, for once this is not a request.'

'I don't need some shrink to talk to, I need some time in the gym, my job and my two ladies to go home to.'

'Falco, you will see the shrink just like everyone else.'

Will was going to argue but the captain stopped him.

'You will see the shrink, or you will go home.'

'Captain, come on I don't need to speak to someone.'

'Yes, you do, Sergeant, all these years and all you have been through and you have never spoken to anyone, and mistakably I let it go because you are such a damn good officer. That stops today, it's time you face your past and your demons and that's the end of it.'

'I don't have a choice.'

'No, and there are about to be more changes. Lieutenant Planter is leaving us for pastures new, our new lieutenant has a good reputation and has plenty of SWAT experience over in California. So no more attitude, you will be answering to him from when he arrives next month. The chief feels it shouldn't be my job to deal with your bullshit, so he is bringing in someone that can handle it.'

'OK, will he be told who I am?'

'He will have access to your work file, Falco, he is known to work his teams hard and expects the best, he is no soft touch like Planter, this guy is SWAT through and through.'

'Sounds like my kind of guy.'

'Well let's see if you feel the same when he has you at your desk for the first stunt you pull.'

Will folded his arms and sighed.

'We done, Captain?'

'Yeah, for now.'

Will left and went into his office, he shut the door, sat down and drank his coffee. He thought about the last eighteen months and what the unit had been through, then he started to consider what impact it would have to have a new lieutenant. He had never really got on with Planter, as good as he was, he wasn't SWAT and so they had had a lot of differences of opinion which led to him pretty much allowing him to run his own team and shouts, even the big ones. He had enjoyed that freedom and he knew that things were about to change. He heard the teams arrive and he prepared himself to break the news to them about Ashborne and the new lieutenant. There was bound to be mixed emotions about both. He went out, they were sat chatting. He went to Tom's office and got him to come out and join the others.

'OK, everyone, if you can all sit down and listen up for a minute.'

They all did so and looked at Will. Tom stood by his door and wondered what kind of news he was going to give them.

'Now, we have all had a rough couple of weeks, it's been worse for some than others, so Captain Bridge has arranged a shrink and all of alpha and bravo will be seeing them.'

'All of us?' Tom asked.

'Yeah, all, including me, Captain's orders. Now I have just been informed that Lieutenant Planter is leaving the unit and we have a new lieutenant starting in a few weeks. He has SWAT experience and apparently works his teams hard, so let's show him why we are the best when he gets here, shall we?'

Will took a breath and looked at them.

'We also have been informed this morning by Detective Park that Ashborne was murdered last night by another prisoner. Palmer's case is now closed, once they get all our reports.'

'She's dead? For real?' Bennett asked.

'Yeah, she is.'

'How did she die?'

'She was stabbed.'

'Good, I hope it fucking hurt.'

'Yeah, me too Bennett, me too.'

Will went back to his office and Tom followed.

'So that's a new one, you seeing a shrink.'

'I don't have a choice, well that's unless I want to be sent home, till I do see one.'

'Well, you know, it might actually be good for you, help you move on from everything. I mean you haven't exactly had an easy time since you took over alpha team.'

'I know, but I have my own way of dealing with things.'

'With Rose here, maybe it's time to try something new?'

'Maybe, we will see soon enough. She is coming today, and I am guessing I will be first on her list.'

Just then their beepers went off.

'Well, let's get back to work, and some kind of normal,' Will said as they left.